VISCOUNTESS

Viscountess

a novel by Taversia

HOLON
PUBLISHING

Viscountess
Copyright © 2013
Taversia.Net

Published by Holon Publishing
& Collective Press

ISBN: 978-0-9853027-9-5

CREDITS :

Cover Model – Taversia
Artwork – Jennifer Smith; Photographer
       Orina Kafe; Digital Artist
Special thanks to Dr. Paul Patton for lending his scientific knowledge and expertise in bringing this story to life.

HOLONPUBLISHING

To my first love. You've inspired me more than you know.

Table of Contents

CHAPTER 1

Psychosis

T wilight filled the sea of sky outside the *Wild Rose*. The airship, large by the wealthiest standards, bobbed slowly as it sailed into the darkening horizon, its many masts bearing flags of every color that flapped farewell to the sun. Stars flashed in and out of clouds through a small circular window on the first level from the top, starboard. Past the reflection of nightlights and milky fly-bys, a richly decorated cabin suite spread from the convex wall. Three tall, white votives rose from a jeweled silver candelabra like frozen fountains, illuminating the main room from their place in the center atop a polished oak desk. Shadows danced across drapes and paintings, enshrining in darkness and orange light the room's only inhabitant.

The young woman sat with perfect, upright posture, red hair gathered about her head like a crown of flames in the flickering candle light. Loose strands licked over her pastel floral dress, seeming to glow against the silken fabric. Her eyes moved fervently over the words and diagrams of a heavy book, glittering with moisture though she rarely blinked. "*Airship Engineering for the Sky Captain of Tomorrow*" headed every page, reigning over detailed pictures of machinery that were swarmed by floating paragraphs. She absently swept a lock of fiery hair behind one ear to meet with the angry bun at the back of her head. Her chair creaked as she shifted her weight restlessly, continuing hungrily through the book as she devoured every bit of text each second would allow.

She held her head at an angle, unwilling to relent a bit of her posture even when alone. While she appreciated the gifts a corset would bestow upon her curves that evening, she was none too pleased as she sat in one while waiting to hear from her father, the captain of their family's vessel, who may at any minute summon her for dinner. The dull ache at the base of her skull trailed down her spine inside the thin steel cage of the corset, her ribs enduring valiantly their imprisonment by fashion. She drew in the occasional deep breath as she read, stubborn and painstaking against the protest of her abdomen.

She read on in silence, completely absorbed by her material. Papers and various utensils cluttered what remained of surface that was not covered by the large, slightly yellow pages and hard leather binding of her volume. She did not even hear the crystal knob on her door click and turn. The door squeaked inward, a breeze exciting the candles' flames into a jig that greeted their guest with bouncing shadows. The girl gasped, slamming the book shut and shoving it to one side, which scattered sheets of paper that fluttered to the floor in hot pursuit of the pens, pencils, and other instruments that had tumbled away from her desk.

"It's Rivkah, miss. Cap'n sent me to bring you downstairs." Rivkah, a woman in her mid-twenties of tight muscle and sun-kissed skin, looked in carefully. Seeing the mess, she opened the door the rest of the way and stepped into the room, amusement shining from her eyes. She stood with gloved hands on her hips, face streaked in ash and grease, her beige buttons and green overalls spotted with the same mess that decorated her laugh lines. "You were reading those tech books again, weren't you?" she asked, grinning.

A sharp glare was the only response she received from the quiet girl who had already risen to her feet, pushing the chair in under the desk behind her. Rivkah chuckled slightly and it was all the younger woman could do to keep from being impetuous in her presence. She thought it particularly humiliating, how a shiphand commoner could make her feel like such a silly little girl. She suspected it had everything to do with Rivkah doing everything she only wished she could.

Rivkah's smirk smoothed, parting for another grin that slowly made its way across her face. "My lady," she said in a lilting voice, "you *know* your father doesn't like you reading through his books… but who saw anything here besides a few ship mice?"

The flame-haired woman scowled. She hated mice, and she hated to be teased. She wanted nothing more than to explain herself; that it was less a matter of her going through her father's things and much more of his opposition to her ever learning how to fly. She often fantasized about operating her own ship, soaring high above the clouds with windswept tresses blowing all about. Even the thought of gritty maintenance work enthralled her.

Rivkah sighed and shook her head. "Now, now… I'm only kidding," she said in response to the hard look. "Come along! It's nearly six o'clock. Let's not keep your father waiting."

Rivkah extended a gloved hand to the visibly disgruntled girl. Her once-white, cowhide mechanical gloves were stained with sooty remnants and smelled faintly of oil. She crinkled her nose, and after a moment's pause, Rivkah seemed to catch onto why. "Oh! I almost forgot," she chuckled, deftly tugging the gloves off her hands and stuffing them into her back pocket. "I've been working on the ship down below all afternoon with the rest of the crew. I guess once you've been at it for hours at a stretch you forget other people aren't covered in the same stuff you are!"

The redhead reluctantly took hold of Rivkah's hand, now bare. She noted the woman's firm grip which surprised her, as it played quite the contrast to the softness of her caramel-mocha skin. It was clear to her that although Rivkah worked long, hard hours pulling her weight alongside the dozen or so other crewmembers (all men, rugged in stature) she was still very much a lady.

She allowed Rivkah to escort her from her room, closing the door behind her as they made their way outside onto the promenade deck, turning left. A brisk wind immediately swept up the skirt of her dress, and a few strands of her hair with that. Adrenaline rushed through her and the ache from her corset flew away with the billowing evening breeze. As they moved along they passed by the rooms of the other aristocratic residents of the ship, presumably all empty as she recalled the sound of opening and closing doors earlier that evening and all throughout her time spent buried in her father's engineering book. Each time she heard footsteps down the hall, she had shut the book partway so as not to be discovered should anyone decide to pop in unexpectedly – a lost cause.

Looking out over the waist-level railing to the right of the open corridor, she took in the view of the setting sun disappearing behind distant clouds. The golden cascade of crepuscular rays ignited the sky like streams of liquid fire washed over the horizon, piercing into the abysmal blue sky with rich cardinal shades of warmth. The slow-advancing expanse of dusk collided with the brilliant glow of daylight receding, and the faintest glimmers of stars were beginning to show face high above. She wished she could frame it right then in that moment; the whole sky snatched from the heavens, and hers to keep.

"Sorry for busting in on you like that, miss," Rivkah interrupted, the silent girl suddenly wrenched back from her moments' musings by her words. "I was told not to knock. I honestly felt bad about it, but your uncle insisted and, well, you know how he is…"

She did.

The girl scowled at the thought of her uncle, whose disposition was that of an angry, old bigot. While her father disapproved of her desire to operate her own ship someday, she had assumed it to be a product of his own desire to protect her. It was her uncle, Acanthus, who harbored the belief that women should not operate or maintain machinery as it was seen by the general aristocratic populace as being highly unladylike, and slowly but surely his outdated manner of thinking seeped its way into the crevices of her father's mind. She hated him for it. Moreover, she hated him for denying her the right to her solitude.

Feeling hopeless and miserable, she looked to the skies as Rivkah walked her to the dining quarter. With the distance so broad and endless, so open and free, she wondered what more to life there was. The women continued along down the corridor, turning up a flight of stairs with the open winds fluttered through their clothes and hair. She remained in sullen contemplation the entire way. They soon approached the double doors that would lead them through the mess hall which divided the communal classes on the ship; crew members from aristocrats.

"There you are, miss." Rivkah smiled, releasing her hand. "I should be off now, but enjoy supper with your family and those other, um, nice people! Oh, and happy birthday!"

For a second, the younger woman wanted to reach out for her, to take her hand again. She watched Rivkah as she walked away, a slight spring in her heels as her boots clomped heavily against the wooden planks of the ship's floorboards. Her curly, jet-black hair bounced with each step until she turned the corner down the corridor at the foot of the stairs and out of sight, leaving her there, alone once more. There was nothing left for her to do but join her father.

She began to reach for the nearest door handle when both doors flung open unexpectedly. Her arms rose in surprise as she loosed a voiceless gasp at the sudden loud burst. Her uncle stood before her now, his usual expression donning his distinctly odd features; contemptuous lips pursed tight and bloodless with years of bitter resentment, bushy furrowed brows prominently low over disapproving inset brown eyes, and a long beaklike nose which accented deep sagging frown wrinkles at the corners of his mouth. His thinning, graying shoulder-length hair was pulled back in its usual greasy braid as he stood there, his tall thin frame quite imposing in his eggplant-purple dinner suit.

"Well, it's about time!" he snarled, exposing a mouthful of large, gummy, tea-stained teeth. He grabbed her arm and began pulling her into the dining area, giving the double doors a shove with his free hand. Just before the doors swung closed, she thought she caught a glimpse of a ship's silhouette approaching behind distant clouds. Her eyes were tired from reading by candlelight; perhaps it was just her imagination. She winced as he gripped her, his long bony fingers digging into her flesh leaving faint red marks on her ivory skin. Without loosening his hold on her arm, he firmly led her over to the very long wooden table now covered by a fine embroidered cloth.

She glanced around at the twelve other people seated six on each side as they talked amongst themselves. All were wearing their finest suits and dresses; dead beasts and salad hats. She hardly knew most of them, having kept to herself as much as she could through each voyage. Rich, upper class passengers would always come and go, so she made it a point to seldom get attached. There were two empty chairs on either side of her father where she and Acanthus routinely sat. Naturally, being the captain of his own ship, her father always seated himself at the head of the table. He looked upon her now with a warm smile.

For everything loathsome her uncle was, her father was unquestionably not. He was a robust, imposing man, as tall as his brother but twice his trouser size. His features were strong and distinguished; a large noble nose set over a perfectly kempt chevron mustache, and jovial laugh lines wreathing brilliant brown eyes under a couplet of handsomely bushy brows. He had a bearded, square jawline, broad with his infectious smile. As overprotective as he was, she adored her father. Acanthus yanked her over by the table and abruptly seized her into the seat adjacent him. Once released, she began massaging her arm where her uncle had gripped it. The dull ache joined the newly realized dull ache down her neck and spine, and she glowered.

"Happy birthday, my dear," her father smiled, gesturing grandly to the feast over the table which she at first failed to notice. In a corset so tightly laced, her appetite was something of minute proportions. Even still, she helped herself to a bit of everything; stale baked bread, mashed sweet potatoes, a variety of mixed herbs and vegetables, and a hot cup of her favorite maple tea.

"Resources are limited," her uncle said, raising a cup of tea to his pale, thin lips. "Your father saw to it that provisions were rationed in accordance with your birthday. You know how difficult it is to find untainted farmlands in these dark times."

"Oh, don't bother the poor girl, Acanthus!" Madame Beatrice reproached, also sipping her tea. She was a corpulent woman of superior age and stunted growth with plump rosy cheeks and beady, bespectacled eyes. "It doesn't take setting foot on open soil to know the risks we take every time we restock our supplies! She has been well-educated of that fact, haven't you dear?"

The girl nodded as the pleasantly plump older woman eyed her, her spectacles resting comfortably on her little round nose. The girl remained silent, taking in a large gulp of her tea. She always felt awkward when people would speak of her in her presence.

Her father chuckled, clasping a large hand around her bare shoulder, the sleeves of her dress held up around her arms by the stringency of her corset. "My daughter has now been in this world for twenty years, to this day," he said, his deep booming voice carrying far and proud. All those seated around the table looked upon him as he spoke, their full attention captured by his sheer force of charisma. "She is an inquisitive mind... much like her mother. I could not be a prouder father."

"Ah, but certainly she takes more after you, Amadeus!" the man seated to her right chimed in, addressing her father by his first name. She did not know this man. He did not know her. Aristocratic schmoozers were all the same.

"Although I never knew your late wife, I would be inclined to agree," joined Madame Beatrice. "She has your taste for adventure; that same look in her eyes you get whenever we embark."

Her father laughed heartily at this, giving her shoulder a firm squeeze. She grimaced, her face now flushed with embarrassment. She wished they would stop talking amongst themselves, as she was the unwilling topic of conversation. It was the sole reason she dreaded her birthdays, and a prime example of why she was often late to any celebration held in her honor.

"Rose was quite the curious one, wasn't she…?" Acanthus smirked. The table fell silent at his words, and her father now looked upon him with faded expression. He returned the gaze with those inset, snake-like eyes of his, the better half of a grin still tugging at the corners of his mouth. "She was a woman of wandering wonder; the unfortunate circumstances which led to her untimely death. I wonder, Amadeus, if your daughter recalls that very day… whether she remembers what happened, that she lost her voice."

The redheaded girl slammed her open palms against the table and stood up from her chair which slid back across the wooden floor. Her hands rattled the silverware with the impact as her eyes pierced into her uncle's now with ferocious, hateful abandon. Her whole body shook with white hot rage, and in a matter of seconds, a series of violent scenarios played out in her mind. Her imagination ran rampant with gruesome, sadistic acts of depravity; of the slow and systematic breaking of fingers to the pealing back of flesh from lean, underdeveloped muscles and tendons. She pictured her uncle's face wrought with inconceivable agony, and the thought loosed a wave of satisfaction that thrashed through her bloodstream which cooled the hot pounding in her heaving breast; all this, in a span of mere seconds.

It was then that she realized she was smiling, despite herself. The guests around the table were very silent and very still, their eyes wide with shock as they all watched her intently. She broke eye contact with her uncle, smile quickly diminished, to survey the room around her. Her moment of subconscious psychosis had passed, and she began to realize what had just happened. Eyes fluttering wildly in bewilderment, it was all she could do to keep herself running from the room once she realized the psychotic spectacle she had just made of herself.

"Acanthus," her father growled, teeth gritted behind curled upper lip. His former hearty demeanor was all but lost. "The next time you mention my late wife at this table, you would do well to speak of her *only* in pleasant terms."

The girl noticed the man seated to her right quietly pushing in his chair, having gotten up in preparation to slip out, presumably unnoticed. *Good riddance*, she thought quietly to herself. He was not the only one. Of the twelve acquaintances seated around the table, only Madame Beatrice, beside her uncle, had not risen from her seat. She wondered if this night could get any worse, with the musky scent of social gaucherie thick in the air.

"You'll have to forgive me, Amadeus," her uncle leered. "It has been a *decade* since your wife's tragic passing and a *decade* since your daughter fell mute! Only she truly knows what happened down there, and I merely suggest—"

It was her father now who rose to his feet, fists slammed against the surface of the table. The celebratory guests had all by this point hurried from the dining hall and the redheaded girl thought it ironic that no sooner had she arrived than her own party had come to an end. There was a brief, uncomfortable silence. Madame Beatrice's eyes fixated upon the two brothers, still unmoved from her spot as they stared each other down. She had a look of morbid fascination plastered across her chubby face. She would surely be entertained with the juicy gossip this incident would reap for weeks to come.

Finally, it was Amadeus to look away first. "Acanthus… Beatrice…" he said, "I think it best you both followed the other guests out. I wish to speak with my daughter, alone."

"The girl has a dark side, *little* brother," Acanthus replied, casting a severe look. "These things go left unchecked long enough, she'll end up just as Rose did. Don't be a fool!"

Heat flushed over her face, but it was no longer with a feeling of embarrassment or anger. She did not know why she felt the sudden need to cry, but still these strange emotions washed over her like waves crashing against a rocky shore. Her eyes trailed back to Madame Beatrice, whom she noticed had turned her gaze to watch her once more. She was standing now, the round older woman giving her a nod of obvious feigned sympathy before turning on her heel to exit the dining area.

"Leave." Amadeus curtly replied.

Muttering inaudibly to himself, Acanthus followed Madame Beatrice out, slamming the doors behind them. Silence settled in the suddenly massive room now, as the girl was left alone with her father. The table was a mess with half-eaten food, spilled cups, and scattered silverware. Amadeus pinched the bridge of his nose between his thumb and index finger, rubbing slightly with a deep sigh. She felt like a great disappointment to him.

"…We *all* harbor darkness inside of us," he said finally, meeting her gaze. "Don't let your uncle's words bother you, my girl. What's important is not that you feel… animosity…"

He stepped toward her, once more clasping a heavy hand down around her shoulder. He was warm, his presence reassuring, and a soft crescent smile played at the corners of his mouth. "It's what you do with these feelings. That is what matters most."

She nodded at him, feeling a little better. Her internal compass seemed too open and complex for her to fully grasp, and she was still unsure of her feelings; particularly that which lead to her sudden outburst. Her father's smile broadened and he gave her shoulder an encouraging squeeze.

"Come with me. I think it's time I gave you your birthday present."

CHAPTER 2

The Key

The young red-haired woman followed her father from the dining quarter to the bow end of the ship; the captain's office, where Amadeus conducted much of the mapping and preparation for each expedition he led. He fumbled with the ring of keys fastened firmly to his belt before thumbing over his master key, extricating it. He turned it in the door lock once, clicking it open, before twisting the handle and pushing open the door.

"Ah, there we are!" he said, putting the key back on its ring. He placed a hand on the small of the girl's back, leading her into the room. She had rarely been allowed entry, and never without her father being there with her. It was just as she had remembered it; a large world globe to the right of his fine oak desk, and an ornate decorative key the size of a young child hanging on the wall behind it. Her father told her it had been an heirloom in her family since long before she was born. The faintest bit of twilight shined through the high circular windows, the room otherwise quite dim.

Her father's desk space was always kept tidy with a single map rolled out over its surface. The bookshelves around the room were full, not a single bit of space between them – with the exception of the one book she had managed to sneak away last week. She walked through the office and over to the sofa upon which she carefully seated herself to ease the strain on her back from her corset. Amadeus smiled at her as she sat with her usual upright posture, gracefully crossing her legs at the ankles.

"You're so much like your mother," Amadeus said, his voice soft and throaty, "If only she could see you now; how you've grown... the beautiful woman you've become."

She smiled back at him, somewhat uncomfortable. As much as she cared for her father, her deep love and respect seldom surfaced to expression. She felt at a loss whenever someone brought up her mother, especially when he was that someone. She tried to picture her face in her mind, from her little rosy lips to her sad, soulful eyes. A twinge of pain shot through her, but not from her corset; a deep aching in her chest she could not identify. Was it even physical? She pushed the feeling back, wiping the image of her mother clean from her mind.

Amadeus frowned, "I'm sorry. It's your birthday, and I shouldn't be giving you any reason to dwell."

She realized then that she had been frowning as well and quickly regained her composure, as though by way of some sheer, unsounded instinct.

"My daughter, the world is a dark and barren place. It has been wrought with plague, blood, and despair since the *Great War*, and that is why we can never return to live on earthen soil. For the state of the world is the reason you were *branded* at birth. It's best to remain up here among the clouds, where it is safest. I know you wish to see the world for more of what it is; beyond our teachings and the pages of old texts, but my dear, what happened to your mother was..."

His throat caught at these words, and he looked away from her for a moment. "This is why I have never permitted you to go wandering alone. This is why I keep such a close eye on you, and why whenever we've gone ashore, I've *never* allowed you to step foot off this ship!" His glistening eyes met hers again as he continued, gravely. "Do you understand me? One day, I won't be around to keep you safe."

As Amadeus spoke, she could not help but feel a profound sense of emptiness welling up inside her. She did her best to search the recesses of her very core, laying back in her bed or staring off into the clouded distance, losing herself to her many thoughts. Despite long hours of this in silence, her feelings remained incomprehensible, leaving only the burning desire to see more than what she knew. What was she, but a living, breathing machine, whose hands were purposed for the operation and maintenance of other machines? She understood machinery in all its common-sensical simplicity, how this fit into that and which tool to use, yet the apparatus of her own heart eluded her.

She hated the inconsistency her emotions presented, and did her best to analyze them from a scientific angle; just psychophysiological phenomena of an individual's state of mind as per the biochemical and electrical effect of environmental stimuli – nothing more. She briefly touched her fingers to the back of her neck, up under fallen tresses of hair, feeling the raised skin – the mark of her birthright.

Amadeus drew in a deep breath, sighing heavily as he stepped toward the oversized key on the wall, removing it from its display. He clutched the decorative metal loops that made up the key's base with both hands, running his large fingers over its intricate design. He fixed his attention around the circular gemstone at the base's center. "Do you remember the bedtime stories your mother would tell some nights when you were very little?" His eyes still ran the length of the key. "Do you remember what she would say about this very instrument? How I told you after she died that the stories were not real?"

The girl nodded eagerly. While she had long since stopped believing in the magical properties this so-called sacred artifact possessed, she still dreamt of its lavish history. It was the only tangible symbol of the stories, the only means of finding and unlocking the fabled Castle in the Sky. Her mother would recount chronicles of the royal family who ruled peacefully among the clouds, and the thousands of earth dwellers who sought to harness the Castle's magic. Rumor of the Castle's existence eventually brought about the invention of sky ships, and many wars were fought over new technology that would propel humankind toward factual discovery of this mysterious bastion. According to the tales, its inhabitants could not come to harm from outside sources, would not age, and were fed indefinitely from a vast, lush garden that produced ripe fruit every day.

Soon, the Castle would be all but forgotten by most as centuries passed, legend fading to clouded myth, the last gathered efforts dying with the construction of airborne vessels. As the memory of the Castle dulled in the minds of the people, ongoing political differences remained, sending the world's nations asunder in a conflict of apocalyptic proportions. Many took to the skies, high above, to escape nuclear fallout from the widespread bombings. Those who lacked the resources to escape on wings and rockets instead found salvation deep underground.

The elusive Castle and its sovereign family mournfully observed the planet's destruction at the hands of its own people. They could no longer deny their own compassion, and finally it was decreed that their precious key be dropped from the heavens as a gift of deliverance from the horrors of humanity, to unlock the secrets of their imperial abode. This could ensure the survival of all humankind, a noble risk to haunt the family for an eternity should the key fall to malevolent intent. To protect themselves after this sacrifice, they separated the twelve gemstones needed to charge the key and hid them in secret places all over the planet. Only one with the dedication to locate and possess all twelve could harness the Castle's power.

"*It is real,*" Amadeus exclaimed, his voice now hushed with the weight of his words. "All of it!"

The girl's eyes grew wide as she stared at her father. He was the most sensible, practical man she had ever known. It was strange that he would say these things even in jest. She looked at him incredulously as he spoke. If it was true, and not a fairytale story her mother told to keep her innocence alive, she wondered why her father would later tell her otherwise. Her mind raced with questions, none of which she could bring herself to ask. She strained as she watched him, eyes growing glossy as she clenched and unclenched her fists in her lap. It was too much.

Amadeus hurriedly stepped to her side, setting the key down over the empty couch cushion next to her. He knelt beside her, taking her hands into his as he looked her in the eyes. Her brows twitched with discomfort.

"My daughter, this is the gift I give to you! This is your birthday present. Please, do not be upset; I know how difficult this must be for you to understand. What I did, I did for the sake of your own safety! I thought if you no longer believed in the fanciful ideals your mother put into your head, that you wouldn't try to run off, chasing down a *legacy* on your own!"

She pulled away from him, but he gripped her hands firmly.

"I couldn't allow you to end up like your mother! You are all that's left of her!"

Again, she pulled away. This time she escaped her father's hold, raising to her feet and making a mad dash for the door. *Why now? Why would he say this now?*

She flung the door wide and ran up the ship's open deck, strong winds catching her hair and whisking her bun loose. Her fiery locks streamed out behind her like a banner of madness. As she sprinted away she could hear her father calling out her name, but she ignored him and snatched up the skirt of her dress so as not to trip. She passed crewmembers and passengers alike, but did not stop to acknowledge any of them as she ran. It was all a blur, her mind racing with possibilities. She began to reminisce, memory taking her.

Recalling the night of her mother's death was a pain endured only in the most vivid of dreams, but she could no longer keep her thoughts at bay as they flooded over her now with the force of a breaking dam. She remembered her mother coming to tuck her into bed, kissing her and whispering "good night," before slipping off the docked ship alone. She remembered following her, watching her from a distance as she brandished the key in front of her. She remembered the strange light that shot from it, guiding her path as she walked along. She remembered – *No! No, I can't!*

Stopping to catch her breath, the girl threw herself against a corridor wall, pressing her back into the wooden planks behind her. She stood with her hands flat on the wall's surface, her breast heaving in short gasps as her expanding ribcage fought a battle with the laces of her corset. She was very dizzy.

"Miss!" She heard Rivkah's smooth, distinct voice call out, "Miss, your father is looking for you!" Her voice grew closer. Through her foggy, lightheaded vision she was able to make out the slender darker-skinned woman's silhouette to her left.

Rivkah came up in front of her, grabbing her by the shoulders, and gave her a light shake, "Why did you run? What's going on with you?"

She shrugged the woman's hands off her shoulders, raising her palms to her face. Her willowy fingers brushed over her forehead and she swayed slightly as she held her face in her hands. The dizziness was not subsiding.

Rivkah frowned. "Are you alright?"

She leaned into Rivkah and did not stop. Rivkah's hands snapped out to catch her, steadying. The sooty mess from Rivkah's overalls smeared across the girl's dress, blackening the pastel flowers of the garment's design as she pressed into her. As wiry as the slightly taller woman was, she was remarkably soft. Dark curly strands of her hair fell over the girl's face and tickled her cheeks as she held her there. She smelled of maple.

"You shouldn't be racing about like that in a corset! Here, turn for me," she said, grabbing her by the waist and spinning her around. She did not expect this abrupt seizing of her person and found her palms firmly planted against the wall once more. For the second time that evening, she was left feeling indignant by the woman's disarmingly assertive nature. "I'm going to loosen this awful thing for you. You can thank me for it later."

She felt Rivkah forcibly tug at the strings of her corset from behind, sending sharp pains through her ribs and spine with each heave. As she yanked and jerked, the girl could not help but imagine a ripcord being released, inflating her body like a big, bulbous parachute.

"Almost... got it!" Rivkah exclaimed, implementing one final tug before the steel panels stitched into the corset parted enough so that she could breathe normally again. She drew an enormous breath, nearly collapsing with a sharp pain in her lungs while relief flooded the rest of her body. The sound of her own breathing startled her. Rarely had she heard so much as a trace that her vocal chords still existed, not having actively used them since her early childhood.

"All better now?" Rivkah asked, a gentle smile dawning her quietly exotic features.

Before the younger girl could respond, Acanthus came bounding toward them, his face stricken with panic as he yelled for their favor. The girls both whirled around to face him, regarding each other with an alarmed side glance as he continued to shout unintelligibly. It seemed neither could make out what he was saying.

There was a loud bang that shuddered through the entire ship like an earthquake. The explosive force hurled powerful shockwaves down the corridor, parts of the wood splitting apart. Acanthus was sent sprawling to the floor before their feet as they struggled to remain upright.

"It... It's the key!" he panted breathlessly as he looked up at them. "The ship is under attack!"

CHAPTER 3

Incursion

Another explosion erupted through the ship's keel, flinging the two women from their feet. They landed adjacent to Acanthus. Rivkah was on her side, and the younger woman on her back. Acanthus had still been trying to stand from the first blast, to no avail.

"What's going on?" Rivkah yelled, trying to be heard over the loud rumbling of the ship. Screams and shouts resounded from all directions. "Sir, *what* key?"

Finally, Acanthus made himself heard over the noise. "Cannon balls! They're firing cannon balls!"

"Who's *they?*"

No sooner had Rivkah spoken than a large shadow was cast overhead through the awning of the promenade deck. The girls' eyes drifted upward as they lay there, darkness moving over the railing as a large, whale-like object steadily came into view. Their eyes widened as they took in the sight of a massive aircraft, twice the size of their ship but similar in build. It had all the makings of an old military vessel as it flew over them, airborne by way of its distended spherical sails. Netted rope spanned over and throughout the ballooned sails for hundreds of yards, securely fastened to the ship as it soared smoothly above them.

The ship itself was darker, its hull lined with cannons which were aimed for further attack. As the ship moved over them, the redheaded girl was able to make out the crudely painted off-white lettering, messily splattered across the ship's exterior; the *S.S. Beulah*. On either side of the lettering, long makeshift ladders tied together with what looked to be bits of rope and wood billowed in the wind, drifting far out from the ship's centreboard. Much like her father's ship, this vessel was water-to-air. Unlike her father's ship, it was armed enough to lay siege to a small city.

Acanthus reached down, extending a hand to his niece to help her off the floor. She turned her attention to him with a glower, but took hold of his bony fingers which closed firmly around hers. She winced slightly as he pulled her up. "Are you hurt, girl?" he asked, sincere concern in his voice.

The redheaded woman brushed herself off and shook her head.

"We have to be quick," he exclaimed. "Your father has the key!"

"Will someone *please* just tell me what is going on?!" Rivkah bellowed, climbing to her feet. Her honey-smooth voice carried over the chaotic resonance through the atmosphere. The younger woman gazed at her, slightly taken aback. As cool and collected as Rivkah was, she rarely raised her voice, and never with command to an aristocrat.

Acanthus narrowed his eyes at her. "We are under attack. You needn't trouble yourself with anything more than that! Assemble the crew. We *must* defend ourselves!"

Rivkah's face contorted with frustration and concern, clearly wrought with worry. She spared one last lingering glance for the girl, still held tightly by her uncle's hand, before turning and sprinting down toward the opposite end of the corridor.

The girl reached out for her, extending her whole arm as if to motion for her to stop, but it was no use. She felt a firm tug on her other arm by her uncle, forcing her to look back at him. He snarled at her calamitously, his eyes ferocious with discontent.

"Your naïve parents have coddled you long enough, brat!"

Her eyes grew wide with her uncle's words. The same white hot sensation that rose up within her at dinner returned in that moment, and it was all she could do to keep herself submitting to the chaotic cravings of her violent mind. Her heart pounded in her chest amid the danger all around her. He seemed to ignore her rage, turning away from her as he took off across the deck, keeping firm hold of the girl's wrist.

"We must find your father immediately!" Acanthus yelled, the two running along past panicked passengers retreating from the blasts. There were so many loud bangs and so much screaming all around her. Her heart felt as though it had been punctured by a knitting pin, and if it were extracted, she would surely bleed out; all of her pent-up emotions, all of her anguish and anxiety, and all of her physical repression—pouring out of her like a fountain fit to burst and spew.

She carried on, breathless with the calamity of her own nerves as Acanthus yanked her along behind him, her arm now numb from the reckless pulling of a madman on the tattered limb of a ragdoll. Her vision was hazy and she began to cough as smoke filled her eyes, nose, and throat. They were in a maze of splinters and twisted metal. Seething fumes from nearby flames stung her eyes and burned her nostrils. She retched, covering her mouth with her free hand as tears streamed down her face.

Fire? the girl thought to herself. It only took her a moment to recognize her grave mistake, the severity of her surroundings plaguing her mind like a sickness eating at her from the inside. *Oh, no... I left the candle still burning in my room...*

"Amadeus, *what have you done...?*" she heard her uncle say under hushed voice. Once they had gotten away from much of the smoke, he stopped suddenly, causing the girl to stumble into his backside. He stood, unaffected by her impact as he continued to hold her up with his ceaseless iron grip. At least he was steady.

The girl collected herself and peered out from behind Acanthus as he watched over the cover of wreckage from a collapsed wall. Her eyes widened with shell-shocked curiosity as she observed several foreign-looking strangers brandishing weapons and wearing strange clothes, executing each passenger they got their hands on. She looked on with intense fascination and dread as one of the intruders ran a sword through the backside of an elder aristocratic woman, the end of the blade protruding from her chest with what she imagined to be bits of the woman's heart dangling from its edge. She trembled. Never before had she seen such violent acts, except in her own terrible fantasies.

Suddenly the man with the sword looked straight at her as she clutched onto the back of her uncle's dinner suit. He grinned a big toothy grin, flaunting a mouthful of gold gleaming ingots where his teeth should have been. Placing a heavy boot against the now dead woman's rear, he pushed her in their direction, her upper body sliding from the blade with a meaty '*schlunk*.' Her corpse reeled toward them, rolling to a stop before their feet. The girl's tremble grew to near convulsion as she clung to her uncle for dear life. Never before would she have pictured herself looking to him for any form of comfort.

"Well looky 'ere, boys," the man said, his voice scratchy and deep as he wiped the blade off on his ugly black and white vertically striped pants, now streaked red, which clashed terribly with the rest of his oddly assembled garb. "We got an audience! And 'ow would you folks like to be part a' the show?"

Acanthus released his hold on the girl in that moment, shoving her down a closed corridor. She stumbled forward, turning back to spare her uncle a glimpse of uncertainty. "Run! Find your father!" he shouted, waving urgently at her. "I will keep them at bay."

"Don't let 'em get away! Kill err'one onboard!" she heard the gold-toothed man say.

She ran. Blood pounded in her ears, and the noises all around her seemed to fade with the drumming in her head. She gasped and panted, her body numb and her mind on autopilot. Everything was a blur from that instant as she raced back to her father's office. She passed bloodied bodies slumped against walls, or spread motionless across floors. Her head was spinning and she thought she might faint.

Finally she reached her destination. The door was shut. Without a second thought, the girl rammed it ajar with her shoulder and crashed to the ground as it swung open, slamming against the inner wall. She propped herself up, eyes darting wildly around the dark room that had been mostly destroyed. The bookcases were toppled over, torn papers and books strewn all about. The desk was overturned; the sofa had been slashed and stuffing was everywhere.

"Well, well. What's this?" she heard a husky voice say. Her eyes followed it as her head spun around, craning to look to her right. In the corner of the room, she saw her father hunched by the wall as he nursed a deep gash in his side. Standing over him was a man in a dark hooded cape, tall and strong, his features obscured by the gloom and smoke.

"D-d-don't t-touch her!" her father wheezed.

She gasped. She wanted to scream, to cry out for the cloaked man to leave her father alone. She clenched her fists in aggravated alarm, desperate to make herself heard. The corners of her mouth twitched involuntarily as her whole body shook with nerves overloaded.

"This must be your daughter then, yes?" The cloaked man smirked from under his hood, a slight chuckle as he made his way toward her. The man moved swiftly, taking the girl by surprise as he appeared over her now. She recoiled with his sudden movement, but she was too late to stop him. With a fistful of the girl's loose orangey-red hair, he hoisted her up and backed her hard against the far wall, the back of her head connecting solidly with a loud thump. She winced, dazed, as he held her there. A large jagged dagger pressed into her neck, and she could smell her father's blood still fresh on the blade.

"D-Demetrius... We had a d-d-deal..." Amadeus coughed, a trickle of blood running down his chin from the corner of his mouth. His skin was ghostly pale, his face covered with beads of perspiration. "L-let her go!"

"That was before I knew you had the *key* onboard," the man now identified as Demetrius retorted, an evil sneer opening his face through the hood as he spoke. "This is the last time I'm going to tell you; show me where you hid it – or I slice her wide."

He pressed the blade into her neck, the harsh steel stinging her skin as it cut into her flesh. She grimaced, her eyes welling up with tears as she narrowed her brows. More rage. She detested this man more than she detested her uncle.

"W-wait!" Amadeus heaved. "I'll... I'll tell you..."

Demetrius smirked, releasing the girl abruptly. She dropped to the floor once more in a twisted heap, propped upright on one arm. She massaged the back of her head and neck with her other hand, crying softly, without making a sound. *What deal?* she thought to herself, her mind racing with panic-induced fervor. *What is happening?!*

Amadeus coughed, extending a shaky finger to the couch. He pointed to the shredded cushions, indicating the key had been stowed underneath. "P-please..." he gagged, more blood falling from his mouth as he tried to speak. "Just t-t-take it and leave us be..."

A deep sinister laugh was all Demetrius spared as he made his way to the couch. He grabbed it deftly by its arm and flipped it over completely using only his right hand, which appeared to be gloved by a metallic, machinelike carapace. Picking the key up off the ground with the same hand, he wielded it like a sword, its gemstone fixed at the base gleaming in the dimly lit room.

"After my men have sufficiently entertained themselves with your passengers, we'll be off your pathetic little ship. And I'll be taking this with me!" he spat, turning the key over in his hand to admire its intricate detail. "I hope that's not a problem."

"Y-You b-b-bastard," Amadeus sputtered.

The girl convulsed as she wept. Her tears stung her eyes as they streamed down her cheeks, pooling around her trembling fingers placed firmly against the floorboards. She dug her nails into the wood, twitching slightly with the sheer magnitude of her careening emotions. She gritted her teeth as she tried desperately to center herself, involuntarily rocking back and forth. How she wished she could do something, anything, to reach outside herself; to stretch thin the fibers of her very being and break free of her own self-imposed prison.

Demetrius held the key out in front of him with his gloved metal hand as the other emerged from the folds of his cloak. His left arm was wrapped from his forearm to his fingers with dark gauzed fabric as he waved it out flat over the gemstone; "*Illumná Çassel tu wa Çuau,*" he chanted. His voice was deep, his words slow. He waited. Nothing happened.

Amadeus chuckled slightly, a resonance emerging as more of a gurgle than a laugh. He choked on his own blood which continued to spill from his mouth, wheezing, as he looked up at the cloaked man. "The g-gemstone is turquoise," he said, breathlessly.

Demetrius snarled. "What the hell is *that* supposed to mean?!"

"S-Surely you h-h-have not forgotten," Amadeus replied, "O-o-only ch-children of the stone can activate it!" He turned his gaze to his daughter, as if to convey hidden intent.

What is he on about? the girl wondered, her face contorted with grief and worry as she continued to sob in silence. She tried to recall important details long forgotten, but to no avail could she remember ever having heard this from her mother.

From under his hood, only the infuriated curling of upper lip could be seen as Demetrius lowered the key to be eye level with the girl on the floor. She watched him, shaking, wondering whether he might try to grab her again. She knew he returned her gaze, though she could not meet his hidden eyes. She felt him staring back at her, sending chills down her spine as he stood there in a moment's pause.

"Your daughter," Demetrius spoke, his back to Amadeus as he continued to face the girl down. "She and Rose shared the same birthday, yes?"

"I-I-It's no use," Amadeus stuttered, "Sh-She cannot speak!"

Oh, All Mother, what is happening? What are they talking about?!

Demetrius tossed her the key. It made a loud clattering noise against the hard wood of the floor and stopped in front of her. The sound of the key falling and the silence that followed brought back the distant shrieks and loud bangs around other parts of the ship, which had previously been drowned out by the incessant pounding in her head. Her heart still raced, adrenaline screaming through her veins. She looked up at the cloaked man, confused.

"Say the words," he said, stepping back to her father's side without looking away from her. He brandished his jagged dagger once more, pressing the point into the wounded man's cheek as he lay slumped against the wall on the floor. He flinched away but Demetrius kept it pressed firmly into his skin. "If you don't, your father will die."

Her eyes grew wide and her pupils dilated. She started to hyperventilate. The corners of her mouth twitched as her tremulous fingers wrapped around the length of the key. She had never touched it before. Her hands clenched and unclenched as she now held that which caused the death of her beloved mother. She strained, working her throat to the best of her ability to make a sound. *Any* sound. Her blood was on fire, her gullet aching and yearning. She pushed with all her might to force a cry from her frail little body, the fuming, fiery essence which threatened to erupt from within her. Try as she might, she could not make a sound.

"Such a selfish little girl you are," Demetrius taunted, "that you would forsake your own father."

No! Please, no! I can do it, I can!

She raised a single hand to her throat, her jaw verging to unhinge with the desperate gaping of her mouth. She pressed against her esophagus as if to give physical account to the profound mental block which kept her from uttering a word. She tried hopelessly to fool her senses, that she might gasp or grunt, that it would be the beginnings so urgently needed to save her father. As her tension ran higher, she could not seize control of her ability to speak.

"No matter," Demetrius smirked wickedly. "If you won't be my vessel, I can simply find someone who *will* be."

No! No, no, no, no, NO!

The girl's eyes met with her father's. Amadeus gave her one final nod, reassuring; apologetic. His eyes were ghastly hues in that icy moment, as though he knew he was about to be left an empty husk. The events which followed were slowed to a surreal dither as she watched in terror, the cruel dagger plunging savagely into his throat, letting loose a fountain of arterial blood. It took all but a fragment of a second, but to her, the movement of time itself had decelerated.

The girl screamed with all her might as she watched her father slump to the floor, his deep red blood pooling out under his head and spilling from the corners of his mouth. She screamed again, horror and agony taking her, as she saw the light fade from his eyes. Her shriek was magnified by the white-hot rage exploding from her core. Even still, her tremendous cries remained locked in silence. Even in the face of death, she could not break free of herself.

She felt her senses shutting down as she began to black out, surrendering herself to her psychosis. It was as if she were suddenly floating, drifting through the blackness all around her. Her ties to this world were now severed. There was nothing to hold her back, nothing to prevent the sanctioning of her own twisted subconscious. Again, she saw horrific things play behind her eyelids – tearing flesh from bone, bone from limb, causing unimaginable trauma to bring the physical world purity. It was great suffering she conceived would be the great equalizer; the perfect cleanser.

Suddenly she was wrenched back from her wicked hallucinations.

With a gust of wind, she snapped back to a cognitive state, the chilly evening air briskly whisking through her hair as she realized that she had been running. She clutched the key with both hands, close to her body, as she made her way aft toward the bridge of the ship. She could no longer hear the screams of passengers. Fires had spread all throughout the expanse of wreckage which spanned as far as she could see. She only stopped running once she had reached the nearest edge of the ship. Looking down, all she could see was an endless breadth of clouds.

"I found 'er!" she heard a deep, scratchy voice cry out. She whirled around to see who it was. Standing a few yards away from her, she saw the man with the golden teeth. He reached into his vertically striped pants and pulled out a pistol, cocking the hammer back. He aimed the firearm at her with a big, golden grin.

She flinched, taking a step backward, the heel of her fine lace boot knocking against the damaged railing. She felt part of it fall away into oblivion, though she dared not turn her gaze. She seldom saw a real gun in person and to have one aimed at her now was almost more than she could take. She held up the giant key in front of her defensively, as if to shield herself from an anticipated bullet.

"Cap'n!" the gold-toothed man called out again, averting his eyes for but a single second in a sidelong glance. "Do ye 'ear me? I got 'er!" He looked back at her, fiendishly.

"Aye, the little bitch darted off after I took care of her father," Demetrius snarled, coming up behind the much shorter man. He stepped to his side, his teeth gritted. "I *need* that key!"

The girl narrowed her eyes, her glance darting between the two of them as she extended the key outward, toward them. She mimicked the same movements she saw Demetrius making with his hands when he had apparently attempted to tap into its power. She mimed desperately, hoping above all hope that she might unlock a powerful counterattack in her honest ignorance.

"The men 'ave all returned to ol' *Beulah*," the gold-toothed man said. "This piece'a scrap'll be goin' up in smoke soon, Cap'n."

Demetrius glowered. "There is nowhere left for you to run, you foolish girl. I'm not interested in playing games. Hand over the key, now!"

The girl's efforts were in vain. Her dried, tear-stained cheeks flushed red with fury. Once again her heart pounded in her chest, adrenaline pumping through her veins as she stared the men down. Winding back the key like a sword, she charged at them with wild determination.

Reacting quickly, the gold-toothed man pulled the trigger.

The bullet spiraled from the barrel of the gun with a loud bang, penetrating her flank with incredible force, knocking her off her feet and throwing her body into the air. She plummeted headlong off the side of the ship.

CHAPTER 4

Bern, the Archer

A black abyss shrouded the girl's subconscious, her mind unsheathed by the confines of her body. She felt weightless and infinite in the dark haze cast over her, without a care in the world. She floated motionlessly; sightlessly, the stillness of her intangible surroundings setting her to endless ease. As she drifted through space, her thoughts took on abstract meaning. She mused not with an understanding of the human language, but now with the many colors of her own emotion; her own sense of being.

She *was*, therefore, she knew she existed – even though her very subsistence was defined by the kaleidoscopic thoughts tumbling through her, not distinguished by anything more than neurons transmitting electrochemical signals. She embraced the cool, quiet dark; the ever slightest glimmer of cavern crystals reflecting light over her optic nerves. Suddenly she felt herself twitch slightly in response to the physical detection of a light source. Though her mind processed her surroundings as much akin to being lost in a cave, she was soon able to piece together more concrete thought formation, such as; *Where am I?*

Certainly, it was not in a cave. Soon she realized her eyes were just closed as the light expanded, washing over her in blaring fiery white, causing her to squint slightly even through shut eyelids with the harshness of the sun's rays. *The sun!* she thought to herself, finally realizing the source of the glare. With this realization came a swiftly mounting wave of heat as her senses steadily returned to her. Much to her dismay, she was regaining consciousness. Slowly but surely, her limbs recovered their sensation. Her arms and legs flinched involuntarily in acknowledgement of the environmental temperature.

She wriggled her fingers, digging into hot, dry sand. Carefully, she turned her body to her right, rolling over onto her side. It was then that all the pain returned with a vengeance, her back and neck stiff, her skin now deeply sunburned, and her side below her ribs palpably injured – to what degree, she knew not. Her long red hair was matted with perspiration, a few of the wet strands falling over her face as she moved with a silent grunt. She felt sticky; grungy. Her dress was torn and dirty. The air was dry and still, a far cry from the breezy winds of the skies above the clouds. No longer facing the sun's severe rays, she wearily began to open her eyes.

Sand. As far as her impaired vision would allow, rolling dunes of golden sand. She cautiously propped herself up on one elbow, wincing with pain. The memory of the night before weighed upon her like a crushing boulder, and she realized then that she was truly alone. Bitter tears welled up in her eyes to combat the dryness of her throat, but her deep sadness produced few droplets as the throes of dehydration began to set in. With an agonized push, she struggled to her feet. She noticed then, to her left, the key partially covered by sand as it lay perfectly intact.

How did I survive the fall? And the gunshot? she pondered, taking a moment to survey her condition. She looked down at her body to examine herself, twisting her torso slightly with a grimace, her hands moving over the taut fabric of her moderately loosened corset. Her fingers brushed over the entry point of the bullet to find that it had been stopped by her corset's steel boning. Part of the paneling was dented and exposed, but otherwise unbroken. She felt around the area further, gritting her teeth with pain as she imagined a tender welted bruise had surfaced on her skin, though she was unable to tell for sure.

Well, that explains the gunshot…

Her eyes drifted downward, resting over the key. She stood there for a moment, considering, before finally reaching down to pick it up. More pain. Ignoring her body's protest, she took the key up in her arms and began to trudge forth toward the sun. As she walked, she could feel the sun's rays slowly cooking her skin, her bare shoulders a deep, throbbing shade of red as she marched on. Although she had little sense of direction for where she was headed, she knew the positioning of the sun would soon tell her east from west as it moved to set. What she could not tell, however, was how much time passed since it had risen.

She walked in complete silence, on and on, the stagnant hot air wearing down on her as she pressed forward. She walked for what felt like hours without seeing so much as the slightest change in her surroundings. Craning her aching neck around to look behind her as she walked, she could see her footprints for miles before they disappeared behind the rise and fall of sand dunes. It was the one advantage that the absence of a breeze afforded her – at least her tracks were left undisturbed so she had somewhat an idea of the distance she had walked. Then her eyes grew wide in that moment, comprehending yet another grave and thoughtless error.

They'll come looking for me.

She stopped walking, whirling around completely to observe the long trail tracks her boots had made in the sand. Sighing hopelessly, she glanced all around. *Now what am I going to do?*

Then, something in the distance caught her eye. More tracks – but they were not her own. She changed route, heading toward the tracks which looked to be another set of boot prints. She trudged onward, the key still cradled in her arms, its load heavier in her weakened state as she dragged her boots drawing ever nearer.

Just a few yards away now, she silently panted, almost limping with exhaustion. She had never known such pain and physical discomfort in all her life. She thought back to her childhood, how simple everything was; how her parents sheltered her from all the world's suffering. How she wished she could go back to those years.

Finally she had reached the imprints in the sand, noting that the boot tracks were larger than her own; two sets of feet she now pursued with weary resolve. She followed them for quite some time, fueled by the hope she would find someone who could help her. The tracks seemed to go on and on. Soon, her surroundings began to show variance as the sand dunes all around displayed the accompaniment of numerous rocks and boulders, and even a dirt trail.

Oh, thank goodness.

Relieved by the change in scenery, she pressed forward feeling a renewed sense of security that she would find some form of civilization soon. But as she walked on, she noticed the prints along the trail stopped up ahead. She wondered why this could be as she cautiously approached, her legs gliding over the footprints like a vagrant in the stride of a safe travel companion. When the tracks came to an end, she decided to continue walking.

As her foot came upon the first bit of dirt trail devoid of the boot imprints she had previously followed, she felt a slight unevenness in the terrain. She was too fatigued to pay this any mind. When she put her full weight down, the ground concaved underneath the pressure, sending her sprawling down a trap hole. Her fall was stopped by a tangling net which closed around her upon impact, leaving her trapped several feet below the broken surface. A downpour of sand followed, and she coughed, raising her arms to protect her face inside the netting.

"Hey, hey," came a low voice a few moments later, "we caught somethin'!"

The girl was unable to see through the confines of the net and the sand in her eyes. She tried to wriggle herself so that she was facing upright. Even then, the man the voice belonged to was not close enough that she would be able to see him.

"Looks like a little lost kitten," came another low voice. She could *hear* the slight smirk which undoubtedly accompanied his words. "Let's get a closer view, eh?"

A few short grunts and she could feel herself being hoisted up out of the hole, the net tightening all around her twisted body with each heaving pull. The two men dragged her out onto the dirt trail, her backside scraping against the ground further ripping her dress. She could not make out their full features. What she did notice was that they each appeared to be quite grungy, their ragged attire encrusted with dirt. Both men were of average build and had not shaved for maybe weeks. Their hair was dirty and unkempt, the rest of their features obscured by the sand in her eyes and her own hair now matted around her face with the tightened net's constriction.

What do they want with me? she thought, her heart racing in her chest. Her breaths came out as soft, silent whimpers as her fear mounted with anticipation of what these men might do to her. This was her first unescorted encounter with an earth dweller, let alone two cretinous would-be captors whose motives were yet unknown. She watched them nervously, her obstructed eyes darting between the two with building dread.

"It's been a while since we had a woman. This is gonna be real good!" one of them said.

"Been a while since we had anything; and don't go gettin' too excited just yet," the other replied, "Quite possible this one's got some hair on 'er. She got a full head a' hair and we haven't seen the rest. She could be a hirsute underneath them clothes fer all we know."

All Mother…!

"Heh. Now look what you've gone and done; you've frightened the kitten…"

"Poor little kitty. Ahh, well; fear ain't gonna change her flavor or nothin', but I do hope she ain't a furry one. No need to fret none, puss," the man said to her with a glint in his eye. By now she had struggled through her confines enough to just barely make out their faces. "It'll all be over soon."

My All Mother; please, help me!

Both men now brandished long knives and began advancing on her. She thrashed about with all her might, rolling around violently in a desperate attempt to fend them off and break free from the net. Her efforts were in vain. The harder she fought, the more tangled she became. Grunting and panting, she wished she could only scream; cry out for help, that someone, anyone, would come to her rescue.

Two arrows cut through the stillness in the air with a crisp whistle and simultaneously pierced through their skulls with a dull, fleshy '*thunk.*' Both men wavered a second or two before collapsing deadweight against the dirt ground—lifeless. It took the girl a few moments to register what had happened. She now lain very still, hearing the jingling of chains coming up from behind her. She tried to quiet her breathing but by this point there was little she could do to keep from hyperventilating in her panicked state.

They're going to kill me! the girl anxiously thought, *I've got to get out of this; oh All Mother, please!* She heard the chains jingle with each clomping footstep, and they were nearly upon her. She shut her eyes tight, teeth gritted as she listened to the sound of her heart pulsating in her chest. The sensation pounded through her head. She felt dizzied; nauseous. There was a slight tug on the netting from behind and she flailed, hopelessly.

"Hold still," a woman's voice soothed, "I'm not going to hurt you."

She could feel the net's ropes gradually snap undone with the sound of a dagger scraping against its hemming. She warily relaxed her tensed body as the mysterious woman went to work, slowly cutting away the means of her imprisonment. Soon enough she was freed, the woman tossing the severed portion of the net to the side. The rest fell away about the girl as she sat upright, turning to look over her shoulder, brushing tatty strands of hair away from her face.

She gazed up at her female savior and took in her striking appearance; deep auburn hair as long as hers, weaved into rows of tight braids which set close to the frame of her scalp. Deep hazel eyes that stood out from lightly tanned skin, further darkened by remnants of soil on her face. Chiseled bone structure complimenting a tall, buxom physique, intimidating in stature with her sleeveless brown duster which fell past her boots to drag on the ground behind her. The boots she wore had thick, clunky chains which crossed at the front, connecting at the back. She returned her dagger to its makeshift sheath strapped to her hip by tied-together belts, the blade slipping neatly through a pair of ornate buckles. Lacing her fingers, she reached her arms up over her head in a stretch.

"You're lucky I came by when I did," she said, arms still raised. As her torso elongated with her stretch, the girl noticed a single bow and quiver peeking out from behind her, strapped to her back. "Those were *subterrans*. They would have eaten you."

The girl's eyes fluttered, not quite grasping what she had said. Her mind was fixed on the woman's quiver; what advanced skill it must take to shoot two arrows from the same bow at once, each hitting their mark with lethal accuracy.

"So? Got a name?"

A name! How was she to give her a name? The girl scrambled around for a moment in silence as the woman stood over her, her hands now resting on her hips as she awaited an answer. She decided to try writing her name with her fingers. Anxiously, she began digging her fingertips into the sand, etching each letter to the best of her ability despite her rattled nerves. She worked quickly, her fingers gliding through displaced sand as she tried her best to make her chickenscratch legible. Once she had finished, she looked back up at the woman who only shook her head.

"I can't read that," she replied plainly.

The girl looked up at her under furrowed brows, cocking her head slightly in confusion.

"I never learned to read, that's why," the woman said without missing a beat. "I take it you must be mute – such a pity. I was hoping you might be able to explain a thing or two about *that*."

She pointed to the key several feet away which had been strewn on the ground once more. The girl flung it aside without realizing upon falling victim to the trap hole. Without standing, she reached over to grab it, cradling it in her arms as before.

"In any case," the woman continued, "my name is Abernathy LaCroix—but I hate it—so, please call me *Bern*. That is, should you ever miraculously find your voice enough to do so."

The girl nodded somberly, forcing a weak, polite smile as she looked up at Bern. Carefully she struggled to her feet, placing the key's hilt firmly on the ground to use as leverage for which to stand. Her knees shook, and she winced with more pain. She thought she might have twisted her ankle, balancing her weight distribution on one foot more than the other to test first. Once she was satisfied that she could at least amble and still keep pace, only then did she stand upright to face the imposing woman before her. Even when standing, Bern still seemed to tower over her.

She smiled, looking the girl over, her hands still on her hips. "Hmm. As worse for wear as you look now, those clothes of yours were very nice at one point. You wouldn't happen to be an aristocrat, would you?"

The girl hesitated, but nodded affirmatively.

"Ha! I knew it!" she said with a grin. But suddenly her smile faded, her eyes focusing on the girl's chest. Adorning her bosom was a small sapphire brooch, baring the emblem of her family's crest. The girl noticed what Bern was looking at and worriedly raised a hand to clasp around it.

"...But you're not *just* an aristocrat... are you," Bern said, now looking very serious as she spoke, "You're from up there! You're a *skylark*... aren't you."

Again, the girl hesitantly nodded. Bern gestured with her eyes, eagerly encouraging her to lower her hand. Her expression was unreadable; disconcerted. She knew not what to think of the much taller woman who saved her just moments ago. It was all happening too fast, but she felt strangely compelled by her prevailing assertiveness. She falteringly let go of her brooch, allowing Bern a closer gander. A few seconds was all it took.

"I... I recognize this symbol. You are nobility; you hold the rank of Viscountess! But what is someone like you doing *alone*, on land, in broad open daylight? Are you trying to get yourself killed?! Surely you know how dangerous it is, especially for someone like you..."

Another nod. She felt her nausea rising, her nerves in a knot.

Bern sighed. "Look. I can take you back to where I'm going. You'll be somewhat safe there; at least far more so than being stranded out here. It's a bit of a walk. Can you handle that?"

The girl could feel more tears welling up in her eyes. She felt very much at a loss, relieved, and overwhelmed all at once. Again her emotions were jumbled up inside her and bursting at the seams, and there was nothing she could say, no amount of reasoning she could express, that would help either Bern or herself to understand. She simply nodded again, in response.

"Okay. Walk directly in front of me, and I'll lead you from behind."

Bern motioned in the direction she wanted her to walk. The girl resituated the key in her arms and steadily resumed stride as before, but with renewed vigor. She glanced over her shoulder, watching Bern with an air of lingering uncertainty. It was then that she noticed the woman's duster trailing over the ground behind her, erasing their tracks in the sand as they continued along the path. The leather fabric had been lined with metal to weigh down its fringe.

"We're fine, Viscountess. Don't worry. Just keep moving."

The Viscountess nodded once more, and the two carried on, amiably, in silence.

CHAPTER 5

Entitled

With deep guzzling swallows, the Viscountess knocked back hurried swigs of lukewarm water from a tin bucket. The water had a slightly minerally aftertaste which would normally have revolted her, but in her state of severe dehydration, the water could not have hit her throat quickly enough to appease her.

"The water we get needs to be boiled," Bern said, sitting across from her in a broken wooden chair. She had since taken off her duster and chained boots, wearing only a man's vest tied at the front with a bootlace through loops and weathered brown overalls. "It isn't the greatest, but it's safe to drink. It's all I have to offer you right now."

There was a small pause, as she watched the girl drink.

"…You've slept most of the day away since we arrived. Do you remember where you are?"

The Viscountess set the tin bucket down on the end table beside the bed she laid in, having downed the last of the water. She thought for a moment, reflecting on the events that followed her initial awakening in the desert; Bern's direction to the small colony of people they now stayed with, a town left mostly untouched in its desolate settlement. She remembered drifting in and out of consciousness, her blackouts brought on by her exhaustion in the intense heat. At one point, she recalled Bern's arm around her, supporting her weight as the two walked.

She glanced around the room they were in, vaguely remembering her surroundings and the proceedings leading up to her being allowed to remain where she now stayed. She remembered the town gate; a barred steel entrance enclosed by a blockade of cement wall. The wall ran the expanse of the whole town, closing its residents in. She imagined this to be a post-war development that must have taken a very long time to build. She also hazily recalled an argument between Bern and a small group of presumed townspeople with paperwork about letting her in. She seemed to remember an instance where her brooch had been grabbed at, and shown. The number '*642*' also stuck out in her mind, though she could not make sense of why…

But where was her *key* in all this? She let out a silent gasp, patting the bed sheets around her. She gazed around the room, stricken with worry as she scanned all corners of the area. Her heart skipped a beat when its presence was not readily apparent in the quaint, rustic living space she assumed to be Bern's home.

"If you are looking for your key, they have taken it," Bern said, her expression flat; her words matter-of-factly. "It's standard procedure for new arrivals, that they be stripped of all their belongings until it is deemed that they are of no risk."

The Viscountess looked down at herself. Her clothes were gone too, now replaced with a peasant's nightgown. Her long red hair fell loose about her shoulders and over her chest, trailing down her back in damp, matted locks. "They took your clothes, too. Don't worry, though… I saw to you myself. You needed a wash, so I gave you a sponge bath and combed out your hair with a rinse. It was nothing, so no need to be embarrassed."

She was mortified. Her arms involuntarily rose up to meet with her body, wrapping around herself protectively, as futile as the act in doing so was. She was aghast over this woman whom she only just met; how she paid such little attention to the importance of social etiquette. Had she no shame? Bern's demeanor suddenly changed as she observed the Viscountess's visible dismay. Her body language, previously read as cordial reserve, contorted to mild annoyance. Their difference in societal class became more and more apparent with each passing moment.

"You needn't think of me as some kind of savage," Bern said sharply, clearly not one to be made to feel the lesser by the insecurities of another; especially when these insecurities were brought on by the remnants of societal hierarchy. "I do what is necessary – just as it was *necessary* that I saved you. I follow a moral code. Do you know what that means?"

The Viscountess slowly shook her head, relaxing her tensed posture as Bern spoke. She could not help but feel somewhat shamed by her own instinctual reaction. She realized in that moment that she was predisposed toward feelings of pride and self-importance. The nobility of the title which now defined her, in the end, was just that – a mere title.

Bern continued, her tone less severe with the Viscountess's rescinded demeanor. "It is my self-appointed duty to patrol the far outskirts of this town, to guide wanderers in need to the safety of our walls. My code is quite simple. I tend to the weak, for I am strong; I deliver the light, for the world is dark. Part of my code entitles me to discernment, as I have the unenviable task of deciding whether the life of another is worth the lives of *two more*."

The Viscountess narrowed her brows, taking in what Bern was saying. *Entitles?* she thought, the word sitting ill with her as she related it to herself, and her own life of privilege.

"I've killed for you, Viscountess," Bern went on, after brief pause, "Could I have aimed my bow to injure, and not slay? Of course I could. But where would that have left your attackers? They'd have suffered in the desert, dying a far more agonizing death from their wounds, or if they lived, they would then be free to continue cannibalizing innocent vagrants as before. Taking this to mind, what *then* would you have had me do differently?"

The woman was very well-spoken. She seemed rehearsed in the justifying of her own actions, as though her way had been questioned many a time before. Even still, there was no arguing with her reasoning. The Viscountess merely lowered he head in a small nod, silently considering. She felt somewhat overwhelmed, her mind broadened in a manner which catered to her emotions and not her mechanical intellect. Never was she in a place to think of such things before. Her mind drifted to her family, and the people whom she shared her space with for years and years...

Though passengers would come and go, there were select few who remained constant through time and travel. *Madame Beatrice*, she thought. As unlikely a prospect as it was to hope for survivors to have somehow escaped from her father's ship, she knew there was no way they could have lived through an aerial explosion, or later, a collision with land. All were probably dead, and there was nothing she could do now but come to terms with that fact. She must have appeared dispirited as she dwelled, because Bern had moved from her seat to kneel by the side of her bed.

"Let's not worry about these things now," she said. Though she had not smiled, her eyes were soft and comforting in that moment, and it was as though her tenderness were all in her gaze. "The pub will be open soon. If you feel enough rested that you might like to join me, I'll be going for a drink. It is the one vice I allow myself; figure I've earned it after today, what do you think? Come with me. It'll do you some good."

The Viscountess had never been allowed to consume alcoholic beverages, her options limited to teas and juices per her father's careful monitoring as advised by her uncle. Acanthus trusted her inebriated judgment about as little as her potential, manning her own vessel while sober. She turned the idea over in her mind for a moment, though it did not take her long to come to a decision, nodding in affirmation.

I could use a drink, she thought to herself, though uncertain of her own whims. The closest she had ever gotten to a drink was a whiff of her father's bourbon once when she was very little. She recalled a burning sensation in her nose that made her eyes water, a most unpleasant experience.

"I'm glad you're willing to come out with me later tonight," Bern said, rising to her feet. She walked out of the room for a moment, passing over the threshold of the open archway connecting the bedroom to the kitchen. There was the sound of the opening and closing of cabinets and clattering pangs followed by abrupt rustling. She returned a few seconds later, a peasant's dress and bodice in hand. "Here," she said, tossing the garments to the Viscountess, who clumsily caught them in her arms. "You'll be needing clothes to wear, so you can have these."

The Viscountess looked down at the slightly wrinkled garments. They looked like they had not been worn in years, the faint scent of mothballs permeating throughout the folds of the fabric.

"I hate dresses," Bern said, with a stern expression. "It belonged to my sister. She... was about your size."

Looking back up at her, the Viscountess searched for traces of bereavement in Bern's hardened features. The woman was a puzzle to her, with many pieces missing. It was terribly hard to read her, but then, she had little handle on sorting out her own feelings as well. She sat there in silence for a moment before shrugging her shoulders slightly, following an apologetic smile and nod. She hoped it would be gesture enough. She felt a little awkward wearing someone else's clothes.

Bern returned the nod. "Well... I'll leave you to get dressed, then. We should try to get there a bit early; wouldn't want to miss the big fight."

CHAPTER 6

The Rogue Musket

Fight?! *What on earth is she talking about?* The Viscountess mulled over Bern's words with feelings of impending doom. She had seen a lot of violence in the past day and she was unsure whether she could handle bearing witness to more, as violent as her own thoughts sometimes were. She walked behind the taller woman, her duster trailing over the ground as before; though it was apparent she now wore it for aesthetic appeal more than anything else. Absent were her bow and quiver. The sun was setting behind the clouds in the distant sky above, and the Viscountess gazed up longingly over the rooftops of residential buildings they passed by. Lit candles sat in each window in preparation for nightfall.

"The dress fits you well," Bern said, without looking back at her. "You look just like her."

She knew she meant her sister when she spoke. Not really certain how to feel about Bern's words, the Viscountess looked down at herself. The bodice fit snuggly around her bust, the sleeves long and off the shoulder, similar to her floral print dress which had been confiscated along with her other belongings. The dress she now wore was long, falling over her boots; the only articles of clothing that had not been taken away. Before they left, Bern told her that prior-owned shoes were often allotted to new residents, as footwear was difficult to come by.

Before too long, they came upon a large well-lit building with double doors. A sign hanging from the awning read: *The Rogue Musket*. They could hear the sounds of rambunctious hoots and chatter from men inside the bar, all talking loudly over a saloon piano playing inside. The Viscountess gulped back a knot in her throat to meet with her knotted nerves.

Bern turned back to look at her finally with raised brow. "Don't look so frightened," she said coolly, "This may be a rowdy bunch, but they're all decent people. You'll be fine."

As they approached, they came by a man leaning against the outer wall of the pub. He tipped his hat, giving them a nod, "Evenin', Berny. Who's yer little ladyfriend here?"

Bern reached an arm around the Viscountess's shoulder, slapping her hand down lightly against her back. The Viscountess winced with pain, her deep sunburn tingling with the stinging sensation of the woman's sudden tap. "She's my date for tonight," she replied, a subtle wry smirk playing at the corners of her mouth. "So, hands off."

The Viscountess flushed red with embarrassment and dismay, which went unnoticed under the burns of her skin. Her discomfort only grew with Bern's odd grin, which she found to be strangely unsettling. This woman hardly smiled since they met, but this particular expression sent chills down the girl's spine. She hoped the date comment was in jest, but she could not tell. Little did it matter anyway as Bern guided her through the double doors of the pub, her hand still on her back, firmly pushing her along.

As they stepped through into the pub, they were greeted with cheers all down the ends of the bar. All eyes were on Bern as glasses raised and hats tipped. She was quite the popular commodity. "Bern!" a man with scraggly shoulder-length hair exclaimed, running from the far end of the bar to greet her. He was shorter than Bern and only slightly taller than the Viscountess, wearing shaggy, dirty clothes which seemed to offset his shaggy, dirty-blonde tresses. Apart from appearing so unkempt in dress, he seemed rather mild in stature with notably soft features. His smooth skin and babyface appeal made it hard for the Viscountess to think of him as a man, but instead, a boy. He played quite the contrast to the rough-and-tumble brutes of the bar. Even the pianist in the corner looked considerably rugged by comparison.

"Hello, Blythe." Bern greeted the man. "Have the fights started?"

"No, you're just in time! It'll be a few minutes yet; everyone's getting drinks," he replied, with the same energetic enthusiasm. "Roland and Alasdair are in the pit. Orel and Kael are sitting this one out though."

"I'm not surprised, with the way Kael fought last week," Bern chuckled. "How is his eye?"

"Better. We caught it early and Orel patched him up pretty good, but it got a little infected. He's since healed up for the most part, but I don't think his sight will ever be the same." Blythe averted his eyes, fixating on the Viscountess in that moment. He looked her up and down, apathetically. "Who's she?"

"She's a Viscountess," Bern replied. "She can't speak."

"Oh," he said, leaving it at that. "Well, follow me. I'll take you to the rest of the boys."

The Viscountess felt somewhat slighted, making her mind up that she did not like this dirty little 'manboy' in shoddy threads. As they walked through the pub she stayed close to Bern, falling in step behind the heavy jingling clomps of her boots against wooded floor. The Viscountess crinkled her nose as they passed by the bar, the various smells and odors permeating through the air enough to make her feel ill. Everyone in the pub looked sweaty, grungy, and generally unkempt – and none of them seemed to mind one another.

As they gradually made their way through the boisterous crowd, the Viscountess trying her best not to accidentally brush against or bump into someone, an abrupt dip in the floorboards came into view. There was a large gathering of men already surrounding the circular crater just several feet away, which appeared to take up most of the pub's space. It was difficult to see around so many bodies, but she supposed it to be a little over six feet deep; maybe seven. She caught a fleeting glimpse of several very tough-looking men assembling at the center of the pit as they passed by, but her attention was immediately drawn away as she almost bumped into Bern from behind, soon realizing that she had come to a stop.

"There they are," she heard Blythe say, who had also stopped from around Bern who was gesturing in a wave over at the far end of the bar. "We've all missed you!"

They approached two other men leaning against the bar perched on stools. One of the men was markedly short, with a stocky build and broad shoulders. He had a deep complexion and a mane of long, dark hair. He was shirtless with a leather vest, and large jagged scars were visible all down and across his impressively muscled chest and abdomen. Much like Blythe, his skin appeared otherwise smooth to the touch, though his features were quite angular; masculine. His left eye looked moderately bruised, a deep cut running the length of his brow.

The other man looked slightly older with a head of short, but bushy, graying hair. His legs were crossed in a gentlemanlike fashion, which looked odd given their surroundings. He seemed of slightly nervous disposition, readjusting his spectacles over the bridge of his nose and thumping his leg in rapid succession. He wore a long-sleeved button-up shirt with trousers, and scuffed brown shoes.

"Yo, Bern!" the shorter man called out, raising a half-full glass of frothy golden beverage the Viscountess presumed to be alcoholic. "How've you been, love?"

"I am *nobody's* love," Bern replied with a scowl.

"Lighten up, honey, you know I like to tease you," he said, setting the glass down. "Everyone's really missed havin' you around. Not many ladyfolk comin' round this bar!"

The Viscountess began to wonder how long Bern had been out of town, roving the surrounding desert plains. Had she really been searching for more people, lost as she? On her own, no less. She looked up at her with continually growing admiration. Rivkah, before her, had been the only other woman she had known to harbor such independent resolve. She longed to be like them both; so confident and self-assured – all the things she was not. In her own silent musings she suddenly realized Bern had stepped aside, and now they were all staring at her. Her eyes fluttered wide with startled apprehension.

"My, my, my," the shorter man said with a disarmingly large grin as he turned his attention away from Bern. He set his drink down, hopping off the bar stool and stepped up to the Viscountess, taking her hand into his, "And who might *this* lovely lady be?"

"She can't speak," Blythe replied flatly, evidently bemused by the man's sudden advances upon her. "I suspect she might be retarded."

The Viscountess almost snarled at him, her nostrils flaring with quiet rage. No one seemed to notice her white hot stare of righteous indignation; not even Blythe, who did not care to so much as look at her. *Just whom does he think he is?!*

"She's not retarded," Bern chimed in, rising to her defense. "Just been through a lot, is all."

"She's so red," the man repeatedly thumping his leg stated, using his index finger to push on his glasses again.

"Perhaps she's 'injun' like you, Kael," Blythe smirked, presumably trying to be funny. No one laughed.

"I found her out wandering the deserts alone. Apparently she's a Viscountess. Since she can't speak to tell me her name, that's just what I've been calling her."

"A Viscountess!" Kael repeated, still holding the girl's hand in his. He raised it to his lips, bowing only slightly given his disadvantage in height. "The pleasure is most assuredly all mine."

If the Viscountess were not so badly sunburned, they may be aware of a ferocious flushing of her cheeks. If ever there were a time she found herself grateful for an affliction she had suffered over the course of her life, this was it.

"Viscountess, I'd like to introduce you to Kael," Bern said with a mild smirk. "He is the resident charmer among our little band of misfits. And the man there, is Orel." She gestured to the man still thumping his leg as he sat on the bar stool.

"Howd'youdo," Orel said with an abrupt jolt of a nod. He pushed his glasses up the bridge of his nose yet again.

Bern glanced around the sea of bustling men, supposedly to introduce her to Blythe more formally. At some point during the introductions he had slipped away, nowhere to be seen. The Viscountess was glad to be rid of him, if only for the moment.

Suddenly there was a loud noise, like a bomb going off. It startled the Viscountess so badly she leapt at Kael, who had not yet released her hand. He readily caught her, taking her up in his arms in a manner reminiscent of a cover for any given trashy romance novel she could think of having read. Everyone in the pub fell silent and even the pianist had abruptly ceased his playing. Once the Viscountess had collected herself enough to disentangle from Kael's hold, she whirled around to face the direction of the sound. Her gaze drifted to the center of the pit where a lone man stood with a smoking gun raised above his head. Instinctively, she then looked up at the ceiling. There were a countless many gunshot holes from years and years of barbaric tradition.

"Gentlemen, and… Lady!" the man announced with a grandiose wave of his arms. Bern chuckled, waving back as all surrounding eyes fell on her in that moment. The Viscountess made a point of it to duck out of sight, though she could feel a few people now watching her, as well. The man continued, "Welcome to our 208th weekly fight night! This number is very important, folks, because tonight signifies our four year anniversary since the founding of *The Rogue Musket* pit!"

Cheers erupted from all around the pub.

"We have eight skilled combatants here for you tonight that won't disappoint, so that's seven matches for your enjoyment! Only one will emerge victorious to claim the illustrious prize of a full week's ration – *and* a one-day permit to explore the coal mines with expressed written consent from the Town Council to keep all that can be carried!"

More cheers and applause. Since as far back as she could remember, the Viscountess never felt the pains of hunger. She never had to worry herself over whether or not she would have food to last her through the end of the week. Her parents had always seen to it that she would never want for anything. To see these people now fight for something she once always had was enough to set her heart to racing. If only she had known.

"Without further ado," the presenter continued, "I give to you the first fight of the evening; Julio 'the Great' versus Francis 'the Destroyer' Cunningham!"

Bern gently tapped the Viscountess on the shoulder. "Come with me," she said. "We're going down there."

What?!

The Viscountess hurried after Bern, who was already on her way out of the pub. Her jingling clomps came in quick succession and the Viscountess tried to match her step. Bern took long strides as she walked, making her way back through the front entrance.

"Leavin' already, Berny?" the man out front asked, as they passed.

"Not just yet, Bill," she replied.

The Viscountess kept in pace, picking up the skirt of her dress as she tried to rush up beside Bern to get her to look at her; that she would see the panic on her face and change her mind, realizing this was a bad idea – or at least tell her what she was up to. The two of them walked hurriedly around the other side of the pub where they came by a staircase descending into the cellar, which was likely where all the wines and other beverages were kept.

Bern made her way down the stairs, stopping at the foot in front of a door with several locks on it. Reaching down for her boots, she took a small silvery key off one of the chains the Viscountess had not noticed before, and began turning the locks. She looked back up at the

Viscountess, who was still at the top of the stairs, frozen with alarm.

"It's okay," Bern reassured. "I've fought before, so I can get us in."

The Viscountess was in awe of this woman. She stepped down the stairs as Bern was opening the door, the two making their way through. Looking around the poorly lit room of the cellar, the Viscountess made strained eye contact with the six other people who were now staring back at her, eyeing she and Bern as if to size them up. She clung to the back of Bern's duster, timidly.

"Well, hello there boys," she said with a smirk. "Did'ja miss me?"

A tall, imposing man with very dark skin stepped forward. He was lean, but powerfully built, and wore darkened beige pants that hung low on his hips with tall black clunky boots. His muscles were smooth and deeply defined; the body of a well-seasoned warrior. "Bern. Back in town, I see," he said, returning her smirk. His voice was velvety and rich. "Surely you're not thinking of fighting tonight – you know *Roland* here would never touch you, and that's hardly fair."

He gestured to another tall, but somewhat shorter man with scraggly brown tresses. He was also leanly muscled, but with a fine tousle of hair running the length of his well-sculpted pecs to the meeting point of his britches, below his navel. He had a cobalt crescent marking etched into his cheek. The Viscountess met with his eyes; piercing blue hues relaxed under bushy brows, which could not detract from the intensity of the man's comforting gaze. He smiled at her. Something trembled inside her; an odd sensation she had never before felt, like the gentle brush of fluttering wings. She felt her face go hot with a blush, and again she was grateful for her sunburn.

These men stood out from the other four figures, standoffish in demeanor, who by now had retreated to the corners in the room to await their turn to fight. There was a brief pause that hung in the air with the muffled sound of the cheering crowd, to accompany blunt noises and grunts behind the closed door at the far end of the cellar. The Viscountess could only assume it led to the open floor of the pit. Still unsure of Bern's intentions, she tugged lightly on the leathery fabric of her duster. Bern shot her an impartial look, then quickly returned her attention to the men in front of her.

"I didn't think *both* of you would be fighting, the same week," Bern said, crossing her arms. "What happened to the cycle rotation; you, one week and Roland, the next?" As Bern crossed her arms, the Viscountess took notice of a line of arrowheads strapped to her belt.

Even behind the town's closed walls, the woman was armed in some way, wherever she went.

At that moment, Roland stepped toward Bern and the Viscountess, leaning in close to Bern's ear, "With me and Alasdair fighting in the same week, it'll double our chances of winning that one-day permit for the coal mines," he said in a hushed tone. He had a distinct manner of speaking, even with his voice lowered; deep, but with a slight lilt to it that the Viscountess liked.

"But that permit is for one person, and one person only!" Bern snapped, speaking in a forcedly hushed tone right back, "Even if one of you did manage to win, only one of us is going through those mines. And if you both get yourselves injured, it won't be *either* of you, and you two are the most able-bodied among us!"

"Ouch," Alasdair chuckled, having moved closer to join their circle, "How'd that taste comin' out of your mouth, Bern? Bet it *burned* your tongue to go and say that."

"Oh, you shut your hole!" she shot back, "All I mean is that the two of you are physically capable of carrying more; you, most of all, Alasdair. You're the biggest. And what if the two of you are paired up against each other? Then what?!"

"Then I take a dive," Roland replied. "We can make it look convincing enough; I'll let Alasdair hit me, and he'll pull the punch. Simple as that."

Bern narrowed her brows, staring him down in silence for a few moments before giving up with an exasperated sigh. "Alright, fine," she murmured. "...But if either one of you screws this up, it's on both your heads!"

"Hey, just relax," Alasdair replied, coolly. "We got this. The two of us came up with the plan while you were out of town on one of your little search-and-rescues. You don't need to be included in every group decision we make."

"No," she said, "but I still appreciate being kept in the loop."

"So, when do you intend on introducing us to the lady here?" Roland interrupted, dropping his subdued tone for a more natural speaking voice. Again, he smiled at the Viscountess.

The Viscountess shyly smiled back at him, awkwardly fidgeting with the folds of her dress. *What has Bern gotten me into?* she thought to herself as these grown men stood before her, indecently dressed, leaving little to an imagination that would otherwise not be running rampant in that very moment.

"I found her on one of the 'little search-and-rescues' that I happen to take quite seriously," she answered Roland, while giving Alasdair a dirty look. "I've taken her under my wing for the time being, so I'm not leaving her alone by herself."

"You got a name, girly?" Alasdair said, ignoring Bern's glare.

"She's mute. I've been referring to her by her title for the time being, until we can find someone who knows how to read so she can write it for us."

"…Her title?" Roland frowned.

"She's a Viscountess."

Just then, the door swung open. A large, heavyset man slumped in the doorway. The presenter's voice could be heard from behind him in the center of the pit. "Congratulations, Mr. Cunningham! You'll move on to the next round, to later be accompanied by the victor of our next match-up… Roland Slater, versus Gorgol!"

The crowd went wild with massive cheers.

"That's you, man! Go knock 'em dead!" Alasdair exclaimed, smacking Roland on the back.

The Viscountess worriedly looked up at Bern.

"Don't worry," Bern reassured. "The death ratio per fight isn't terribly high."

CHAPTER 7

Roland, the Ram

The Viscountess watched from the metal railing overlooking the pit alongside Bern, Kael, and Orel. Men all around her were cheering and bumping each other, and it was all she could do to keep from pushing back every time someone sharply brushed against her sunburns. She furrowed her brows in disdain for the boisterous crowd, feeling ill as the stagnant stench of body odor assaulted her from every direction.

A few times now, she had swallowed back the urge to vomit. There was nothing she could recall being more fearful of throughout her youth than involuntarily evacuating the contents of her insides. She remembered reading somewhere that her profound aversion to vomiting had a name; 'emetophobia,' and thus she felt justified never having outgrown this fear, with the knowledge that there were other people who hated it as much as she did.

Despite her unpleasant surroundings, the Viscountess tried to focus on the two fighters in the pit as they now circled each other, both with intense expressions engraved into their features. She watched Roland's movements very carefully in junction with the fighter known only as Gorgol; a much larger brute of a man who barely moved at all. The top half of his steely body remained stiff with his defensive stance as his legs glided smoothly over the bloodstained floor of the pit. Roland followed suit, his movements more erratic than his combatant's steady ebb.

Their circling closed in, both fighters moving ever nearer as they gauged each others' intent. The Viscountess's heart raced with anticipation as she looked on. It was almost like a dance; two people swept up in each others' flow with each step. Suddenly the balance was broken as the first strike shot out, catching Roland in the forearm as he raised it to block Gorgol's fist. He returned the attack with a counterstrike, swinging the elbow of his other arm wildly at Gorgol's head. It connected solidly with his temple, his neck snapping to the side with the impact.

The crowd cheered loudly; "First blood!" they chanted. They must have done this hundreds of times before. The Viscountess gasped, startled by the swiftness of the blow. Roland hopped back in retreat as Gorgol swung violently in retaliation. Again, they circled. A trickle of blood trailed down Gorgol's brow as they studied each others' faces, neither showing any signs of emotion. Bern placed her hand over the Viscountess's which had been clenched around the bar of the railing, her knuckles white with her grip. The Viscountess tore her attention away, now conscious of her numbing constriction, loosening her hold as Bern leaned in close to her ear.

"He is playing it safe," she shouted. She could barely be heard over the roar of the pub. "In a fight, it's best to take advantage of your opponent when his guard is down, then back off before he has a chance to recover. At least until you've got his pattern down – or until you've weakened his defenses."

The Viscountess redirected her attention back to the pit, taking in Bern's words. She watched as Roland continued to bob lightly on the heels of his boots with his fists raised in front of him. Again Gorgol lashed out, his powerful swing once more connecting with Roland's forearm, raised to block from his face. This time Roland deflected the blow, swiping the beastly man's fist to the side. He shifted his footing in the same motion, twisting his torso around with his other arm extended. A solid punch slammed into the other side of Gorgol's head with an audible crack that echoed over the crowd's growing roars.

"Nice haymaker!" Kael exclaimed, clapping enthusiastically. His cheeks were flushed and he looked to be considerably drunker than before. Even so, the Viscountess imagined that she would not have understood him if he were sober.

Gorgol was on the offensive now, swinging wildly at Roland who continued to bob and weave through most of the onslaught, blocking and deflecting what blows he could not avoid. The Viscountess darted her eyes between the two combatants, trying to keep up with their movements. It was all happening so fast now that she could hardly keep track. Just then Roland spun around, just as Gorgol had lunged forward. He unleashed a lightning-fast kick, shattering Gorgol's jaw. The sheer force of the impact knocked the larger man off his feet and sent him careening to the floor of the pit, a geyser of blood sprayed across the ground from his mouth.

"What a roundhouse!" Kael yelled, "That's m'man down there!"

The rest of the crowd erupted in cheers, louder than ever, which caused the Viscountess to cover her ears with her hands. *How lovely*, she silently grimaced. *A headache to accompany my nausea.* Then someone scraped against her sunburn from behind and it was all she could do to keep from attempting a 'homemaker-hayhouse' of her own.

"His frustration is making him reckless," she heard Bern say. The Viscountess lowered her hands and looked up at her. Bern leaned in close once more, "He knows Roland is faster than he is. If he can get up after that last kick, he'll try something dirty to gain the upper hand. Roland had better be careful…"

The Viscountess glanced back to the pit, just as Gorgol was climbing to his feet. She furrowed her brows worriedly now, taking consideration to Bern's warning. She hoped that Roland would be wary of this, though she was uncertain as to what form of foul play could be executed in a closed arena. Then it occurred to her; *Are there even any rules?*

No sooner had Gorgol picked himself up than he was already charging toward Roland once again, fists clenched. Roland was ready for the bloodied brute, keeping light on his feet as he rapidly approached. Then Gorgol stopped suddenly, just out of arms' reach. He wound back his arm in the same instant and hurled a cloud of sand at Roland's face. Among the constant cheers of the crowd were some boos now, as Roland jumped backward to avoid sand getting in his eyes.

"See? What'd I tell you," Bern shouted, again leaning in. "That sort of poor sportsmanship in the pit is frowned upon, but unfortunately allowed. Anything goes."

"I wouldn't even have let the bastard get up," Kael gritted.

"Probably would have taken a knife in, if the fighters were not thoroughly searched first," the Viscountess could barely hear Orel say.

He had been so quiet, she nearly forgot him standing at Kael's other side. "They want these fights to go on for as long as possible, which is probably the only reason why weapons are disallowed." The Viscountess had turned to look over at him to better hear him speak. The man was swaying and constantly shifting his weight. She was amazed at his profound inability to ever be still.

"Look! Look, there!" Bern yelled, smacking the Viscountess on her very burnt shoulder. She gasped and grimaced, but returned her attention to the fight. Her eyes immediately fell over Gorgol's other fist as bits of sand slipped through the cracks of his fingers. He had another round of this makeshift ammunition to throw. Before Roland could react, Gorgol had launched his other handful, and this time he did not miss.

Instinctively Roland raised his arms to shield his face from projectile sand, but all too late as remnants still blinded him. He was rendered momentarily paralyzed. Gorgol wasted no time in taking advantage, plunging his fist deep into the pit of Roland's stomach. The force of the blow partially lifted him from the ground and he emitted a deep guttural groan, audible over the ruckus of the crowd. He was unable to get his guard lowered in time. As his muscles spasmed and contracted, Gorgol dug another fast punch near his navel and just under his ribcage.

The Viscountess's eyes grew wide with dread as she watched Roland gag and sputter, collapsing onto the floor of the pit in a fetal heap. Bern slammed the palms of her hands against the railing in anger, while Kael cursed loudly and shouted words the Viscountess only read in books but seldom heard spoken. It was all far too much for her to process. She was clutching the railing so hard her hands had gone numb long before she recognized that she was gripping it again. *Get up! Please, get up!* she voicelessly begged.

Roland wrapped his arms around his abdomen, a tendril of spit dangling from the corner of his mouth as he looked up and squinted through the sand in his eyes. Gorgol threw his leg at his head, the side of his boot cracking against Roland's jaw, sprawling him out over the canvas of the arena like a toppled spittoon. He writhed in pain, and the crowd loved every brutal second of it. The Viscountess could hardly stand what was happening. She felt dizzied with the mock and mirth of her surroundings, drunk with her own insuppressible rage. This was unacceptable.

Gorgol stomped down hard onto Roland's exposed midsection, burying the sole of his boot in his gut. His whole body convulsed with the impact, a small stream of blood spurting from his mouth. The Viscountess felt her body start to go limp. The room was now spinning all around her, except for Gorgol who remained clear in her sights. There was a moment of this, before she again lost herself to violent musings of inflicting torturous, inconceivable pain. Suddenly—*darkness*. Had she fainted? What was happening to her?

These questions were pushed back into the far recesses of her mind as she surrendered herself to this floating sensation; this darkness that now enveloped her. The unpleasant ambiance which set the tone for the pub, from the loud noises to the harsh smells, seemed to dissipate into the nothingness along with her. She wished it would all just go away; everything that transpired in the past twenty-four hours, all of it gone. She longed to return to a time before the attack, when she was just a skylark, the *Castle in the Sky* was just a myth, and the key was just an old family heirloom. *The key!* she thought to herself, in the midst of the absence. *It is my responsibility! My father! They took it from me!*

She opened her eyes. The reality and horror of her situation came as quickly as the ground beneath her backside as she was thrown from Gorgol's shoulders. He cried out in agony, the end of an arrowhead protruding from his eye socket. It became wholly apparent to her that she had another blackout time-lapse. She laid there, confused and in shock, several feet from Roland who was turned on his side now and looking directly at her. His piercing gaze was unreadable to her; was he angry? Concerned? Did he know what she had done?

The crowd seemed unpredictable as well, a strange mixture of cheers and jeers swept together amid chaotic, unintelligible discourse. Gorgol fumbled with the arrowhead, his fingers slipping on his own blood pooling out around it, gushing from the wound. Finally he managed to grab solid hold of it, yanking it out forcibly and discarding it to the ground with shaky hands. The Viscountess glimpsed all around her, from Roland to Gorgol, then finally up at the crowd where Kael and Orel stood by the railing, their expressions a combination of shock and immersed interest. Where Bern had once stood, now was Blythe, a strange impish grin plastered across his face. Bern was nowhere to be found.

"You fucking bitch!" Gorgol howled, his dirty face a mess with his own blood as he glared at her now through his one good eye. The

Viscountess refocused her attention upon him as he strode toward her, his hands still shaking in front of his body. "I'll *kill* you! I'll rip you apart!" He was mad with fury. His fingers twitched with a perceived desire to snap her neck, or perhaps gouge her eyes into the back of her skull. Her blood ran cold at the thought, heart pounding in her chest.

He was almost upon her now, a mere second from snatching her up in his hands and making her the recipient to her own darkest fantasies. She flinched back, huddled on the floor of the pit as she shut her eyes tight with dreaded anticipation. She heard the sounds of scrapes and blunt thuds, feeling a quick brush of air whisk past her. The thudding noises continued, none of which she felt against her person. Hesitantly she reopened her eyes, as Roland was straddled over Gorgol, repeatedly slamming the back of his head into the ground with his hands wrapped around his big, trunk of a neck.

"Enough! That's enough!" the man presenting the fights yelled, racing toward them. He was followed by two large, brutish-looking men. By then, Gorgol's body had long fallen limp; lifeless. Was he dead? The Viscountess could not tell. Her whole body shook with trepidation. Roland dismounted Gorgol's still mass and stood partially upright, hunching over slightly in pain. "Both fighters are disqualified from the tournament for this girl's intervention!"

The Viscountess wished a deep fissure would part the earth beneath her and swallow her whole.

The presenter continued, "Outside physical disruptions *and* weapons are strictly prohibited from all bouts! There are no exceptions to this rule, and disciplinary action will be taken accordingly." The crowd cheered its approval, as one of the men that had followed the presenter onto the arena floor began dragging Gorgol back to the cellar by his legs. The other man reached down and grabbed the Viscountess by the arm, wrenching it behind her back as he lifted her to her feet. She gasped with pain and alarm, looking to Roland as the man shoved her along. Roland limply followed, his eyes looking very worn and tired; defeated.

She felt awful. She wished she knew what had happened; what it was that came over her. Of all the times she had hallucinated or experienced a blackout, never before had she actually succumbed to committing acts of violence. She knew now that she was physically capable of such things – and this frightened her. They made their way off the arena floor and back through the cellar, where the Viscountess was surprised to see that Bern was waiting for her. She shot her a quick sidelong glance before directing her attention to the man running the show.

"Wait," Bern said, "She's with me! *I* brought her into this town; *I* brought her into this pub. She is my responsibility, so let me deal with her myself!"

Her eyes were fiery and intense as she looked up at the larger man restraining the Viscountess, then back at the presenter, almost challengingly. The other man dragged Gorgol toward the middle of the cellar where the combatants were either waiting to fight, or still recovering from having fought. Already among these men was Roland, who was speaking mutedly between sharp breaths and wheezes, with Alasdair, who periodically met with the Viscountess's eyes in short intervals. He appeared very stern and straight-faced which only alluded to the gravity of the situation as the two men sat there along a bench in a far corner of the room.

"Bern, my dear," the presenter addressed her, his tone condescending. "You know your little ventures are *not* supported by the town council. You may be revered among the people, but this little stunt puts you in just as much hot water, as it does this new girl of yours!"

"Governor, sir," Bern pleaded, through gritted teeth, "*Please* just let me have a word with—"

"There is nothing to discuss, and certainly not now; not in the middle of fight night!" he snapped. He turned away from her, looking toward Roland and Alasdair, who were still locked in quiet exchange. "Alasdair, you and Cranos are up next; get over here!"

Alasdair turned to look at him, then gave Roland a nod and a quick pat on the shoulder before getting up from his seat and making his approach. Following him was another tall, but intimidatingly broad man who seemed to appear out of nowhere as he stepped out from behind an aisled wine rack. The Viscountess did not care to observe his features, her eyes fixed between Bern and Roland and distracted by the painful hold the man behind her had on her arm.

Bern suddenly grabbed at the Governor's forearm. "Just hear me out," she said, pleadingly. There was a strange look in her eyes as her brows narrowed with determination. She looked conflicted, but resolute. "I'm... most certain that we can work out a deal to your utmost satisfaction."

A deal...? the Viscountess contemplated. She looked him up and down, gauging his reaction to Bern's dire insistence while taking in the man's odd characteristics for the first time, now that she was up close and personal with him. He was shorter than she, but not Kael; a stout, chubby man with a bulbously pointed nose and long crooked teeth, visible as he now sneered. Somehow he reminded her of an overgrown sewer rat, though she had never seen one live. There was a brief pause as he considered Bern's words.

"...I see..." the Governor shone his ugly grin. "Okay; I'll hear you out. We'll... *talk*. During this next fight." He shook Bern's hand from his arm, his eyes never once leaving hers as he spoke, "Just be mindful that I *could* bring this up with the council, and they would not be so lenient..."

At that, the Viscountess felt the brute release his hold on her arm. She snatched it back, resentfully massaging it as she distanced herself from him and the Governor, and the other brute who by now had returned to their side. She found Bern's cover once again. Though she did not understand this woman, she was beginning to feel very safe with her despite the various quirks that did not sit well in her mind where she was concerned. At this point, the Viscountess was willing to overlook any perceived oddities that Bern might have had. She knew she had her back, even despite their difference in class, and that was well enough for her.

"Roland, why don't you take the Viscountess outside for a bit of fresh air?" Bern suggested, nodding to him from the opposite end of the room. He looked up at her in dull expression as he sat there, wordlessly. She continued, "You look like you could use a bit, yourself."

Alasdair was still looking very grave through all of this, and the Viscountess could not help but wonder what it was that he and Roland were discussing before, as he continued to make fleeting glances in her direction. He came up next to Bern, clasping his hand around the woman's shoulder as he passed. "You sure you know what you're doing?" he asked.

"Don't worry about it. Just fight." Bern replied.

As they all began to pile out of the cellar room and either onto the pit floor, or to another area unbeknownst to the Viscountess, she timidly decided to take it upon herself to approach Roland, who had not moved from his spot on the bench from across the room. She fidgeted with her fingers in her hands as she strode toward him, feeling quite ill, stepping around the unconscious (or dead) Gorgol, and moving through the few other fighters. She stopped a few feet in front of him, and slowly he raised his head to look up at her as he slouched.

"Guess I gotta take you outside then, huh," he said as he wearily straightened himself out and rose to his feet. "Alright then, come along. Just know that I *would* have beaten him on my own."

CHAPTER 8

A Warrior's Wish

The Viscountess sat with Roland outside, in silence, by the light emanating from within the pub. With their backs to the cool cobblestone of the pub's walls, she could feel the warmth from the light through the windows overhead. She sat on the earthy ground with her legs folded elegantly underneath her body, her hands resting in her lap while she continued to fidget. She could hear the muffled sounds of men cheering from inside, and it was enough to keep her mind as restless as her fingers.

Roland had not said a word since they stepped out into the night together. He rested his elbows on his knees, his legs spread out as he focused on breathing. His head drooped between his legs in his hunched-over posture, and the Viscountess felt the strong desire to comfort him. She wished she were bold enough to place a hand to the back of his neck; to run her fingers through his tousled hair, that she might soothe him. This was an act reserved only for the brazen; the most audacious of consorts – someone like Bern. Why could she not be more like Bern?

"Y'know," Roland wheezed, "I've never talked to anyone who, well, couldn't talk back before… I don't really know what to say to you."

The Viscountess gazed up at him through lowered lashes. His eyes were so blue, as he looked back at her. The cobalt crescent scar under his left eye scrunched with his equally crescent smile. She wondered what he was thinking; what he was feeling. *Please don't hate me*, she thought silently, wishing only that she could tell him. She wanted nothing more than to explain herself somehow. *If I had known what I was doing would have eliminated you from your fight, I would have restrained myself!* She grimaced.

…If I could have restrained myself…

"Think I might've cracked a rib," Roland chuckled, followed by a sharp wince to interrupt his own laugh.

Without thinking, the Viscountess reached over and touched her hand to his side. He lifted an arm off his knee, pivoting his upper body toward her, and as he turned, her fingers gently glided across his midsection. His skin was warm and taut with firm muscle, though his body was relaxed as her fingertips lightly grazed over fine hairs. She flinched back, withdrawing her hand suddenly in embarrassment. *What are you doing with this half-clothed common man?!* she questioned herself.

…You depraved, daft little harlot…!

"No, no," Roland said, "It's alright. Really." He smiled at her, seeming to take light of her poor impulse control. All the reassurance in the world could not make her feel any less mortified by having just groped him, though she appreciated his concern for her otherwise delicate sensibilities.

She felt her face go hot as she returned her fidgeting hands to her lap, averting her eyes from him. She settled her gaze upon the expanse of night sky, the stars above shining brightly in the absence of light. The candles set on windowsills of houses throughout the town had since long been put out, The Rogue Musket being the only lit building on the block. She wondered what time it was, and for how much longer the fights would drag on. How she wished she could return to the skies, or at the very least, Bern's abode.

"Looks like I'm developing a nasty bruise," Roland smirked. "Check it out."

The Viscountess turned to face him. Immediately her eyes were drawn to the discolored raised welt forming from the inside of his ribs, around his abdomen. She could not help but smile back at him, an idea formulating in her mind. Without a moment's hesitation, she loosened the strings of her bodice from behind and swiveled it up her torso with the top part of her dress. With her midriff now exposed, she turned to the side so that her bruised flank was in full view. She delighted in Roland's shocked expression, his blue eyes wide with surprise.

"And just how in the world did *that* happen?!" he gawked. "You're not a brawler too, are you...?"

Don't be silly! Of course not! the Viscountess thought, shaking her head with a sardonic grin. The very idea was absurd to her.

"Oh. Well, that's good," Roland replied, as if she had actually spoken. He seemed strangely relieved by this, somehow. "But, it shouldn't surprise me if you were. Not with the way you hopped over that railing and into the pit like some kind of wildcat!"

The Viscountess stared blankly at him, *I really did that?*

"How Gorgol didn't even notice you 'til you'd jumped on his back, I'll never know," he continued. "And then when you stuck that... What was that pointy thing anyway; an arrowhead, or something? Did you take that from Bern?"

The Viscountess shrugged her sunburned shoulders at him, helplessly. She had no recollection of doing the things he now described to her.

"...I should never have let him get up," he frowned, suddenly preoccupied as he looked away from her. "It's the gentleman's code; to kick a man when he's down is to negate ones' own sense of honor. When I fight, I'd like to think myself honorable... but it's hard not to become jaded when someone so easily turns your strength into a weakness."

...What do you mean...? the Viscountess frowned.

"What I mean to say is that I pride myself, in that I am just. I'm a just man, and when an unjust man is able to exploit my principles simply because he, himself, has none..." Roland trailed off, taking a moment to sigh and catch his breath. He was clearly getting himself worked up. The Viscountess surged up the courage in that moment to reach for him, again. As she rested a delicate hand upon his shoulder, he turned his head to face her. The intensity in his eyes smoothed into a soft gaze, but did not lose their magnetism. He smiled a disarming smile.

The Viscountess felt that same fluttery feeling as before, earlier in the evening. She found it all the more difficult to maintain eye contact with the man for very long. His eyes drew her in like the hot steam rolling off still waters' surface; warm, and soothing. She could not linger there, submerged in the depths, as the heat would render her faint; delirious, with the tides of her own surrender. He overwhelmed her with his open, inviting eyes. It was as though, if only for a brief instant, he was without human constraint; without guard. Vulnerable.

"I'm crazy, y'know," Roland said suddenly, breaking the silence as he looked at her intently.

The Viscountess furrowed her brows, puzzled by this odd statement. She did not know how to take his words, and as they hung in the air in a moment's pause, she realized that he was quite serious. She urged him on with her stare, pleading for reason.

"It's true. It feels like I lose sense of reality sometimes, when it just seems like the world is on my shoulders. And then I get anxious, and it feels like I can barely breathe, like now, and then fighting is all I have! It's the one thing that grounds me, and keeps me in the 'here and now,' y'know what I mean? If I'm not brooding over the past, I'm dreading what's to come. But when I fight, it forces me to focus only on what's in front of me. Right *here* – right *now*."

The Viscountess cocked a brow at his words. *You cannot truly believe this makes you crazy*, she thought. *You are empathetic... but, certainly not crazy!*

Roland continued, "I feel like a monster alone on the edge of society, preying and stalking like a lone wolf... So what do you think of that? I'll bet no one's told you anything like this before. I mean, what kind of person would come out and admit to feeling not quite human? What defines a person as 'human,' anyway? Their feelings? ...Because I got lots of those. I just can't, for the life of me, figure out how to express them. I'm no good at seeking out the company of others, much less that of a *beautiful* woman."

The last of his words were spoken with a slight inflection, not unlike a young child softly 'ooo'ing at a shiny new toy for which he would tend well to. He gave her a small, slow nod which she took as indication enough that he was referring to her. She hung on his every word, her heart racing. She felt all the more drawn to this man with each passing moment. As he spoke, she could feel a common ground building between them. It was like nothing she had ever felt before.

"I don't know why I'm telling you all of this," he said, with a sigh. "It's not like you can really talk back to me so I know what you're thinking. It's funny; the first girl I bare my soul to, and she can't say a damned thing about it. Maybe part of it is *because* you can't say anything back. Is that wrong?"

No… I understand, completely…

"Look; see, the thing is… I get lonely. I don't mind being alone… but I can't stand being lonely. It's hard, because I know I have so much to offer—beyond camaraderie. Something deeper, and more meaningful. To have a real, emotional and romantic relationship with something small, soft, and delicate. To be trusted enough to be allowed to touch them. To be wanted to be touched by them. To see myself as something worthy, by seeing myself through their eyes…"

All Mother, that's beautiful.

"…But in the end it just felt like it always has. They see me as this horrible monster, and I see the way they see me. It makes me sick with rage, self-loathing, and misanthropy. That's the way it's always been, and that's why I never open up to *anyone*. But, I'll stop… I probably sound like some kind of bellyaching sod to you."

She wanted to pour into him like a waterfall colliding into stone, etching away at the rocky surface by the pressure of her infinite stream. She wanted to know the monster inside him; to see it firsthand, and beckon it into the forefront of his subsistence. The very thought of another person feeling the inexplicable emotions that she felt, herself, was almost too much for her to process. Could this man truly know what it was she struggled with? Was she really that much closer to understanding the 'darkness' inside of her, through him?

She remembered her uncle's words; "The girl has a dark side," but what did he mean? She dwelled on this thought for a short while, and soon she was left thinking of her father, and everyone else on her home ship. The tears came as sudden as summer rain. She buried her face in her hands and silently cried.

"Oh, umm, hey…" Roland said, his voice cracking with apprehension. "I… I didn't make you cry, did I? Damn. I'm sorry, I didn't mean to!" He sighed, thumping the back of his head against the wall behind him, "Just another reason why I shouldn't talk about myself, I guess."

As he spoke, the Viscountess was already inching herself closer to him, still sobbing with her face in her hands. She laid her head on his shoulder as a means of expressing both the empathy she felt for him, and the sadness she felt for herself. Even among a gathering of many, she knew she was ultimately alone. Roland presented as a ray of hope; that perhaps she did not have to be.

Without hesitation, he put his arm around her, drawing her into him. He smelled strangely of cayenne. She just cried as he held her close. This somehow made it all okay again – at least for now. "I'm sorry," Roland repeated softly, clasping a hand around the outside of her shoulder. He had large, rough hands, and she could feel the coolness of his bare palm on her skin. It was comforting to her.

"Wow, you're very warm," he said, his voice still soft as he spoke in low tone. "You were out there in the desert for quite some time, weren't you... I'll bet you've been through hell and back, haven't you..."

My family is dead! The town council has taken the key! It is the only way I can get back into the sky... I must find the Castle. Please; please, help me! the Viscountess wept, lowering her hands from her face to look up at him. Her eyes felt puffy, her cheeks streaked with tears.

"Hey, it's gonna be okay. You're safe now," Roland smiled, brushing strands of her hair away from her face with his fingers. "I can protect you. And I know Alasdair, and Abernathy, and the others will help care for you, too. You're in good hands."

No, I cannot stay here! she pleaded. *I need to find the key! My... My mother would have wanted me to continue her quest...*

"I wish there were something I could say to appease you," he frowned. "Look, maybe I shouldn't have dumped all my troubles onto you like that. You have more than your fair share, yourself, it seems. I appreciate you listening, even if you had little choice."

"Hey, there you guys are!" Kael exclaimed, rounding the corner. Roland quickly slipped his arm back from around the Viscountess and straightened out his posture, placing both hands in his lap. This unsettled the Viscountess a bit, but she was too distracted by Kael's sudden intrusion to pay it much mind. He was clearly still drunk, staggering a bit as he caught his balance against the pub's wall. "Alasdair won his fights! Why weren't you in there watching with us?!"

"Needed some fresh air," Roland muttered. "...Or did you not see me get my ass handed to me?"

"You would'a beat him!" Kael shouted. He was a very loud and obnoxious drunk, which further compensated for his stunted height. He flexed his bulging bicep as he spoke; "M'man's got the moves, aye, Viscountess?" he said, winking with his good eye. This looked strange.

"You're drunk. What've you had, tonight?"

"Bah! Just wine. Y'know what they say, don't you? A bottle of wine a day is good for your heart!"

"That's not what they say," Roland replied. "I'm glad Alasdair won, though. We need to round up the others after he redeems the prize, so we can decide our course of action. How's he doing? Did he come out of it okay?"

"Two broken ribs, a busted lip, and a sprained knee."

"Oh, man… There's no way he's going to be able to scavenge the mines in that condition. How much time do we have, before the offer expires? Did the Governor say?"

"I dunno, but Bern's been… *talkin'* to him…"

Roland's face noticeably paled. His whole demeanor abruptly changed, his body, rigid. He appeared almost angry. "I'll never understand that woman."

Kael laughed boisterously. "What's wrong, Roland? You jealous or somethin'?"

"*Hell no!*" he shot back. "Would you drink out of a glass that's been cleaned with somebody else's spit? I know a lot of guys don't give it much thought one way or the other, but I'm not one of them! Bern has my respect as a tactician. It's her methods that make my skin crawl."

The Viscountess felt very at a loss. Perhaps there was more to Bern than she initially thought.

CHAPTER 9

In Sickness, And In Health

Two days had passed since that night at The Rogue Musket. Bern insisted that deliberation as to their next course of action take place only at a time where everyone could be available. This meant rounding up Kael, Orel, and Blythe, as well as Roland and Alasdair, all together at once. The Viscountess was bedridden during this time, drifting in and out of consciousness. She felt feverish and dizzy, her body riddled with cold sweats and tremors. Her plight in the desert and her exposure to so many unfamiliar bodies and places had finally caught up with her.

She had experienced sickness before, but never the lucid, psychedelic upheaval of her mind from her physical body as she did now. The room was spinning. Even from behind shut eyelids, she could feel it. An explosion of colors and visual vibrations soared before her, her limbs both heavy and weightless at the same time. As she drifted through these strange sensations, she could feel the presence of those around her. They were all there in the next room, talking heatedly among themselves. Did they know she was conscious of it? She tried to home in on the conversation.

"Alasdair is unfit to go through the coal mines," she heard Bern say. "It should be me."

"No, Abernathy! Absolutely not," Roland's voice came in booming retort. He sounded angry. "You didn't participate in the pit fights this time; *we* did. It should be one of *us*. I work in those mines for a living, damn it! I came out of my fight a little banged up, but I'm *still* stronger than you, and I know where all the turns are."

There was a loud bang, followed by the rattling of glass. "Look, you misogynistic oaf; you wouldn't be in the good condition you're in if it wasn't for the Viscountess – the girl I brought here, to *Fyndridge*. If she hadn't jumped into the pit like she had, there would be no argument! You would be a mangled mess, and I'd already be on my way!"

"Hey guys, let's just settle down for a minute," a notably deeper voice spoke out. It took her a moment, but eventually the Viscountess recognized it as belonging to Alasdair. "I may be hurt real bad, but I'm still the one who actually won this permit. I feel that I should have the most say in who's gonna be the man for the job… Excuse the expression, Bern."

"How about we take a vote on it?" another chimed in. Again, the Viscountess had to rack her brain to remember who this voice belonged to. It was difficult to hear individual people speak back at The Rogue Musket, as voices were drowned out amid the raucous of the crowd.

"No, Orel, how 'bout we don't?" Roland curtly responded.

"Come now, let us be reasonable, yes?" Kael said, his voice more easily recognizable. It had a distinctly deep rasp, albeit a decibel higher than the other men who spoke. "We can do this without fighting about it. Personally, I don't like to see our tall, tantalizing temptress here put in situations that can potentially bring her harm, y'know what I mean?"

"You are far more likely to come to harm, than I, at this very moment, Kael," Bern growled.

"I think Bern should go, too," Blythe spoke up. Even in her state of incapacitated infirmity, the Viscountess could still recognize his high-pitched squeak. She had not before realized it, but this was part of what annoyed her about him, among many other inferiorities. "No offense," he continued, "but as much as Roland may know the ins and outs of the coal mines, none of us have even *half* the worldly experience that Bern has. She's an explorer, so, shouldn't it stand to reason that she be the one to go through? Brute strength isn't everything. She'd have the discernment to know what to carry back out with her, I'd think."

"And I wouldn't?!" Roland snarled. "Does *Bern* know the difference between lignite and anthracite? Which types of coal have the highest carbon content? Do you even know there's a distinction?"

Bern sighed in exasperation. "Coal is not what I'm after, you dung beetle!"

There was a pause. The sudden stillness of the room, though lasting only a few short beats, set the Viscountess's heart to racing as she tried to anticipate what was to come. The diminutive silence was deafening. It served as indication enough that Bern's intentions separated her from her companions. There must have been something she knew that she was not telling them.

"What else do you think you're gonna find in those mines, Abernathy?" Roland asked. His words were careful, and slow. "I've scoured every nook and cranny since I was a boy, and not *once* have I ever found anything besides a whole lot'a rocks, coal, and dirt. Just what do you think you know that we don't...?"

"She found me," Blythe said. "I'd be dead if she hadn't come along when she did. Just like she had with that *princess* or whatever, in the next room!"

The Viscountess neighed like a disgruntled mare.

"Not that I don't agree with ya', Blythe..." she heard Kael say, his tone strangely coddling, "but you're biased, y'know? I'm all for havin' faith in Bern's abilities, I mean, she is quite the able-bodied body, and an enticing one at that..."

"Not interested, Kael," Bern interjected.

"...even so, fact of the matter is, a person's easier to find in a desert than any buried treasure in a mine. At least in a desert, you can see your hand in front of your face. It's gonna be pitch black in there! How you gonna see anything? A lantern only goes so far."

"Fine, whatever," Blythe sighed, angrily. "You guys figure it out. I'm stepping outside for a bit."

"C'mon Blythe, wait, just listen man—!" Kael beseeched.

The Viscountess heard a series of stomping footsteps, followed by the opening and abrupt closing of wooden door. She wondered why Kael even bothered appeasing him.

"You're not going in there," Roland said. "It's too big of a risk; especially when you consistently keep things from the rest of us! And then you come back, demanding to be involved in plans that me and Alasdair already set in motion. The night we were gonna carry out those plans! I'm sick of this garbage, Abernathy. No more; it ends here."

"Right, because this has *everything* to do with your concern for my safety, and *nothing* to do with your own stupid big man complex," Bern shot back. "And you call me 'Abernathy' one more time. See what happens!"

"For the last damn time, this is not a decision either of you get to make!" came Alasdair's deep, booming voice. His rich, velvety tone was such that even without yelling, he still captured everyone's attention. "I thought we were gathering here to discuss our options. I'm still the one who won this permit. Period."

The Viscountess heard a brief rustling of paper.

"Now, if there's anyone who's going through those mines, it'll be someone who knows what they're doing. I trust Roland to get us what we need. When was the last time you had running water, Bern? A hot shower, maybe?" Alasdair spoke with resolute sincerity. His voice softened as he went on, "The thing is, our resources are slim. We need the coal to burn, for our water heaters… for cooking up a hot meal… for operating machinery… The Rogue Musket and the homes of the councilmen are the only places with an active water and heat system. You know how big this is. We can't afford to squander this opportunity."

There was another pause that hung in the air. Somehow, the Viscountess could feel Bern's resentful scowl, though she could not see her. She tried to turn her head; to open her eyes, but attempting to do so proved too exhausting for her to manage. Opening her eyes even slightly caused an overwhelming stinging sensation from behind her heavy lids. She was confined to the bed Bern had set for her.

"Not to be a boor," again Orel finally spoke. The Viscountess had nearly forgotten he was even still in the room. "…but, I feel it necessary to point out; for the past two days since the pit fights, Roland has been experiencing the repercussions from his internal hemorrhaging. Carrying an exorbitant amount of weight in and out of the mines is very ill advised. He won't be fully recovered for a long while yet." His voice was erratic and excitable as ever.

"You gave me medical treatment, Orel! I'm fine!" Roland angrily spat.

"Until you burst a blood vessel and bleed to death from the inside, out," retorted Bern.

"Whoa, whoa… Hold up," Alasdair said, "You didn't say *anything* about any of that!"

"I'm just still a little winded from the fight; it's no big deal…" The Viscountess could hear Roland's heavy pacing footsteps as he spoke, "Two days is more than enough time for recovery. I've had worse. So have you. Hell, so has Orel! Too many shots to the head, and now the man can't sit still. Look at him twitching! He's still the best damn doctor we got in this backward town…"

"All the more reason why you should listen to what he has to say, and let me handle this," Bern calmly replied. She sighed weightily, "I don't understand why you still can't trust me, even after all this time!"

"…You *know* why…" Roland said.

Another pause, to accompany the building tension of the room. There was so much to be read between the lines that the Viscountess could hardly keep up. It was clear to her that this group of people shared a lot of history together, and that even despite their quarrels, they remained a team. She remembered how often her father and uncle would argue with one another. How, as much as she detested her uncle, there was something her father had seen in him that she did not. Perhaps this was just another one of those times.

"Roland, man, I'm sorry…" Alasdair sighed, "I don't think it'd be such a good idea to send you in there if you're really that injured. By the sound of it, it seems like I'm in better shape than you are. Even *with* my broken ribs."

"I said I'm *fine*," Roland roared. "It's nothing!"

His shouts startled the Viscountess. She jolted considerably, her heart skipping a beat with her body's sudden involuntary movement. This was getting awkward, and she was growing restless. She wished she could figure out how to sit upright again. If only she were not so utterly exhausted. It was becoming increasingly difficult for her to focus on what they were saying.

"…If you weren't such a… maybe then we could…"

She recognized Bern's voice, but once more, things were getting hazy. Was she losing consciousness again? She felt so hot; her eyelids, so heavy. If she tried to open them before, there was no way she was making the attempt again. Not anytime soon.

"…working yourself up… should sit down… —fore you have another…"

Who was speaking? What were they even saying? Was the discussion over? The Viscountess could not retain her focus any longer. She could feel herself slowly starting to drift away. It was as though her mind, once surfaced briefly, could only return to the depths of her watery recesses. She was left, swimming in abstract thought, her body remaining but her mind floating far, far away by its own undertow.

The last thing she heard before completely succumbing to her drowsiness was Bern.

"…I have the *key*."

CHAPTER 10

Orel, the Scales

The Viscountess reawakened to the sound of footsteps. The room was dark. She could sense the absence of light from behind her eyelids. It must have been just past midnight for there to be so little luminosity – which meant that Bern was wasting no time in taking the fullest advantage of that day permit, and would be leaving soon.

She tried opening her eyes. She still felt hot and dizzy, but much better than before. Slowly, she turned her body toward facing the rest of the room. With the bed in the corner, she could see everything through the darkness; the threshold leading into the kitchen, the barren walls of the room, and what meager furniture Bern had. She wondered where Bern slept, realizing she had not gotten to see the rest of the house's layout.

Bern's unmistakable steps suddenly became louder. The Viscountess realized she would soon be upon her. She lay motionless in the bed, shutting her eyes again, only partly, so that she could scarcely still see. Bern rounded the corner of the threshold, coming into view. She had the key strapped to her back by the leather of her quiver. Her arrows and bow were not to be found. With a flourish of her sleeveless duster, the Viscountess saw that her belt still borne a collection of her arrowheads. Her hair was tied back in its usual braided rows, close to her scalp, but in a knotted bun at the back of her head. It looked like a coil of deep auburn snakes, looped and intertwined in a tangled fray.

Bern reached back behind her, tugging the leather strap over her shoulder and forward, until the key flipped around to resemble an elegant mandolin; like her mother's. In that moment, Bern took on her form, standing there while she held the key which was perhaps only slightly larger than a traditional instrument in likeness. The Viscountess recalled when her mother would play for her, softly strumming along to a song she would make up then and there. She sang lullabies to her as she played, and so she would drift seamlessly off to sleep.

This was no time to be reminiscing. She watched carefully in the dark. Occasionally, Bern would shoot her quick glances to be sure that she was still sleeping while she went about her business. She watched the woman grab a knapsack off a coat hanger and begin stuffing things into it; a first aid kit, a small lantern, a bundle of strange-looking tubes with string attached, and a spool of rope. Then she disappeared into the kitchen, quietly opening cabinets and rustling through her pantry, probably gathering a supply of food and water.

The Viscountess wondered when the last time she ate might have been. She vaguely recalled Bern spooning her mouthfuls of soup (potato bisque, if she remembered correctly) while she was delirious with sickness. Why was she caring for her, at all? If she wanted to kill her, she could have done that back in the open desert. *She must be keeping me alive to use me for something,* the Viscountess thought silently to herself. *But what...?*

She watched as Bern suddenly held the key, still on its strap, out in front of her. "*Illumná pressia orr wa kleitijd,*" she chanted. A beam of soft blue light filled the room, shooting through the only window visible across the threshold, into the kitchen. It was unlike anything she had ever before seen, and by Bern's startled reaction, she knew the experience was new for her, as well. Bern gasped, hesitating a moment, her eyes lingering on that perfect luminescent saber piercing into the northern distance beyond the pane's glass. Its faint glow seemed to pulsate visibly through the key's metal – now rendered translucent as blue veins beneath porcelain skin.

"I knew it...!" Bern mouthed, quietly. Her voice was then, but a whisper, "I *knew* there was a gemstone hidden somewhere in those mines!"

The Viscountess's eyes would have grown wide by that point, had Bern not quickly glanced in her direction. The Viscountess kept her gaze through lowered lashes raised over partly closed lids. Remaining but a moment longer, Bern steadily backed out of the room, keeping her eyes on the girl, moving briskly. It was not until she had disappeared from view around the threshold, that she took her eyes off her. She reached the door of the kitchen and the light followed her.

"Née ma!" she said. The light abruptly went out.

The Viscountess could hear Bern leave, and once more she was left in darkness. It took her eyes a moment to readjust to the dimmed surroundings of the room while she heard Bern exit through one more door in the hallway; the front of the house. *I have to follow her!* she thought to herself. She swung her legs out of bed and threw the blanket off her body, not bothering to change out of the long white nightgown she was wearing. Unsteady on her feet, she ambled into the kitchen where her boots were left and stumbled onto the floor beside them. She clumsily began putting them on.

This was reasonable enough dress to her. No one would see her in undergarments at this hour, and even then, her regard for decency had waned. She moved through the kitchen door, left open with Bern's hasty departure. Once she had reached the front door, she first peered into its peephole, checking for signs of Bern nearby. Satisfied she was far gone on her way, the Viscountess opened the door and closed it behind her. She did not look back. All she had on her mind then was a northbound trek where the light had pointed.

As she hurriedly marched onward, picking up the skirt of her gown over her boots, she thought about all of the horrible things she wanted to do to Bern. She thought about how angry her betrayal had made her; how such a common woman could deceive someone of her own stature. She gazed around the surrounding housing structures, seething with the tail end of her sickness, and with her white hot resolve. As off balance as she was, she *would* overcome it.

The town was very still in the gloom of the night. The only sounds heard were her own trudging footsteps. The houses were almost indistinguishable, all looking quite rundown and architecturally repetitive, as she carried on. The only foliage from all around consisted of dead or dying dry grass and the lifeless husks of trees. From blocks and blocks of residential buildings, there ran that same wall she recognized before, which encircled the entire area for as far as she could see. The wall was taller than the tallest building she had seen in the town; *The Rogue Musket.*

She soon came upon the large steel gate which marked the town's entrance. She peered out around the side of a building, observing Bern from several yards away as she stood in front of that gate. Several heavily armed men stood guard in her way. She watched her pull a sheet of paper from her knapsack, presenting it to one of them to look over. It took but a minute for him to nod in acknowledgement, making a gesture with the end of one of his swords, at the men around him. She counted them—about eight. Perhaps nine? Her heart was pounding in her breast.

They began to push the gate open, which was large enough that half the men standing guard had to struggle with it. They opened it just enough that Bern could slip through. Then they began pulling it closed once more. The Viscountess's mind raced as she tried to come up with a way outside the town's walls without being detected. The odds seemed hopelessly stacked against her. If only she could scale the wall somehow...

"Psstt," she heard a voice. Her heart leapt into her throat.

Slowly turning around, she came face to face with Orel. He was peering out from another building adjacent to her. Waving frantically, he motioned for her to fall back and join him. The Viscountess hesitantly made her way toward him, unsure of whether he could be trusted. But then, what choice did she have? He had spotted her, watching; following. She kept low, ducking out of view as quickly as she could as she slinked up beside him, her back to the wall.

"I saw you leave, after Bern," he twitched. "My home is just down the street from hers. Knowing that woman, I supposed she would depart for the mines the first chance she got. I stayed up to watch for her, and then when I saw you..."

As Orel tapered off, the Viscountess looked him over carefully. The man had dark purple rings around his eyes that she had not before noticed. They were visible from behind the lenses of his glasses, and indication enough that he was quite accustomed to depriving himself of sleep. He continuously tapped his foot on the ground as he dithered, his body shaking with an endless reserve of nervous energy in his shoddy tailored suit vest.

"...That *key* Bern found is not just a coincidence. It belongs to you, does it not?"

The Viscountess nodded vigorously, and without thinking. It was then that she realized how frightened she was; how she had not let her natural inclinations kick in. Although she was very familiar with sneaking around under the noses of her superiors, never had she done so among those whose temperaments could not be predicted. Common savages were not to be trusted. The ideals of her uncle, once perceived as bigoted and outdated, were beginning to make more sense. She saw how her father could be at least moderately influenced by his way of thinking.

"Listen to me, and listen carefully Viscountess," Orel said, anxiously pushing his spectacles up the bridge of his nose with two fingers. "In my practice, I treat more men from mining related injuries than I do fighters, from the pit. The mines are *very* dangerous, and not just because they are outside the perimeter of Fyndridge's wall. I've heard horror stories of subterran scavengers, rogue machinery, and even skylark pirates infiltrating our mines – be it to rob us of our resources, or to seek refuge from the desert wasteland surrounding this place! Are you aware that Fyndridge is a docking station for ships? Not waterbound, mind you."

The Viscountess shook her head. Why was he telling her all of this?

"We're a big supplier for the aristocracies. We have a landing pad built for ships out by the mines. It's about a mile, east from the gated entrance." He pointed to the massive steel gate bordered by the concrete wall that spanned the whole town. "It is the only way in and out of here, but only miners, guards, and council are permitted to come and go as they choose... except Bern. And I don't trust her."

Orel twitched and convulsed harshly with the last of his words. The man's foot tapping became more erratic as he continued to speak, "I watch. I listen. I am quiet most times, because if I am to find balance and order in this backward town, I *must* take in my surroundings and consider them carefully. Does this make any sense to you at all...?" he asked, visibly struggling now to stiffen his lively leg.

The Viscountess shrugged her shoulders a bit. *No. And it concerns me, that you're a doctor.*

"I know what you will be getting yourself into if you choose to do what I think that you are thinking about doing! I want to be absolutely certain that you know the risks involved; that you could be seriously injured, or killed, and nobody would know it – myself excluded, assuming you don't come back. You need to know, before we proceed. Before I *help* you."

She looked at him long and hard. Here this girl stood, the only garments of hers remaining in her possession being the boots on her feet. Her long red hair was a wild, tangled mess around her head. The stillness of the air unsettled her. She was subconsciously drawn to the disruption of the folds in the nightgown she now wore; that which once belonged to Bern's sister. She idly clutched and twisted the fabric as Orel spoke to her. She knew her face must have looked perpetually flushed, with the burns from the desert sun, and he must have thought her quite mad.

"Bern brought you in during daylight hours, did she not?" Orel asked after a brief lull. "...These men guarding the gate are nightshift, which means they've probably heard of your admission but are scarce on the details. All they would have been told is that you are a Viscountess, escorted here by Bern. They wouldn't know that you had been found, wandering aimlessly. We can play it off like you're merely visiting; that you *aren't* a rescue. Quite the contrary; your ship is docked by the mines right now, and you must be returning to your crew. You had to come to town for an overnight stay, because you weren't feeling well. You're fine now. I've checked you out, and I am now showing you back. Agreed?"

Wait a minute! I'm in a nightgown! And what if they recognize me from the pit fights?!

The Viscountess flinched, trying to protest by way of body language, but Orel had taken her by the arm and was now already guiding her out from the building they had been hiding behind. He made a casual stroll up the dirt road, headed toward the massive gate. As they drew nearer, the Viscountess fretfully resigned her gaze to the lit torches lining the uppermost part of the surrounding wall, avoiding eye contact with any guards they now approached.

"Your belongings would be in the holding area by the entrance, straight ahead," Orel whispered, gesturing past the guards, who were undoubtedly aware of their steady approach. His words came out as a jumbled rush of tension. "Stop fidgeting; it looks suspicious. I know you've been through a lot, but you need to trust me. Walk like the noblewoman you know you are!"

It was hard to take the man seriously when he himself was twitching and jolting with each step. She could not tell whether he was just nervous, or involuntarily demonstrating the severity of his apparent past head injury.

"Doctor Fischer," one of the guards said, greeting Orel with a curt nod. "What brings you out at this hour?" His voice was somehow soothing over the sound of crackling fire from the wall mounted torches overhead.

Now that they were closer, the Viscountess took in their appearances, each guard dressed indistinguishably from the other; a large stiff hat with a badge on it, a coat of deep blue buttoned down the front, and off-white pantlegs ballooning out over the tall black boots they were stuffed into, which came up to their knees. On the guards' coats was another badge, identical to the one on their hats—in case their authority was not readily apparent.

"I have the visiting Viscountess with me," Orel replied, gulping back to steady his voice, "She came down with a high fever, and I've been tending to her needs. She is well enough now to gather up her belongings and return to her ship."

The guard raised his brow and eyed the Viscountess, unnervingly. "That's funny; I don't recall hearing about a ship being docked outside… Your insignia, my Lady, please," he said, his tone forceful.

"…Insignia?" Orel gaped.

"Please present the insignia which bares your family emblem; the proof of your birthright," the guard clarified, speaking to the Viscountess directly. "Without it, you'll just have to remain here the rest of the night, until morning."

"We, uhh, it was impounded with the rest of her belongings!" Orel exclaimed, with a slight twitch in his upper lip, obviously struggling to maintain his state of calm. "This is the protocol, as I understand it; how we avoid the possibility of infection, how we ensure the safety of visitors and inhabitants alike, how—"

"I'm sorry, Doctor Fischer, but we have our orders."

The Viscountess touched a hand to Orel's arm. He glanced at her, and as he did, she turned around so that her back was now facing the guards. She remembered instances where she would forget to wear her brooch, or even in heightened circumstances where the brooch did not matter altogether. She recalled being in a marketplace, once, when she was very young. She had been with her mother. There were guards everywhere, but even with such heavy security precautions, a riot still broke out. Someone had stolen a sack of potatoes. She remembered vividly, despite it having been so long ago; tall bodies bumping into her, her mother's grasp on her hand loosening and slipping away, screams and shouts coming from all directions.

It took her nearly an hour to be reunited with her mother, by a guard whose initial belief was that she had stolen the brooch she bore. She cried and urged, and it was not until she had shamefully turned around and pulled back her hair, presenting her branded neck, that he would help her at all. The whole ordeal was quite traumatic for her at the time, and only served to reinforce that she was never again to leave her father's ship. To this day, displaying the back of her neck in such a way made her feel violated. Still, she lifted her hair.

The guard awkwardly shifted his weight from one foot to the other, taking in the various shapes which make up the symbol of her birthright – a four-pointed star within a diamond, a curved line running through and out its center. He seemed to recognize the markings, regarding her with a slight nod.

"Viscountess; right this way, please," he said, moving toward the nearest building by the gate.

Orel shot her a sidelong glance, his mouth twitching into a small, quick grin before falling into step behind the guard. She watched the other guards as she followed behind him, their faces all solemn but for one guard, who appeared to be scowling at her. She put this out of her mind, refocusing her attention on the ring of keys the uniformed man now fumbled with, moving his sheathed sword out of the way on his belt to slip the ring off its loop. It took him but a moment to find the correct key, slipping it into the door and hurriedly unlocking it.

They stepped into the building, and for a moment, the Viscountess thought the walls were made up entirely of filing cabinets. It was a very dimly lit room, gently swaying lanterns illuminating the floor from the ceiling. What light there was made her somewhat dizzy, as it bounced off the cabinets and around the room, with the lanterns' sway. She wondered how many people, both visitors and residents alike, never got back their belongings. It suddenly occurred to her; *How am I to know which cabinet contains my clothes?!*

"The dayshift guards who checked you in would have given you a number," the guard said, as if reading through her troubled expression. "If you can remember it, you may gather your things out of the cabinet assigned to you."

Orel clasped a hand around her shoulder, leaning in close to whisper in her ear. "We don't have a whole lot of time. Think about it; do you remember anything at all from your admittance into Fyndridge…? You *had* to have been with Bern when you would've received a number—"

"Doctor Fischer, if it's indecency the Lady is worried about," the guard interrupted, "she can either return to the infirmary where I *suspect* she was under your care as you say, and wait there 'til morning, or she can pick out her cabinet. A dayshift guard would be better suited to assist her."

"Just, please!" Orel shouted, holding his palm out in front of the guard's face, twitching nervously. "Let her think!"

The Viscountess could tell the guard was growing more impatient, and perhaps more suspicious, with each passing moment. She racked her brain as she tried to recall the events preceding her reawakening for the first time in Bern's home. All she could remember was Bern shouldering her weight, as people clamored around her while she vouched for her entry into town. Her brooch was shown, paperwork was waved around, and then – a number.

'642.'

She rushed past walls and aisles of numbered cabinets, quickly making her way toward the compartment with that number on it. Though her recollection was vague, she knew she heard something about this when Bern was handing over her belongings after she had gotten her settled into bed. She had continued to drift in and out of consciousness, but the Viscountess was certain she picked up on that much. Sure enough, the filing cabinet contained each of her garments which had apparently been washed clean, as per an undoubted set of quarantine regulations.

"Phew; what a relief you remembered!" Orel uneasily chuckled.

"I'll allow the Lady a few minutes to change into her clothes," the guard said, brusquely. "Doctor, if you will follow me back out, please…"

"Oh, uhh, sure! Right; that sounds fine." Orel pushed his glasses up the bridge of his nose as he regarded the Viscountess with a final quick nod, before following the guard back out of the building. The door slammed shut behind them.

…I suppose they expect me to just change right here, then…

The Viscountess quickly kicked her boots off and slid the silky fabric of her stockings up her legs, underneath the nightgown. She was careful so as not to elongate the runs in the fabric, from her knees to her thighs. She then stepped into her tattered floral dress, pulling it up around her waist, not bothering to remove the nightgown beneath the garment. She gritted her teeth as the sleeves of the dress met with her arms to hang off her shoulders. Her skin was still raw with her sunburns, but she knew she needed to hurry. She fastened her corset so that it was firm around her ribcage, but loose enough that it did not constrict her. Then she tore the lace lining from the ends of her dress to tie up her hair. Her brooch was nowhere to be found.

After slipping her boots back onto her feet, the Viscountess rushed toward the door, deciding not to dwell on the loss of her family emblem. No sooner had she reached the knob that the door swung open suddenly. Startled, the Viscountess flinched back to avoid being struck. Three guards stood before her. Among those, were the man who saw her into the building, and the man who greeted her with a scowl.

"Good," the scowling guard said. "She managed to dress herself."

Not even a knock…? I'll never get used to this…

"If you are ready, Viscountess," the guard with the ring of keys said, taking her by the arm and guiding her out of the building, "You will be escorted back to your ship by these two gentlemen here… for your own safety."

The Viscountess's heart skipped a beat. She looked around for Orel, whose expression was just as alarmed as she was sure of her own to be. She wondered what could have happened over the course of time she had been changing, to so drastically alter the guards' dispositions. What words had been exchanged while she was indisposed? None of that mattered, now. She knew that when the guards would escort her to the mines only to find that there was no docked ship, she and Orel would both be under fire.

The several other guards on duty began flipping the many latches on the gate, unfastening the chains and turning the bolts, until it could be pulled open by its massive handles. With a single unified heave, they lugged the gate ajar enough that the Viscountess and her two impromptu escorts could pass through. Orel gulped, and allotted her a reassuring nod, though it was obvious he was panicking on the inside. Her heart thumped erratically in her chest, as she too tried to maintain her composure.

"Why the scared look, sweetheart?" the scowling guard said with a look that was not quite a sneer, but not quite a smile either. He had very ugly teeth. "We're here to protect you."

The Viscountess had no time to be appalled by his addressing her so informally, as both appointed escorts; he and the other guard, took hold of her, each on one arm. They firmly guided her out of town. She looked back at Orel, whose eyes darted all around, occasionally settling back on her. His body twitched and convulsed violently, to which the other guards paid no mind as this was something he was known to do regardless. Even so, she had a very bad feeling about this entire development, watching with her neck craned as the guards pushed the gate shut once more.

As they walked along the path, the soft glow of light emitting from the town began to fall away. The other guard, whose teeth were not quite so aesthetically displeasing, held up a lantern to light the expanse of desert in front of them. The Viscountess tried to keep calm, the tight grip each man held on her arms, less than friendly, and made worse by her already throbbing skin.

"That doc's some kinda whackjob, isn't he," the guard with the lantern and the slightly nicer teeth stated casually. "Too bad he's the only doc in town."

"Heh, yeah, I can't believe the guy used to fight," the other replied. "Wasn't half bad, as I recall. Won most of his matches… 'til good ol' Gorgol did him in; damn near gave him a concussion."

The Viscountess's blood ran cold with the mention of Gorgol. Could they have been at the last fight night? *Could they know?!* She drew in a shaky breath.

"He's so jumpy, and tense; even before goin' comatose. A'course, I'd prob'ly be too… if I were a gangly little maltworm like him." The guard chuckled, raising his lantern as they continued to walk along.

The terrain was beginning to look less and less like a dirt path and more of a rolling desert, the further they got from town. The Viscountess felt like a prisoner, rather an escort, the firm grip each man had on her arms painfully apparent. She wriggled her wrists, trying to pull away, or at least incite looseness in grip. Neither man relaxed, instead holding on more tightly.

"What's the matter, sweetheart?" the guard with the teeth scowled, viciously. "You're not gettin' scared, are you? You certainly didn't *look* scared plunging that arrowhead into Gorgol's eye…"

The Viscountess turned, and twisted, desperate to break free of them. She could hear her heart pounding in her ears like a war drum.

"She too good to talk to us, or somethin'?"

"No. She's *retarded*. I remember overhearing Bern talkin' with the Governor about it during the pit fights. What I don't know is why that excuses her from maiming my only brother!"

With that, both guards released her, throwing her to the ground. Her left shoulder skidded across the sand, the sudden impact scraping her skin. She voicelessly cried out in pain as she looked up at the men with fiery anger and frozen fear.

"Whoa, look at her eyes! Just like a wild animal..."

"Set down the lantern for a minute," the guard with the teeth said, brows narrowed as he stared the Viscountess down. His eyes were dark and expressionless, as if not all there.

The other guard complied, setting the lantern on the ground between them before lunging around the Viscountess to grab at her arms. He wrenched them both behind her back, forcing her to sit upright. She kicked out at the man before her, terrified and enraged. One of her boots caught him solidly in the shin.

"Little *bitch!*" he snarled, backhanding her powerfully across the face.

CHAPTER 11

Sagittarius Shooting Blind

The Viscountess had never been struck before in her whole life; not by her uncle, nor her father and mother, nor anyone, purposefully or otherwise. There was a ringing in her left ear from the point of impact, followed by an intense stinging sensation that spread from her cheek throughout her face. Her left eye throbbed, and felt as though it would pop out of its socket. All she could see was a blinding white nothingness before all her sensations suddenly shut down and she could feel no more. Even the ringing in her ear faded into a soft humming in the back of her mind. She was slipping away again, giving into the tides of her chaotic and unpredictable nature.

She wanted to take out all her pent-up rage on these two men. She knew they were taking advantage of her right that very moment, even as her mind separated from her physical body, left to mingle with her basest of instincts. What would she do to them, she wondered? She fantasized about breaking bone from ligaments, snapping tendons from muscle; the slow, systematic tearing of cartilage by the applying of weight until a crushing pop is released. A wave of euphoria washed over her with these violent thoughts. She felt a profound calm. The deed had been done.

She reawakened from her psychosis, soon very aware of her legs pumping the sand beneath her feet. She had swept up the skirt of her dress, and in her other hand was the lantern. As she sprinted as fast as her legs would carry her, she could hear the distant agonized screams of both guards through the darkness. As terrified as she was, it was like music to her ears.

"My nose! All Mother, my nose! What the *fuck* did you *say* to me, you cunt?! I'll *kill* you! Do you fuckin' hear me?!"

"Oh, All Mother… I can't see! It huuurrts… please, help me!"

She hoped she was moving in the right direction, operating purely on her own intuition. She tried to push back feelings of uncertainty, focusing only on carrying herself as far away from her attackers as possible. She panted as she ran, holding the lantern far out in front of her, watching the light dance over the endless golden dunes of sand. The guards' cries grew more distant with each bounding stride. Her heart felt as though it would burst through the steel boning of her corset, having long since sunk to her stomach.

…But then, it did stop a bullet, she mused, so as not to dwell on the limiting frailty of her body.

It then occurred to her that she may, or may not, have just fended off two burly men twice her size – and it was not until she started down this line of thinking that she even noticed the blood coating her hands, staining her dress and the handle of the lantern. Perhaps she were a far more abled body than she accredited herself to being. She wondered what she had done this time, and some small part of her worried about the sense of satisfaction she felt thinking about it.

A mine shaft suddenly came into view, its rail tracks leading in from around a constructed landing pad, which stretched far and wide in the absence of a ship. It was there she saw Bern standing just outside its entrance, with the bright beam of light running through the key's shank and shooting out from its end. The Viscountess collapsed to the ground with deliberate intent, throwing her skirt over the lantern to conceal her own light. She was still panting heavily, trying desperately to calm her heart's rapid pace as she just concentrated on breathing. She sat motionless, several yards away, watching the soft blue hue in all its brilliance as it extended far into the tunnel of the mine. It curved out of sight, igniting the walls with its lustrous sheen. She assessed it to being as powerful a light source as the sun, though it soothed her to watch it.

Bern began her steady tread into and through the shaft of the mine. As the key's light grew dim with her progression, the Viscountess knew it was time for her to make her move. By now she had caught her breath, standing up partway but still crouching low as she moved across the desert plains. She made her way toward the opening with her arm shielding the lantern from giving off too much light. Once she was close enough to peer inside, the tinge of blue glow still danced along the mine's inner walls, even long after Bern had turned a corner. She suspected the mines would be pitch black without it, save for her meager lantern fire which would only allot her the ability to see her own hand in front of her face; perhaps also the immediate tracks on the ground.

The Viscountess wondered how miners functioned with so little light to work by, day in and day out. She recalled reading once in one of her father's books that miners only had lanterns by which to see; a concept that was simply unfathomable to her. At least the friendly skies offered moonlit nights, which she much preferred to the stygian, closed-in surroundings she now endured as she carefully stepped through, into the mine shaft. If not for the key illuminating the excavation, she knew she would be feeling quite claustrophobic.

She heard Bern's jingling footsteps echo throughout the mines, the sound reverberating off the walls to reside with her. The Viscountess was careful about where she stepped, and how quickly she moved, trying to keep pace while remaining a few rounded corners behind the woman she so loathed. Her mind lingered a little on that profound sense of loathing; that same feeling she had every time her uncle would be condescending toward her, or push her to talk about her mother. How she missed her mother, so...

Her mind wandered as she carried onward in steady pursuit. She found herself reminiscing of happier days when she was still a child; her mother filling her head with whimsical tales of lovers. Two smitten creatures met with adversity; poetic rapturous abandon – something her analytical mind, though young and impressionable, was hard-pressed to grasp. Her father had traded away, or sold most of her mother's belongings at her uncle's counsel. This included the romance and fantasy novels she so loved. She loathed her uncle. She loathed Bern.

Her mother loathed no one, even after what had happened to her. Even as she lay dying, her blood pooling out around her as it filled the cracks in the ground, all she could do was smile softly and—No! *No; she's gone now! She's gone, and I hate, and nothing can stop me **hating!***

The Viscountess ground her teeth, clutching the handle of the lantern so tightly her knuckles had become white and bloodless with the force of her grip. Could this be what her uncle meant? Could this be her 'dark side'?

She came upon an area where the tracks she walked over were no longer bordered by rocky earth. She became very aware of her own heartbeat, holding her breath as she balanced herself carefully. While the tracks were not narrow, she knew that if she took just a couple of steps in either direction, she would plummet a couple dozen feet into the jagged rocks below. The wood of the tracks creaked in some places as she gingerly applied her full weight unto her boot. If she had all but the small flame in the lantern to go by, she would have surely fallen by now.

Large cylindrical pillars lined the cavernous rocky walls of the mine, from all around. The Viscountess soon began to smell sulfur, the scent gradually becoming more overpowering as she continued along. It was a musty, acrid odor she was only marginally familiar with the few times she had managed to slip away from the aristocratic women. Such women included the likes of Madame Beatrice, whom her uncle had appointed to her in the hopes that she would pick up a trade skill; anything to keep her nose out of her father's books. Such trade skills consisted of knitting, sewing, and baking pies – *never* working below the deck, putting her bookish mechanical knowledge to practice. She enjoyed watching Rivkah, and came to like the sulfuric, sooty smells her work produced. Thinking of this made her nostalgic.

Bern's hazel eyes were ferociously menacing, and dire. It was not until the Viscountess had rounded another corner, coming face to face with the woman who stood several feet before her, that she even realized she had not heard her jingling footsteps for quite some time. There, she stood before her. Seeing her expression so suddenly startled the Viscountess, and she fell back onto the ground with a silent gasp, her heart seeming to leap into her throat. Her lantern smashed against a rock, the glass breaking; fire instantly snuffed out by the sharpness of the air.

Bern thrust the key out in front of her, pointing its end at the Viscountess's chest. "*Zeü povis!*" she bellowed. The light radiating through, and out of the key, instantly fizzled out with a loud, rumbling pop. Then – silence. Everything went black.

The Viscountess exhaled shakily, having shut her eyes tight in a flinch. A few seconds passed, and nothing happened. When she opened her eyes, it was quiet, her surroundings still pitch black. She could feel the cool, moist earth beneath her bottom, and the wooden planks of the tracks under her legs and the palms of her hands. She could feel a splinter in one of her fingers. This was as much proof of her consciousness as anything else. She was shaken, but relatively unharmed.

"*Réii ma!*" Bern exclaimed. The soft blue light burst into being, once again. It filled the dark space in every corner; every nook and cranny, and not a shadow could be found so close to its source. The key's light beam resumed its course, spilling out into the other direction; down the uncharted passageway, opposite Bern's gaze. Her eyes fixated, instead, on the Viscountess.

"...You're a Sagittarius, then," Bern said simply, her face baring no trace of remorse or sympathy. "Otherwise, my directive would have been fulfilled."

The Viscountess shot her a venomous glare, bemused and enraged by the woman's strange words. Bern lowered the key to her side, returning her gaze with a stony glower of her own.

"It is not my intent that you be harmed, Viscountess... Just that you return to the surface, and make your way back to Fyndridge, where it's safe. This is no place for a skylark."

Bern stroked her fingers over the smooth, bulbous surface of the turquoise gemstone fixed at the center of the key's base. It gleamed translucently with the key, as an odd colorless swirl of pulsating energy followed her fingertips beneath the stone's exterior. The Viscountess watched her carefully, slowly beginning to rise to her feet. She gritted her teeth, brows narrowed over eyes widened; a look of contemptuous outrage – of bitter hate.

"I would not raise arms against you; don't you see...?!" Bern continued, evidently a bit unnerved by the Viscountess's willful obsession. "Look, I don't know how much of this stuff you know, or if you were even aware, to begin with, of the significance this powerful instrument holds! The fate of the entire *world* depends on me! I simply don't have time to explain it to you. If I can't coerce you into leaving by commanding this gem's life force against you... then I can only *ask* you. Please, turn back."

The Viscountess's whole body shook with the sheer ferocity of her blinding rage. She stood with her fists at her sides, trembling uncontrollably. She could feel her nails cutting into the creases of her palms, drawing blood to intermingle with previous stains not her own. She could feel herself on the verge of another blackout. As sick with her own fury as she was, it took every ounce of willpower she had to keep her burning mind from another descent.

"All Mother, you look so much like her," Bern uttered, brows drooped with distant longing behind a hardened veneer. "I beg of you... don't make me do this. Please."

Steadily, Bern gripped the shank of the key with both hands, slowly winding it back and raising it over her head. The beam of light followed with it, its course unchanged. The undeniable ache in her eyes lasted all but a few seconds, and then it was gone. That moment was passed, and now all that remained was the quiet space between them and her intent to strike. The Viscountess could hear a very soft whirring sound coming from the light of the key, or perhaps it was the gemstone set into its base. She was close enough now that she could hear it in the deafening silence that hung in the air. Strangely enough, she also smelled the sweet scent of lavender.

Suddenly, an inhuman guttural screeching noise echoed throughout the mines. A brief pause followed, and then more chilling shrieks in rapid succession. Bern's tanned face went ghostly white as she lowered the key. A lumbering stampede of scrapes and footsteps could be heard, steadily growing louder as they neared. The Viscountess whirled around, hiking up the skirt of her dress and fell back a few steps, alongside Bern. What she saw next, was too much to take.

The Viscountess blacked out.

CHAPTER 12

A Knight's Rescue

Her ears were ringing. She could hear the faint cries of someone calling out to her; a man's voice, perhaps, but she could barely make it out. It was muffled by the ringing sensation, her ears both wet and cold. Was she underwater? No; she could still breathe, though her gulps of air were sharp and pained, each inhale like a needle piercing the pincushion of her heart. Her left leg throbbed, useless and immobile; numb, below the knee. The back of her head ached as she also felt cool liquid pooling out around her scalp to meet with the wetness in her ears. She twitched her right ankle and wiggled the fingers on both her hands. At least she could feel that much.

Little by little, the Viscountess noticed a heaviness being lifted from her chest. She would not have registered the presence of any pressure to begin with, if not for the gradual lessening of weight. Her body was mostly deadened of all sensation, save for some minor stirring here and there. She could hear the faint rumbling and displacement of rocks. After a few minutes of this, she remembered where she was. It took her the last several pounds of pressure being removed, for her to realize she had been buried under rock and coal. The feeling of needles piercing her heart each time she drew in a breath dissipated, and she gasped almost involuntarily. Bitter air filled her lungs, followed by harsh, retching coughs, that pushed the air back out again.

She tried to roll herself off her back, but her strength had all but disappeared. She felt rough, sooty hands close around her wrists. They pulled her partway off the ground, one hand sliding up underneath her to support her back, the other slipping around the backs of her knees. Slowly and steadily, she felt herself being raised off the ground completely. As she was hoisted up, she felt the cool liquid empty from her ears and trickle down her jawline and neck.

Then, that deep muffled voice; "Visc…tess, c…n … …ear me?!"

…*What?* she thought, trying to make sense of the words.

The liquid having drained from her ears, she slowly began to regain her hearing, though the ringing sensation still remained.

"Can you *hear* me, Viscountess? C'mon, girl, wake up! You gotta be okay…"

Roland…?

She tried to open her eyes. Her vision was blurred as she looked up at Roland's obscured features, illuminated by the light of a lantern which now rested over her corset. Its thin handlebar was clenched between his teeth while he carried her in his arms. Even in this dire situation, it was hard for her not to smile. She wondered how badly she was wounded.

"Yeh— Yes! Now stay with me!" he breathlessly exclaimed. He sounded more than a little amusing to her, trying frantically to speak while holding a lantern in his mouth. "You're going to be just fine. I'll get you outta here."

How did you even find me…? Suddenly, her heart leapt into her throat as her mind caught up with her, remembering the series of events that played out before she lost consciousness.

Where is Bern? Where is the key?!

The Viscountess twisted in Roland's arms, her panic returning to her faster than the feeling in her body. Her limbs flailed uselessly, and without force. Roland redistributed her weight slightly, adjusting her back to her original position with relative ease.

"You're safe now; I've got you!" Roland reassured. "There's nothing to worry about. Orel is gonna patch you up, and—"

The Viscountess twisted again, with more feeling this time.

"It's okay! I've *got* you!" he repeated. "As soon as Orel told me what happened, I came when I could. I'm only sorry it's taken me so long. We're not allowed to begin a day's work until dawn. Not without the supervisor, regulating workflow…"

It's dawn, already…?

"I had to slip away from the rest of my excavation crew to find you. We don't go down this way, in these mines. Stumbling upon you was just a bit of dumb luck. No sign of Bern yet, though..."

He frowned through his teeth at his mention of Bern, brows furrowed with disdain. As the Viscountess looked up at him, she detected a peculiar array of emotions having crossed his features. She could not put her finger on it, but it set her ill at ease. She decided to turn it over in her mind for the time being, dropping her gaze from his face to the lantern dangling just below his chin. As her eyes drooped downward, she noticed the trail of blood from outside her peripheral vision, having trickled into her line of sight from her collarbone, down her chest. It stained her corset and floral dress. She realized then, that her eardrums had burst.

This was the cause for the ringing sensation in her ears and the wetness she felt. The back of her head must have been struck by a fallen bit of rock, also wet with her own blood and tingly with likely impact. Could there have been a loud blast? She mused over this for a moment, but her thoughts were strained and hazy. She decided now was not the time to dwell, leaning her head into Roland's chest through his shirt. He smelled faintly of cayenne. *How strange,* she thought.

"Oh, no. Listen," Roland said, stopping dead in his tracks suddenly, and holding her very still. "Do you hear that?"

The Viscountess held her breath, straining to hear. All she could register was the sound of his voice, and when she listened carefully, the faintest beating of his heart through his chest. Though, even this was almost completely drowned out by the ringing in her ears which had not stopped. She raised her head to look up at him again. He suddenly looked very ill.

Without warning, he dropped the handle of the lantern from his mouth, setting its lamp over her body, and started in on a clumsy jog. The Viscountess jostled around in his arms a bit as he rushed, the erratic movement sending sharp pains through her left leg and head. Roland panted as he ran, beginning to sweat from his body's exertion.

"The... props are... creaking...!" he said, in between breaths.

The Viscountess thought for a moment. She recalled seeing pillars along the walls of the mines earlier, when she had been following Bern. It was then that she realized they were all that separated the ceiling, from the ground. They were about to experience a cave in.

"When the props... start talkin'..." Roland panted, "...the miners start... walkin'!"

The Viscountess felt like she was on a mechanical bull, the only level of reference she had to what that might be like, being the stories she remembered overhearing; the crewmen from her father's ship, each bragging about how long they could last without being thrown off. The machine bull would shake and bump them, and they would each hold on as tightly as they could. They seemed to have a lot of fun at the saloons they would visit from surviving settlements around the world over the course of their travels. They would often leave to explore the town they were in after finishing their duties aboard the ship, once docked. Even Rivkah would sometimes go, and the Viscountess always wished she were able to join her.

"Don't you do that; don't you fall asleep!" she heard Roland say, forcing his words out in one labored breath. She had closed her eyes, almost drifting out of consciousness all over again, lost with her thoughts. "I need... you to hold... the light!"

The Viscountess opened her eyes. Her arms were tucked limply around her chest. Weakly, she crossed her right arm over her upper body, shakily grabbing at the handle of the lantern cradled on top of her, and lifted it. As Roland ran, she tried to hold it steady out in front of him.

I can do this... Just have to focus... she thought to herself, trying to keep her mind sharp in spite of its dizzied lack of clarity.

Roland was puffing hard, struggling to hold her in his arms. A couple of times, he had to stop and bounce her up higher to reestablish his grasp. The Viscountess could feel his muscles bulging with the strain of her weight. His shirt had become very damp against her cheek, clinging to his body with his sweat. The aroma of cayenne permeating from his clothes became much more poignant, mingling with the sulfuric mustiness of the air. All she could make out around him was the light from the lantern, illuminating his features. She wondered how he was able to see where he was going with so little light.

"You see... the mice...?" Roland gasped. "Leadin' us... back...!"

Mice? There are mice in these mines?!

The Viscountess cringed. She hated mice. Mice would occasionally find themselves aboard her father's ship, stowing away in the lower cabins during which time the ship was docked. They carried diseases with them, and she recalled a time when one of the crewmembers had been bitten. It took him twenty-four days to die. She really, really hated mice.

There was a faint rumbling resounding over the ringing in her ears, now. To Roland, it must have sounded a lot louder. His breathing became hoarser, and the Viscountess could feel the pounding of his heart through his chest with her cheek pressed up against him. It skipped a couple of beats as he ran faster than ever now, knocking her around in his increasingly shaky arms. The lantern the Viscountess clutched loosely in her hand swiveled and swayed with the bumping.

"Oh, All Mother… It's happening…! No, no… no!"

The Viscountess could now hear loud cracks and rumbles which drowned out the sound of ringing in her ears. She felt dirt fall on her face, from the ceiling. Roland tripped over something on the ground, his legs frantically struggling to recapture his footing; to no avail. He came tumbling down over the tracks, the Viscountess rolling out of his arms and sprawling out over the wooded panels alongside him. Before hitting the ground, she managed to curl herself around the lantern, shielding it from breaking. She laid there a moment, unable to sit up. She could feel a light, scratchy scurrying of tiny mouse paws run over her, and she began to cry.

It was almost as if she were too tired for the fear to have set in completely, before, but it was overtaking her now. She was tired, thirsty, frightened, and seriously wounded. It took one of her greatest phobias scampering across her fallen body for her to regain consciousness of her surroundings enough to know that she may be buried alive—and then she would die. She sobbed, voicelessly. She felt as if she had failed her father, her mother. Herself.

She felt a cold, clammy hand clasp around her wrist, then roughly work its way up her arm. Roland kneaded sightlessly through the dark, crawling up beside her. He grabbed the lantern away from her, propping her up with his other hand as he reached around, behind her head.

"You have to stand…!" he said, breathlessly. "C'mon; put your arms… around my neck!"

She weakly did so, draping her arms over his broad shoulders and lacing her fingers to crown. Roland heaved, standing her up as he stood with her. She leaned into him, unable to put any weight on her left leg. Being upright was a rush to her head, his face spinning through the black nothingness in front of her. More clumps of dirt fell about her head and shoulders.

"When I say to hold your breath, you *hold* it! Do you understand me?!" Roland shouted.

She nodded up at him. More dirt clumps, as the rumbling continued to grow even louder.

"Raise your arms high above your head; as high as you can!" he said, raising his. "Now hold—!"

The Viscountess raised her arms, holding her breath just as the ceiling came down around them.

CHAPTER 13

Trials & Tribulations

Cool air funneled around the Viscountess's fingers. There must have been a ventilation system overhead. She wriggled them around, trying to loosen the dirt around her hands. Her body and arms were completely buried, the tips of her fingers being her only point of mobility. She tried to move her body out of the imprisonment of dirt that surrounded her, raising her knees through the soil and shifting her head; all, completely covered. She was firmly trapped, and unable to breathe. Her heart raced in her chest. Her fear was almost crippling.

What seemed like minutes, passed. She was suffocating. Just then, she felt unfamiliar hands around her fingers, digging out her wrists. Steadily and with great haste, they unearthed her arms to her elbows. Several hands clasped around her limbs while others still dug. She felt herself being raised as dirt began to fall away from her, little by little. Her face surfaced, and she gasped automatically. The air once more rushing into her lungs made her feel so lightheaded she felt as though her body were floating. Every nerve tingled inside her. She heard voices now, over the continued ringing in her ears, trying to make them out. None of them were recognizable.

"A *woman!*" one of them said. "How'd she get into these mines?! She ain't no scavenger, is she…?"

"No," said another. "Look at her clothes! Those are—*were*—some fine threads…"

"So what is she doin' here?"

An extra voice; "Don't know, but we need to get the doc out here as soon's we can," the man said. "Looks like she's hurt real bad…"

The Viscountess was set out over the ground, from which she had been plucked like the roots of a turnip. She felt very strange. The pain was faded, at least in that moment, and now all that remained was the cold, faraway twinge of her body's numb surrender.

"Was she with yeh, Roland?" a gruff man's voice questioned.

"Yes… Hnnggh… yes, sir…!" Roland groaned. The Viscountess turned her head toward his voice, her vision blurry with her own tears; a mixture of emotion and natural bodily function, as her eyes watered to wash away dirt. She was covered from head to boot. As she fixed her gaze through a dizzied fog, she could just make out Roland's form. He was on the ground beside her, set free of the pounds of collapsed dirt and rubble moments before she was. She could make out the curvature of his back as he swayed on his knees, doubled over and clutching his stomach. He had overexerted himself, the injuries he sustained from fighting, worsened.

"Yeh shouldn't have broken off from the group; yeh know we don't go past the sulfur buildup," the gruff voice scolded him.

The Viscountess closed her eyes, unable to keep them open for very long. Her head was spinning; her lungs, on fire. All she could do was breathe.

"Put 'em both on stretchers and let's get 'em back toward the surface," the gruff voice instructed the other men, presumably all miners. "They can recuperate at the check-in station by the entrance while we get Doctor Fischer out here… We should probably alert the Governor, too…"

Some other words might have been exchanged, and the Viscountess barely felt her arms and legs being taken up as she was lifted, and put onto a firm, thinly cushioned surface. It was like a strange feeling of weightlessness in such a dazed state, as she was carried off by two men on the rigid plank she rested upon. The cool air circulating through the mine helped to further placate her, and again she felt herself unable to keep from drifting out of consciousness all over…

…When she opened her eyes, it was as if she had merely blinked. There was a dim light source, lanterns hanging along the rocky ceiling in this part of the mine. Roland was seated on a small wooden stool, crouched over her with a canteen of water. He tipped it into her mouth, and her arms rose up unconsciously for her hands to clasp around it.

She drank deep, the mineral-rich lukewarm fluid washing down her throat and soaking her pallet. She gasped, choking a bit, some of the water dribbling down her chin and carrying dried dirt with its trickle. Roland was just as covered in dirt as she was, his once white shirt now brown with soot. His piercing blue eyes stood out now more than ever as he looked at her with a strangely startled gaze.

"You spoke," Roland said. He appeared utterly fascinated, his wide stare dancing from her eyes to her mouth as he held the canteen steady for her. "I didn't know you could speak."

The Viscountess tried to make sense of what he was saying. *I don't; I can't,* she thought, downing the last of the water in a final heaping gulp. *I… when…?! I think I'd know it, if I had.*

"In your sleep, you mentioned Bern. And a few other things, too… Something about her *sister*…? That key she seemed so excited about; it belonged to you, then."

Yes! Yes!! Please; you must help me get it back! the Viscountess pleaded, pushing the canteen away and grabbing at his wrists. *We have to find her! We have to find out where she went!*

"Hey, take it easy…" Roland soothed. He placed his rough hands over the Viscountess's shoulders and eased her back down. She did not realize she was even sitting up partway; demonstration of her animated severity. He cracked a slight crescent smile. "…At least now I know you're actually *capable* of speaking. I guess that means one day, maybe you'll speak to me, right…? Heh. Maybe even thank me for rescuing you back there, huh?"

He started to chuckle, but stopped abruptly with a sharp wince, wrapping his arms around his midsection once more. The Viscountess watched him, suddenly feeling quite guilty for his pain. At the same time, her flutters had returned, with the knowledge that she was still alive because of him. At this point, it was only second nature for her to slide her hand over the surface of the stretcher she still laid upon, meeting it with his. Her hand was small and delicate by comparison, her fingers moving over his knuckles and curling around the inside of his thumb. He gave it a light squeeze, rubbing his thumb over her wrist comfortingly. Her heart leapt.

Even with the simplest of actions, the elation she felt was near overwhelming; unlike anything she had ever experienced before. If only she were not so weak. The thought of rising to throw her arms around his neck played out vividly in her mind. She fantasized over him enveloping her in a tight embrace, the two of them kissing so rough, so passionate, so fierce that if lips parted from mouth for even a second the consequence would only be more grabbing and clawing with the need to be closer. Their arms; their hands, working to draw the other nearer, though even flesh on flesh could not adequately satiate the raw need to interweave their bodies like fibrous, firm vines up a chiseled stone wall.

"Viscountess… Do you really think common folk are all *scum*…?" Roland asked, abruptly.

The question caught her off guard, wrenching her from her musings with force comparable to the collapse of a rocky ceiling; something she was now familiar with, to compare. It disturbed her somehow that she had to think about it before she was able to give a straight answer. Was she really so biased, as her uncle? She took a moment to contemplate this, looking away from Roland so as not to meet with his eyes. After all, he, himself, was 'common folk,' and not moments before, she was a proper aristocratic skylark whose lasciviousness almost got the better of her. Even then, she wondered how he would have known this in her. She was certain she did no such thing as voice her innermost thoughts and feelings. Those were private; personal—*revealing*.

"I see…" Roland sighed, disappointedly. He pulled away from her hand, sitting back in the stool as he looked her over. She returned his gaze, unable to stop herself looking back at him, her eyes drifting up to meet with icy blue hues, now cold and distant with expressed disenchantment. "Honestly, I didn't take you for the kind of woman to be so… *opinionated*, in this way."

It took all her strength to sit up, propping herself on her elbows for support. She met him eyelevel, her expression pleading and uncertain. She felt at a loss; confused, and troubled. She wanted only to please him, this man whom she barely knew; this man who had saved her life. Class had nothing to do with it then, and it should not have anything to do with *anything* now. She wrestled with the conflicting surges of her emotions and her logical sensibilities. Looking into Roland's eyes now, however, it was as if they were for once in harmony.

The Viscountess reached for him again, refusing to back down. Gingerly, she leaned over while balancing herself upright on her knees, distributing weight more on her right leg. As drained and sickly as she felt, she wanted nothing more than to reassure him, placing both her hands over his cheeks. She could feel his light, rough stubble grazing her palms through the residual dirt caked on his face and coating the lining of creases in her hands. She looked at him with all the sincerity she felt in her heart, hoping that this would be enough; hoping her body language would translate her sentiments in some way. He returned her gaze, his icy stare melting into weary warmth.

"...I wonder what Bern was hoping to achieve, in telling you she had a sister," Roland said, simply; an appreciated effort in changing the subject. "She's never had a sister, so I don't know why she would have told you something like that..."

For reasons not all that clear to the Viscountess, this bit of knowledge sat particularly ill with her, beyond the suggestion as to Bern having lied. She wished she could put her finger on exactly what it was that troubled her, but her mind drew a blank as she tried to psychoanalyze her own negative response upon hearing this. She could not understand why she would feel so strongly about Bern's sister being fabricated. It should be chalked up to reasons more why she was not to be trusted, and simply left at that, should it not?

"Hey, no need to look so forlorn over that," Roland reassured, his crescent smile returning. "She's a liar, and a thief, and we're gonna find your key and get it back for you. I promise."

More flutters. She studied his face, drinking in the every last of his features, from the cobalt crescent scar under his left eye, stretched thin with his clever, bewitching smile, to the crowfeet lines at the outermost corners of his lids. Though the lines in his face were deepened by the soot, his features rather obscured, the darkened complexion he borne only served to intensify his already striking blue eyes. She could get lost in those eyes; like swimming through crystal clear pools of water, their surface reflecting such light to the depths that even as she plunged headlong into him, lost as she was, she would fear no more—for she could forevermore see.

His hands rose up to meet with hers, still held lovingly to his cheeks. He covered her hands completely in his, leaning in closer to her; and her, to him. Her heart raced and her body tingled. She was as a stoked flame, emanating the heat of a fiery need now burning within her. She could feel his hot breath now, his mouth parted slightly as he hovered over her lips. She watched his gaze drop from her eyes, then back again. She realized, only then, that he had been taking her in with his eyes, as well. She felt vulnerable and bare, almost uncomfortably so, in such a state of physical decline. She wished she were more in her element.

The look in his eyes truly intimidated her. He felt so open and real, so wide-eyed and giving. She wanted nothing more than to take of him, and give herself in turn. It was hard to maintain eye contact with him. She felt as if he could see straight into her soul. He grabbed her, quickly. She could feel his hands around her waist now, albeit barely, through the taut fabric of her steel boned corset. Her hands glided away from his cheeks and still further back, lacing to crown once more around the nape of his neck. Her arms now rested over his shoulders; his lips, so close. *What are you waiting for?* she thought to herself, eagerly.

...You've always wondered what it would be like.

"Ah-*heh*-hem!" a gruff voice cleared itself. Roland pulled away from the Viscountess with fervorous abandon, simultaneously shoving her back down onto the stretcher. She tumbled against it, falling backward into her previous laying position. 'Unsettled' was not the word for what she was now feeling. This was the second time he had abruptly ceased the showing of interest in her, upon the interruption of another. Was he ashamed?

"You doin' okay, I see?" the man asked, with a bit of a playful lilt in his thick, gravelly voice. The Viscountess turned her head toward its source, realizing she had not yet taken in her surroundings. In her moment of reawakening, Roland was all she had cared to see.

Roland had swiveled the stool around so that he was now facing in the direction the imposing voice had come from. As she looked beyond him, she saw a very broad man with his arms crossed over his chest. His belly protruded far out in front of him, and half his face was hidden under a thick woolly beard; mostly white, with a varied collection of graying strands. He wore a silvery hardhat with an assortment of dents and scratches marking all along its surface.

"Where's yer helmet, boy?" he asked, not waiting for Roland to answer his previous question. It must have been rhetorical.

"I, uhh, ...I guess I must have lost it while I was running, sir..." Roland replied, haphazardly. "Doctor Fischer informed me of a girl, who may have gotten lost in the mines. I... Well, I guess I found her. Will the doc be comin' out here soon? She's definitely hurt real bad." His response seemed almost deflective. The Viscountess did not like being referred to as just, 'a girl.'

"I know Orel's a good friend a' yers, Roland. No need to be so formal about it," the gruff man said, before turning his attention to the Viscountess. She nervously averted her eyes. She heard the man chuckle, possibly at her having turned her gaze. Between Roland and this man, she felt increasingly self-conscious. "So, another redhead, huh?" he continued. "Got a thing for 'em, don't yeh? She kinda looks like the last girl you were—"

"*Okay*, Arnie, yes! Yes, she does," Roland cut him off, seeming embarrassed. "We don't have to talk about that right now, though, do we?"

The Viscountess cocked a brow over this statement. *Another redhead? Last girl…?!*

"Roland, m'boy," Arnie continued, unfazed, "I'm gonna level with yeh here fer a minute. Not as yer supervisor, but as a *friendly advisor*… Yer one of the best damn miners we got out here—Pardonin' the strong language, ma'am—and with that in mind, we can't afford to lose yeh."

The Viscountess regarded his offhanded, if polite inclusion of concern for her sensibilities favorably. She eased herself a bit, despite the *redhead* comment, realizing she had been quite tense since he first came into the bit of space they rested in. As the two spoke, she decided to take this time to get a sense for where she was.

"…That being said," he continued, "I'm concerned about what the Governor will have to say about yer little rescue mission, bein' that it took yeh away from yer work. And now we're short on meetin' our quota of coal supply for the town!"

Roland sighed. "Can't we just tell him about the cave in and leave it at that? I mean, does he really gotta know about *the girl* being here…? Besides, it's not our fault if we fall short of supply for the day because of environmental situations outside our control!"

As the Viscountess looked around, she tried to ignore the welling resentment she felt over Roland's continued referral, to her, as 'girl.' She felt as if this were all she was to him. She tried to put this insecurity out of her mind, soon realizing they were still within a part of the mine. She noticed the surroundings of the check-in station were very cluttered. There were various boxes stacked on top of each other, and papers scattered seemingly without order over a desk behind the stool Roland sat on. On the far stony wall by the makeshift threshold, the Viscountess noticed a board with punched timecards. It all looked very strange and foreign to her.

"Yeah, but yeh know the Governor just ain't gonna see it that way," Arnie sternly replied, after a moment's pause. "Even *he* knows yer condition, and that yeh still came to work today…"

"Just, please; he can't know about the girl," Roland urged.

"Hey, wait a tick! Ain't she the little lady who jumped in on Gorgol when you was fightin' him? …Can't be; can it?!" Arnie looked her over, eyes wide, his gruff voice raising a few cracked decibels in poorly controlled excitement. "The Governor told everybody in the crowd that night that she was gonna be 'properly dealt with' as he put it. Ain't never heard a time when that didn't mean some kinda maimin' and killin'…"

"Which is exactly why we can't say anything to him about her *now*, sir! She got off, the first time. She won't be so lucky, the next. Orel told me the guards gave him some trouble over her, last night… *Please*…"

There was an uncomfortable silence that hung in the air. The Viscountess began to feel her physical tensions returning. Perhaps Roland was withholding his feelings for her, in both expression and in the manner he spoke, because he was trying to protect her. Why else would he have gone to such great lengths to save her? Of course, it also stood to reason that his sense of honor bound him to reciprocity, and he was merely adhering to his code. Perhaps she was fantasizing the whole thing, per her own wishful thinking. She was sure she could torture herself like this indefinitely, if she tried.

"…You got a name, miss?" Arnie inquired, genially.

"She… uhh, well," Roland glanced back at the Viscountess, apologetically. "She's a mute."

"A mute…?"

"That means she can't speak. We know she's a Viscountess."

Arnie frowned. "Ahh. Pity she can't speak. She looks like she'd have a good voice on 'er."

Roland only smiled, awkwardly. The Viscountess was unsure of how to feel, her emotions an exhaustive jumble of uncertainty. For a split moment, she wished she could just bury herself in one of her father's books and return to her little conjectural safety box of absolutes and repetition. At least in the world of science and mechanics, there were few grey areas to be had; it either was, or it was not. Emotions were *complicated*.

"Sir," a man covered in dirt and wearing a hardhat approached. "Doctor Fischer is here."

"Good," Arnie replied. "Tell the boys they're not to utter a *word* about the girl, or details of the cave in. Yeh hear me? We had a collapse in the mine and that's all anyone needs to know. Everyone is okay; no black carriage will be dispatched back into town, today."

Black carriage...? the Viscountess pondered, wondering what significance this held.

The man in the hardhat nodded curtly, turning on his heel and out of sight down the mine passageway, opposite whence he came. Orel took his place, standing in the threshold. He looked much worse for wear than when the Viscountess first encountered him earlier. He looked shaken and moderately roughed up. His glasses hung crookedly over his nose, held together with a small wad of gum. His eyes were puffy and bloodshot. He had shiny discolored bruises swelling around both his cheekbones, under his right eye slightly more than his left.

"Orel, man, what'd they do to you?!" Roland exclaimed, brows narrowed angrily. "You look worse than before!"

The Viscountess could not help but feel a little guilty upon seeing Orel standing there, a bit of a mess. If not for her, the guards would not have given him so much trouble.

"Roland, Viscountess. *Ernie*, was it?" he greeted them, shakily.

"It's Arnie," Arnie corrected. "Good day, Doctor Fischer."

"Howd'youdo...! My bruises are nothing to worry about! They're from when you saw me last, Roland, but they've had time to swell. Speaking of bruises, you each look to be in far worse shape than I." Orel started to push his glasses up the bridge of his nose with his fingers, but seemed to remember the gum holding them together, and quickly took his hand away. "Er, right then; I'll go ahead and check Roland out first. Something tells me the Viscountess will take more of my time. I'll inspect you... somewhere with a little more lighting, perhaps...?"

"Oh. Right, sure," Roland agreed, getting up off the stool carefully. His posture was stooped low, and as he stood, his stomach made an audible, slushy growling noise. "...That can't be good."

"We just need to make sure you have the appropriate medication," Orel said. "...And that you're not bleeding out, internally."

"Oh, is that all," he sardonically replied.

The Viscountess watched Roland follow Orel around the corner and up the mine passageway toward the entrance. There was a brief, somewhat awkward pause as her eyes met with Arnie's.

"Well, my hands are tied with all this chaos goin' on at the moment," he said, breaking the silence. He seemed to take the eye contact as an open invitation to socialize, despite knowing full well the Viscountess could not engage him in conversation, herself. "I have a report to fill out, so I should be doin' that, but I can't for the life of me figger out what a little thing like yeh'd be doin' here? Do yeh even know anything about minin'…?"

She shook her head, slowly sitting up partway to prop herself up on her elbows again.

"Well, then! Yer in luck!" he gloated, crossing around the desk and over to the stool where Roland had sat. He plopped himself down like a sack of potatoes, the stool disappearing completely underneath his much larger frame. "Yer talkin' to the man who singlehandedly started this little mining operation! Got it off the ground 'bout thirty years back. I'm proud to say that without it, the town's trade would be pretty nonexistent. It's because of these mines that we're able to just barely keep ourselves on the grid, for outsiders. It'd be damn near *impossible* to have what meager things we got goin' for us, otherwise… Ain't gonna find too many materials like wood an' iron in the middle of a desert!"

The Viscountess nodded, somewhat absently. There were strange noises that sounded like they were coming from outside the mine, like loud thumps and muffled shouts, but Arnie seemed not to notice. She wondered how long it would be before Orel finished up with Roland, glancing around the heavily shadowed area of the check-in station. Being so close to the entrance, she could tell the sun must have risen by now. Even the lanterns lining the ceiling would be scarce lighting, if not for the faintest gleam of daylight coming in from the mine's shaft.

"Minin' is serious business, y'know… If yeh ain't careful, there've been serious injuries workin' these mines. Lost a few of my men, *and* their boys."

Boys? There are children going to work, in these mines?

"This wudn't the first cave in; won't be the last neither. The lucky ones come out of it with a few lost fingers or toes, here n' there. The luckier, still, a few scars maybe. I'll show yeh mine!"

Before the Viscountess had time to protest, Arnie had already swiveled the stool around in a fit of overzealous enthusiasm and lifted the back of his shirt, dropping his trousers to the split of his buttocks to reveal his very wide backside, in all its entirety. The sudden display both horrified and repulsed her, and it was all she could do to maintain her composure; as composed as a person could be, lying on a stretcher whilst covered in dirt and soot. Even so, she took in the expanse of hairy backside before her, unsightly that it was. There was an array of deep scars, some long and others short. Most of them had a faint cobalt tint, much like the scar under Roland's left eye. It almost looked as though someone had whipped him.

"Some of these scars I got when I was around yer age; or Roland's, at least. I dunno how old yeh are. Yeh look like you'd be around his age. Maybe a little younger, eh?" He tapped the top of his hardhat with his knuckles. "Had a few rocks fall on my head before too, but so long's I'm wearin' this, I'm usually okay. Still hurts when it happens, though!"

The Viscountess remembered her own head injury and touched her fingers to the back of her head, through her thick mane of red hair. When she did so, a wave of sharp pain shot through her skull. It was like an arrow piercing into bone, running through to her brain. She grimaced, dizzied, and laid her head back down. Arnie seemed to be too wound up and excited over what he was talking about to notice.

"Do yeh know why these scars look a little bluish?" he asked, rhetorically. "…It's 'cause bits of coal got trapped under my skin! And then my skin healed over it! Pretty nifty, eh?"

He seemed a little too excited about this for the Viscountess to understand. She just smiled and nodded politely, all the while thinking him quite odd. *To his credit,* she thought quietly, *this is certainly a man, impassioned by his work.* She had also passively wondered about the cobalt scar underneath Roland's eye. It was beginning to make a little more sense, as she found it to be an attractive feature on him— though, perhaps, not on Arnie. Still, she hoped any cuts she might have sustained did not result in such a scar.

"We call it a coal miners' tattoo! We wear 'em proudly, since they mark our survival from close encounters; cave ins, explosives, fallen rubble, faulty machinery… you name it! Occasionally yeh run into mice, which yeh gotta watch out for. If they bite yeh, well, who knows what the little buggers're carryin'!"

As he went on, he dropped his voice suddenly, becoming a little more dire. Despite his disposition having changed, he maintained the same enthusiasm with which he spoke.

"…Our biggest hindrance are subterran *degenerate*s lurkin' around in here, though. We've closed off most of the areas that have 'em, but sometimes they still get through. They're out wanderin' the desert plains, mostly, but in the mines they feed off a the mice. Usually they eat 'em whole, but if we find a half-eaten carcass lyin' around, that's when we gotta close off another area for the sake a' safety. Those damn things're dangerous."

The mention of degenerates made the Viscountess feel ill. She was not certain as to what they were, or why she reacted so strongly to the mention of them, but she hoped he would change the subject soon. What little she knew, she learned from having read post-war texts and eavesdropping over aristocratic hearsay.

"The boys would be boardin' up the area we found yeh in now, if that passageway hadn't caved in. Can never be too careful, yeh know what I mean? Oh… An' sorry, again, for my crass language. I don't find myself in the company of very many ladies."

I wonder why that might be, the Viscountess smirked.

Orel suddenly reappeared in the threshold. "Viscountess," he said, his voice shaky. "I will see you now. Come with me." He looked unusually stricken.

"I'll talk to yeh later, I guess," Arnie grinned. "Gotta be gettin' to my paperwork anyhow."

The Viscountess sat upright, wincing with pain as a dizzying rush of vertigo struck her all at once. She ached all over, and it took her great effort to stand. She did so, still, balancing most of her weight on her right leg, her left, still fairly numb. When she stepped forward, shifting her weight slightly, an overwhelming tingling sensation shot up her hip. She moved herself around the desk and crossed over to Orel, who took her by the hand and slipped her arm over, and around his shoulder. She welcomed the support.

He was much taller than the Viscountess, her arm reaching up awkwardly as he held her steady around the waist. "All the Governor and the guards or anyone else in Fyndridge know right now is that you ran away from town and have not come back," he said in a hushed voice, twitching and convulsing with every step. His nerves were shot. He looked far more the wreck than before, when he had gone to inspect Roland.

Where is Roland…? the Viscountess wondered, Orel's sudden, unusually nervous disposition setting her ill at ease. *What's wrong? What happened?*

"You are probably assumed dead by the town council, but if you go back, you're a liability and you are certain to be killed. Especially if the Governor catches wind of this little trip to the mines. But, we have bigger trouble now…"

The Viscountess watched him carefully. His features were contorted in a twist of nerves and strain, the veins in his neck and forehead visibly pulsing with his own tension. His face looked almost sickly beneath his various bruises, and he was sweating profusely. She felt his body tremble as he walked slowly, half carrying her, and half dragging her along. With his free hand, he combed his fingers through the graying strands of his messy black hair.

"Th-There's a man," he stammered, through clenched teeth. "He's wearing a cloak, and he has a… a glove made out of metal! Almost like it's a part of his arm!"

In that moment, her blood ran cold. She remembered the man, who somehow knew her father and mother; the man whose furtive history comprised a deal. She remembered him killing her father in front of her, just before a blackout saw her fleeing.

Demetrius…! she glowered. She wanted so much to rip into him slowly, with systematic precision. She wanted to make him bleed out, just as he had done to her father.

"He ambushed us with his men while I was examining Roland. He killed all the miners outside, and some of the guards who were patrolling the outer perimeter, before they could alert anyone else! He wants *you*, Viscountess. If I don't bring you before him now, he'll kill Roland; and he'll kill him if I bring anyone else with me, too. He says he's looking for the key!"

How did he find me? How does he know I'm here?!

"He… He saw the light, Viscountess. The light from the key, earlier this morning, as Bern was entering the mines. You must be able to see that light from a mile up! It's what alerted me to when Bern was leaving her house; the flash of light I saw, coming out her window."

The Viscountess's heart pounded with anxiety. The pressure was on. She wished she could run back to Arnie and let him know what was happening, but she knew they could not risk anyone else knowing what was going on just outside the mine entrance. She had to keep calm.

"J-Just stay close to me," Orel stuttered, teeth gritted. "We won't let them take you!"

They made their way through to the exit, stepping out of the mine's shaft. The first thing the Viscountess saw was the crudely painted off-white lettering on the side of the docked ship, which took up the entirety of the massive landing pad; the *S.S. Beulah*. The darkly tinted ship was enormous, dwarfing her father's in size by at least two times over. Its ballooned sails rested, partly deflated over the mast of the ship on long, thick wooden planks that ran from its nose to its posterior. She arbitrarily took in the rest of its intimidating features; miles of rope fastened around the blimpish fixtures overhead, the hull lined with cannons, windows lining each of the cabins, and pirates descending the ramp, dropped from the deck and onto the landing pad.

Then, the Viscountess's eyes fell on the man in the cloak; Demetrius. He had his arms crossed under the thick woolen fabric of its shroud, as he stood toweringly tall beside the familiar gold-toothed man in the black and white vertically striped pants. The much shorter man had Roland on his knees, holding him in a headlock with a knife pressed to his throat. Roland's lip was bloodied. He must have struggled. Scattered all around them were the lifeless bodies of men in hardhats; other miners, including a couple of guards from town. Standing a few steps behind Demetrius and the gold-toothed man were a dozen or so other pirates. They were each oddly dressed, with their hands on their weapons, remaining at the ready.

You sinister, creepy bastard, the Viscountess snarled, feeling her adrenaline pumping through her veins. She was nearly shaking just as much as Orel by this point, but not with shot nerves brought on by the anxiety of an inescapable state of affairs. She had a bloodlust.

"Aha, you've survived the fall, after all," Demetrius smirked, evilly. "I don't know how you've managed that, but if you hand over the key now, we'll leave you, and everyone else we *haven't* killed, alive. Now, how does that sound?"

The Viscountess clenched her fists, her nails digging into her bloodied, dirty palms. Demetrius stepped aside, suddenly. Behind him was a bound and tied down Rivkah. She had thick trails of dried blood running from her mouth which hung ajar, to her blouse. Someone had cut out her tongue.

CHAPTER 14

Caged

The Viscountess awoke in a puddle of her own filth. The smell of urine intermingling with the stagnant stench of fecal matter roused her into a state of half consciousness, and it was just not a very good situation for her at all.

"Wakey, wakey," came a woefully familiar voice, scratchy and deep with malcontent.

A massive wash of ice cold water splashed over her suddenly. She sat upright with a start, shivering and eyes wide open. She realized then that she was in a small holding cell with three other women. Rivkah was one of them. As she looked up still, her eyes fell over the man with gold ingot teeth, neither sneering nor frowning as he looked down at her with a toothy mug. He held a large, overturned wooden bucket in front of his vertically striped pants, still dripping with some of the water he had thrown over her.

"Ye be the daughter of the 'Great Adventurer,' Amadeus?!" he cackled, coarsely. His ugly laugh was followed by a hacking, wheezy cough, which was then followed by a hocking spit. The phlegmy ball landed at her boots with a splat against the metal flooring of the cell. "Out a' err'one on that ship done burned to the ground, I'd never a' guessed it, lookin' at'cha now! I done shat myself *and* pissed me trousers… but never at the same time!"

The Viscountess looked down at herself and surveyed her condition. She could only hear out of her right ear. The skirt of her floral dress was hiked up around her waist, revealing her torn stockings and a bruise on her upper left thigh roughly the size and coloration of an eggplant. The dirt and soot covering her body was now a sopping wet, muddy mixture of excrement and bile. In her unconscious state, she had evacuated the contents of both her bladder and bowels. She could not fathom how long she had been lying like this, but as the odor assaulted her senses, she felt the retching heaves of bile rise up into her throat. Try as she might, she could not stop herself turning to vomit, the acidic fluids burning her nose and esophagus on their way out.

As the gold-toothed man burst into a fit of hysterics, cackling and hacking over her reduced state, the Viscountess collapsed into deep, shaking sobs. She felt repulsive and ashamed, unable to keep in the lowest misery she had ever known. Her sobs were guttural; almost animalistic. She felt like a wounded beast, as sick in the head as her state and appearance suggested her to be. Maybe she *was* 'retarded.' Maybe the branding on the back of her neck was just a symbol that meant nothing at all – a scar of a past existence she would never again come to know.

She heard the sounds she was making; the sobbing cries that broke her waking silence for the first time in over a decade. It did not sound like her, but then, she was uncertain of what she should sound like after so much time. Once more, it had taken one of her greatest phobias to send her over the edge. She looked at the contents of her insides, spilled out over the metal flooring beside her. She realized then that this must have been the second time or so, since her confinement. As she sobbed, she thought of her father and mother; how she dishonored them both. How she failed them. The thoughts became jumbled madness in her head. She could no longer think straight.

I'm sorry; I'm so sorry… I'm a failure… Favorite dress. This was mother's favorite dress! It's ruined, and so is everything! Everything's ruined, and it's all my fault! I could have done more… I could have done so much more, to save you, mother; I'm sorry! I was young, and stupid, and I'm still stupid, and I deserve this; I deserve all of it…

All she could do was despair as she bawled there on the cold, hard, wet floor. Her mind was wrought with the silent ravings of a woman reduced to within an inch of her sanity. She barely heard the gold-toothed man leave over the sounds of her own wretched cries.

So stupid, so disgusting… I am nothing I—

"That is Gertie. He is rather dreadful, do you not think?" one of the women spoke, suddenly.

The Viscountess calmed her shaking sobs enough to slowly glance up at her, catching a better look than she had before. The woman looked very strange and otherworldly, with skin so milky white in the dimly lit confines of their holding cell, that it practically glowed. She appeared almost translucent as the light hit her through the metal bars, the shadows falling upon her in harsh broken lines. Between the shadows were the grayest eyes she had ever seen; not a hint of pigment, yet they sparkled like diamonds, wide and captivating. Her expression was relaxed; tranquil, even, but her eyes had a froglike quality to them that made her appear perpetually startled. She was bizarrely beautiful.

Her hair was very fine, cascading over her slender shoulders like yarn, and just as white as her milky skin. She wore a modest pale blue shawl made from knitted wool, otherwise seamless if not for the moth-eaten holes which made the spaces in between all the larger. For someone locked up in a cage, she did not seem that much worse for wear.

"I have not the faintest idea why a man so chary as Demetrius would allow that pirate to be near him," she continued. The Viscountess felt somewhat soothed by her voice. It was light and melodious, and pleasantly soft. "He is so bumbling, and he acts so predominantly out of fear. Not like your friend, Miss Rivkah... They severed, and cauterized her tongue just yesterday. She has had much to say about you, to us, but not as much to say about you, to Demetrius, or any of his crew. That is probably why they cut it out. They supposed that if she was not going to use it to help them, that she did not need it."

The Viscountess unsteadily turned her head to look at Rivkah, who was sitting in a corner of the cell with her arms wrapped tightly around her legs. They were pulled up close to her chest. Rivkah regarded her weakly, her mouth still hanging ever so slightly ajar. Her eyes were glossy and cheerless as she returned her gaze. The blood on her dirtied blouse had long since dried, and she was almost as filthy as the Viscountess, covered in coals and soot, just as the night their ship had gone aflame. It then occurred to her that Rivkah had not changed clothes, having been held this way in the *S. S. Beulah* the entire time.

"So, *you're* the Viscountess," the other woman said. Much the contrast to the softly musical voice of the woman who spoke before her, she had a deeply smooth monotone cadence. It had a droll diffidence to it, as though she were unmoved, if slightly amused by the Viscountess's shameful situation. She had to crane her neck around to see her. She was seated in the back corner of the holding cell, behind her and a little off to the side. Her features were obscured in the dark, unbroken shadows cast over her in this corner. "Well… It certainly does seem like you've been through a share of your own personal hell. Welcome back to the realm of the living. I would suspect, given your current condition, that you would rather not have joined us though. But, *then* I'm just projecting…"

The Viscountess was dumbstruck by how they could greet her in this way, given her humiliating state. How could they excuse the putrid stagnancy in the air? How could they forgive she, the noblewoman; the living example of higher standards? She had a responsibility to those many people of lesser standing; of lesser worth, to be a moniker of sorts. With her birthright, she was to be the symbol of cleanliness, poise, and virtue. It was her duty to set an example for commoners and kinfolk alike.

I'm a monster… she quietly despaired, falling back into her cycle of self-deprecating misery. *I could not save my friends, and I could not save my own mother. This is all my fault! Oh All Mother, what if they're dead…? I could never forgive myself, I'd—*

"That is Ovocula," the white frog-eyed woman said, gesturing to the other, shrouded in shadow.

…What…?

"Have you not ever heard of such a peculiar name before? Not simple, like mine. I am called Gwendolyn—Gwendolyn Amber Rose O'Bannion of Galvinsglade. But just Gwendolyn is fine."

"Gwendolyn, dear," Ovocula said, sardonically, "if 'just Gwendolyn' were fine, you wouldn't be introducing yourself that very same way to *every* new person you meet."

"I apologize, Miss Ovocula. I do not mean to grate on your already shot nerves."

"In any case," she continued, brushing over the last of her rapport, "I doubt it matters all that much who you are, or from where you hail, when you're locked up in here. It's just too bad Rivkah couldn't tell us what *your* name was before Demetrius cut out her tongue. I suppose none of us thought it very important at the time… Rivkah seemed pretty confident of your demise. Of course, from how I hear things went down, I'm sure you thought the same of her. But, again; projecting. Gwendolyn says I do that." She sounded vinegary, despite Gwendolyn's sincerity.

"It is somewhat unpleasant that you should take my words out of their original context, Miss Ovocula. I find it stressful that you seem to misunderstand me so frequently, and all the more so when your misunderstanding is… *projected*, unto another, as fact."

"Oh, for the love of—!"

"Since we bring it up again," Gwendolyn talked over her, pleasant as can be, "I simply meant that Miss Ovocula is rather pessimistic in her world view. And that this affects her general disposition when faced with less than adequate conditions. In my experience, someone who is negative all of the time is not going to be able to consider clearly, the fact of the matter. Their judgments would be clouded by their own negative energy – and then they project it, before they know the truth."

"Less than adequate…? Negative energy?!" though remaining smooth spoken, Ovocula's voice carried with her agitation. "Are you daft, or do you really not remember where we are right now? I'd say our current situation is a little more terrible than being 'less than adequate,' for goodness' sake! And besides, the same can be said of someone who is incessantly cheerful!"

"The truth," Gwendolyn said, remaining amicably detached, "is that they are not going to kill us. They may torture us if we do not comply with their demands, but to put it simply, they need us for something. I do not know what that something is, but Demetrius would surely have killed Miss Rivkah if she were not of questionable value."

"Gwendolyn, what did you do with my bread ration?" Ovocula asked, changing the subject suddenly. "Now that the smel— umm," she glanced quickly at the Viscountess, "I mean, now that I've… gotten a little more used to our surroundings, I think I can finally stomach something to eat. Where did you put it?"

"I bequeathed it unto my mouth," Gwendolyn replied, quite solemnly. "And then my tongue beheld it. And then I ate of it."

Ovocula sighed, and grimaced. "Of *course* you did."

"You had given it to me. Do you not remember? It was shortly before you had become sick, and immediately after you had become sick all over the Visc—"

"*Okay!* Yes! I remember; *thank* you!"

The Viscountess wilted with shame. She felt far less than noble, and all the more less than human. Her glazed, puffy eyes drifted resignedly over to Rivkah, whom she noticed had still been watching her. Her eyes, though sad, were comforting; understanding. Her eyes, though tired, shown a bottomless well of worldly wisdom and a small burning fire that refused to die. Her exotic golden brown eyes, willful and strong, replenished the Viscountess. They instilled within her an ember of hope. She was so thankful to see her again, alive.

"Say, Miss Rivkah," Gwendolyn said, thoughtfully, "I do not suppose you might happen to have a parchment of some kind? And a writing utensil, as well, perhaps?"

"A writing utensil, and parchment?!" Ovocula repeated, incredulously. "You *can't* be serious. Why would a skylark engineer just happen to have these things tucked away in their drawers?"

Rivkah patted around for a few seconds, checking each of her pockets. Eventually she slipped a hand into one of her back compartments, pulling out a small, folded piece of paper. It was dirty and crumpled, but when she began to unfold it with her grimy, gloveless hands, the Viscountess could clearly make out the outlines for what appeared to be a new ship design. Had Rivkah been planning to construct a vessel of her own? She was surprised, and almost appalled. If her uncle had known, he would surely have had her removed from the crew. Perhaps she was a bit jealous? She banished the thought from her mind, unable to deny her astonishment at the very least.

"I don't get it," Ovocula said, plainly aghast. "An *engineer* wouldn't know how to even read, let alone write! That's just a bunch of pictures of arrows, pointing to ship parts. Are those construction plans...?"

"An earth dweller engineer may not be able to read," Gwendolyn replied, "but a *skylark* engineer most certainly could! Miss Rivkah cannot tell us what the Viscountess's name is, and neither can she, herself, what with her *elective mutism*..."

"Elective mutism...? How in the world—?"

"My uncle was a psychologist. I would clean his study as a young girl. Often times, I would clean *during* his sessions. The walls were thin, and I could hear just about everything; from histrionics, to nymphomania. I have learned a lot from his practice, and I remember one instance where a man who came to see him suffered the same symptoms as the Viscountess. My uncle called it elective mutism. I remember him quite well, because he was a very odd man."

The Viscountess raised a brow to that statement, thinking Gwendolyn quite odd, herself.

"Anyway," she continued, "I supposed that once Demetrius decides he is finished with Mister Doctor Orel, the other pirates will bring him back here again. And then we can have him read her name off to us once Rivkah has written it! Does this sound… adequate?"

Rivkah nodded with a tired, but genuine smile, spreading the parchment over the floor and smoothing out the tears and wrinkles. She then took a small coal pebble caught in the folds of her clothing, and began to write it out.

The Viscountess felt relieved to know that Orel was still living, apparently locked in with them the whole time she was unconscious. It did not even matter to her that he would have been present for her unwitting self soiling. She needed to know that Roland was alive as well. And if so, where was he? Had they let him go, or taken him too? She tried only to focus on their kind gesture for now, happy for the chance to finally hear her own name spoken back to her after so much time. She watched as Rivkah spelled out the last crudely drawn letter.

Suddenly, the sound of a door slamming open, followed by loud clomping footsteps were heard from outside their holding cell. Rivkah quickly crumpled the paper and thrust it back into her pocket. As the door swung around, just out of view, a spilling of light washed in through the bars. The Viscountess craned her head around as the shadows momentarily lifted. She took in Ovocula's appearance. She wore an elegant black gown that was only moderately soiled and tattered, fitted with lace and beautiful embroidery all along its velvety fabric; all of it, black. She wore a black ribbon pulled tight around her neck, an oval brass locket dangling from its loop to the meeting of her collarbones.

She looked to be about the Viscountess's age, with wavy ebony hair framing a doll-like porcelain face. She had plump, full lips, long eyelashes, and beautiful emerald green eyes. Her cheeks were rosy; unusually splotchy, in bursts of pinks and reds that did not appear to have a rhyme to reason. She donned an expression wrought with worry, her eyes following the sounds of the approaching footsteps. Then the light dissipated as the door swung closed once more.

Soon, three men came into view; two tall, and one familiarly short. The taller pirates each had one of Orel's legs locked under their arms as they dragged his limp body over the wooden planks which made up the floor outside their cell. The shorter man, Gertie, lead them closer as he twirled a ring of keys around one of his fat, stubby fingers. He grinned toothily, the gleam from his golden sneer looming in the dimness of the surrounding ship compartment.

"I'm sure y'all are propp'ly acquainted now, aye?" Gertie said, with a wheezy chuckle. He turned the key in the lock on the other side of the bars. The Viscountess had not realized there was even a door there, until some of the bars separated from the others. "Guess ye can reacquaint 'cherselves with this limp noodle we got 'ere!"

Gertie stepped aside, and as he did, the two other men flung Orel into the holding cell with the Viscountess and the other women. He came toppling beside her as he impacted the metal flooring with a muddled pang. Just as they were shutting the door, Rivkah stood suddenly and charged into it. She let out an angry gurgling growl. It was raw, and human; pained, and furious, as she lashed out with clawed fingers. She raked them across the face of one of the pirates, drawing blood. The Viscountess looked on, shocked, as the man shouted obscenities and clutched the side of his cheek, his fingers covering his eye.

"Stupid bitch!" Gertie said, securing the lock on the door.

"Let me in there," the man growled. "I'm gonna learn 'er a lesson!"

"Oh, yeh'll learn 'er real good awright. Thought she 'ad learned to behave when the Cap'n cut out that perdy little tongue! Tsk, tsk... We'll do 'er one better—but, later! We gots other stuff to worry about right now; like them canopies o'er us, needin' more gas fer liftoff. Let's get to it!"

The man begrudgingly complied, all three turning to leave. The door swung open one last time, letting in a wash of light. Just as the door was closing again the Viscountess got a good look at Orel, turning him over to see if he was still breathing. He was a bloodied, beaten mess before her. His glasses were absent from his face. Both of his eyes were bruised and swollen shut.

CHAPTER 15

Triad of Fire

Hours passed. At one point, the Viscountess experienced a feeling of brief weightlessness, as though she had woken from a dream in which she were falling. She silently took this as indication enough that the ship had departed from land, and was once more airborne. The wooden planks which made up the floor outside the cell had begun to creak. A short while following, Orel finally stirred, his leg twitching and convulsing as he wheezed, breathlessly.

"He needs water," Gwendolyn said, extending a very pale arm to the Viscountess as she held out a tarnished brass cup. "I have some left in here; give this to him, if you would, please."

The Viscountess took the cup from her and raised Orel's head with her other hand. Carefully, she tipped it to his lips. He was receptive, drinking very weakly, but slowly taking in the cool fluid. Some of the water trickled down his chin, and he coughed abruptly, sputtering and gasping. The Viscountess set the cup down beside herself and wiped his mouth with the back of her hand, deciding against using her dress in the sordid state it was in. He panted and wheezed, seeming not to mind the foul odor permeating throughout the cell.

"Welcome back, Mister Doctor Orel," Gwendolyn calmly greeted him, her melodious voice as unchanged as her disposition. "If you could assess your state for us please, perhaps then we may be able to properly care for you in light of your new injuries."

The Viscountess could hear Ovocula scoff in the shadows. Rivkah merely exchanged glances with her, allotting a small shrug. She nodded back, and returned her gaze to Orel whose bottom lip was quivering, as though he were trying to get his mouth to work well enough to speak.

"My... arms are broken..." he said, weakly. His voice was almost a whisper.

"What did he say?" Ovocula asked.

Rivkah turned in her direction, raising a finger to her lips. "Shhh!" she advised.

"I have... two cracked ribs..." Orel continued, "A sprained ankle... think my nose is broke... and I... can't see. They hit me so... many times... May have... blood clot."

"A *blood* clot," Ovocula repeated. "What's that...?"

"Whatever it is, I suspect it is something very not good," Gwendolyn said, almost gravely. She began tearing the ends of her very plain dress in long, clothen strips. "We should tie these off around his arms and make a sling. It is not much, but it will do for the time being." Then she tore off another long strip, her legs now exposed up to her milky white calves. The Viscountess noticed that she was barefoot. "We should wrap this one around his head. For pressure. Daddy says that pressure helps with headaches. I would believe that Orel probably has one."

Gwendolyn handed off the torn pieces of her dress to the Viscountess, who only looked down at them in her hands, not really sure what to do. She hesitated a moment, before Rivkah finally snapped her fingers to garner her attention. She turned to look at her. Rivkah was holding her arm out, waiting for the strips of cloth to be passed over to her. The Viscountess smiled somewhat apologetically, feeling all the more useless and embarrassed as she placed them in her far more capable hands. From there, Rivkah took hold of Orel and began bandaging him up.

"As you know, Mister Doctor Orel," Gwendolyn began, "we have been locked up this way for quite some time. I am uncertain as to how many days, exactly—"

"Seven days; today marks a week," Ovocula interrupted.

They were aboard during the attack on my father's ship! the Viscountess thought, taking mental note of the amount of time having passed. *Unless... How long had I been out...?*

"Thank you, Miss Ovocula. Yes, that does sound about right. Of which, you and the Viscountess and that... other man, have spent with us for the better part of a day. You will have to excuse me, but since he has not been in here with us, I have not been able to catch up on his name. You have only spoken of him briefly, and I believe I saw him once whilst being escorted to the Lucy Liu."

Roland! the Viscountess silently gasped. It had to be him. It just had to be.

"…You mean, the loo? The *toilet?*"

"Ahh. Yes. Thank you, once again, Miss Ovocula. I overheard one of our pirate captors referring to it as a… a loopty loo! That is it! I thought it rather amusing. I must say, I have never before heard of such a thing. Daddy always calls it his throne, but never before have I—"

"You're getting off topic, Gwendolyn; for the love of All Mother…!"

"Yes. Right. I apologize. Where was I…? Oh! When I saw that man, I overheard some of the conversation entailing… something about returning to town, and asking if anyone might have seen a woman with a giant key. I thought it to be quite odd. I vaguely remember stories involving such a thing, as a child. Anyway, I heard Demetrius telling him they would kill the 'pretty little redhead,' whom I can only assume would be the Viscountess, if he did not return within the hour. Seeing as how she remains with us, I would suppose he has long since returned."

The Viscountess listened intently, her eyes darting around the cell at each of the women. A wave of relief washed over her, the more and more certain she was that it was Roland of whom she spoke. Her eyes fell back upon Rivkah, who had finished with Orel's makeshift arm slings.

"But, that doesn't make any sense," Ovocula said, after a pause. "Why would they trust him with such a thing? Couldn't he just alert all the guards in town, and come back with a small army…? And besides, I thought you were *so* convinced that they needed us badly enough *not* to kill us!"

"I assume he would not wish to risk calling in the reinforcements of his people. And I also assume that when Demetrius said something about no longer needing her if the woman with the key suited his needs… he meant it. Something about two Sages being unnecessary."

"What…" Orel weakly tried to speak, "What… Sage…?"

"She is a *Sagittarius*…!" Ovocula exclaimed, as though she were suddenly struck by lightning.

"I must be begging your pardon, Miss Ovocula, but what does this mean?"

"It must have something to do with why we've been kept here! *Sage* is another word for Sagittarius. Demetrius is *collecting* us... Don't you see?! The Viscountess is a Sagittarius. I am a Leo. Orel, what are you?"

"Don't..." Orel coughed, "I don't... know."

Ovocula crawled out of the shadows, moving past the Viscountess and making her way between Rivkah and Orel. Her emerald green eyes were alive with intrigue, brows narrowed and intense. She gathered her dress up around her, avoiding the mucky puddle where the Viscountess had lain. "What month were you born in?" she asked. "And, what day?"

"September... September 30th..."

"Aha!" Ovocula smiled, loftily. "You're a Libra."

"I do not understand," Gwendolyn frowned. "Why is it that Demetrius would want to collect people, simply by birth? It seems rather... *odd.*"

"It must have something to do with the key, I guess. I've never heard of these stories told to you in your youth, but it seems that we're a lot more expendable than you initially thought! So long as no one *better* comes along with one of our signs, we're safe, but until then..." Ovocula trailed off. "Orel, you said the key initially belonged to the Viscountess, right?"

"Y-... Yes."

"I think we need to find out more about this. We need to know why the key was in the Viscountess's possession in the first place, and then we need to know what exactly she knows about it. We need to act as a team, here!"

Ovocula spoke with a passion that seemed to take everyone by surprise, a brief wide-eyed silence hanging in the air over her fervent words. The Viscountess felt uncomfortable being spoken about, as if she were not even there. She hated it from the other aristocrats who had once boarded her father's ship, and she did not like it now. At the same time, she was conflicted; grateful to be the subject of a conversation which had nothing to do with her dirtied, loathsomely soiled form.

"Why, Miss Ovocula," Gwendolyn smiled, "It is quite unlike you to be so buoyant about our situation. Almost as though someone flipped a switch in your brainwomb, and now you are as a fanciful mother bird, regurgitating the hymns of kinship and togetherness into the eager mouths of her young, and I must say, it is quite refreshing."

"...That's gross," Ovocula replied.

"Her... Her birthright..." Orel wheezed, as Rivkah finished tying off the last torn piece of cloth around his head. "The Viscountess's... birthright."

The Viscountess tensed up with the wave of anxiety that suddenly surged through her at the mention of her branding. *No, Orel, please don't...*

"Most noble men and women have a birthright; a branding, yes?" Gwendolyn replied. "What about it, Mister Doctor Orel?"

"I... I recognized it... when I saw it..." he replied, shakily. He drew in a thorny breath through his mouth, his nasal cavity blocked by his own dried blood. Once he had gathered himself enough, he sat upright and eased himself against the wall next to Rivkah. "While I do not remember your family name," he continued, making uncomfortable eye contact with the Viscountess despite his inability to clearly see, "I remember... your mother. Rose. Named for your father's ship; the *Wild Rose.* Does... Does this sound familiar to you, Viscountess?"

She reluctantly nodded, not liking the direction this conversation was taking.

"I remember... because once, long ago, she came to me... your mother... She experienced certain... *complications,* following the birth of her child—you. Though I never met you then, you must have only been a couple of years old... I was a... young lad, at the time. Still an adolescent. I was practicing in another town, under an old man who... used strange, and rather... *new age* medicinal remedies... His methods were... unpractical. *Crystal healing.* I knew they would not work. He ran a faith-based sanatorium. He believed... by the power of the crystals... that he could heal your mother's postpartum disease. Something about... relating the crystals to the power... of the gemstones. From the *Castle in the Sky.*"

One of Orel's eyes was swollen completely shut, the other glazed over and red, only opening partway beneath the bruising to make out her shape. The Viscountess looked back, wrought with stress. "I know it was your mother... She bore the same unmistakable symbol, on a brooch, as the one on the back of your neck."

"But, that is just an old children's tale, I thought," Gwendolyn softly interjected. "The magic key, fabled to unlock an enchanted castle nestled among clouds..."

"...Which can only be operated with one of twelve gemstones by the person whose astrological sign matches that of the stone." Ovocula said, aghast. "My All Mother, I *have* heard these stories before! It's been so long! Goodness; I must have been barely old enough to walk when I first heard of this... Or, well, at least not yet potty trained." She shot the Viscountess a quick, barely noticeable glance. Or perhaps the Viscountess were merely paranoid; a result of the stressful conversation.

"That means the woman who now bears the key," Ovocula continued, "also bears one of these gemstones; the turquoise Stone of the Sage. That means... this could actually be *real*."

"How do you know so much about astrology, Miss Ovocula?"

Ovocula returned Gwendolyn's inquiry with a smug, green-eyed grin. "It's just always been a sort of wistful passion of mine. I like to feel connected to the world around me, and I do so by the stars. What about you, then? Do you know what your sign is?"

Gwendolyn smiled. "I am an Aries. But I do not know what that means."

"How *interesting*," Ovocula replied with a lilt in her voice, her green eyes twinkling with fascination. She looked positively creepy.

Orel frowned. "Why... is this interesting...?"

"Gwendolyn is an Aries. I am a Leo. The Viscountess is a Sagittarius. Together, by the signs of the sun, we make up a triad of fire! Of the twelve signs in astrology, these three are the symbols of *fire*. Three more, for *water*, another three, for *earth*, and then there are also three *air* signs!"

"So...?" he replied.

The light in Ovocula's eyes immediately went out with Orel's simple airy response. "I dunno, I guess I just thought it was... kinda neat. But, nevermind," she curtly retorted. "I'll just go back to silently brooding in my little corner of the cell and remind myself that this is what happens when I divulge my interests to people."

The Viscountess watched Ovocula slink back into the shadows, once more gathering up her dress around her as she scooted herself out of clear view. Orel just gave a small, twitchy shrug and twiddled his thumbs in his interlaced fingers as they rested in his lap. There was an uncomfortable silence that hung in the air following Ovocula's affronted retreat.

"...In what month, and on what day, were *you* born, Miss Rivkah?" Gwendolyn pleasantly smiled, clearing the air with her whimsical and equally pleasant disposition.

It was apparent that Rivkah wanted to respond in words,

instinctively moving her mouth to speak as though somehow forgetting, if only momentarily, that her tongue was missing. She frowned dejectedly, the slightest fleeting glimpse of defeat dimming her eyes. Then she looked down at her hands, bare and covered in soot. Suddenly, she held up one finger in front of her face.

"One…?" Gwendolyn replied. "The first month of the year; January?"

Rivkah responded with an open mouthed grin, nodding slow; affirmatively. She then held up her hand in a wave, presenting all five of her fingers.

"Oh, I see! January 5th is when you were born, then. Miss Ovocula… what does this mean?"

Another unpleasant air of silence. Finally, Ovocula responded. "Capricorn… An earth sign."

"Oh, I see!" Gwendolyn repeated. "How… ironic it is, Miss Rivkah, that you are an earth sign when you have spent so much of your life sailing the friendly skies! Why, that is just the opposite of earth, now is it not!"

Ovocula sighed weightily in exasperation, from the safety of the shadows.

The Viscountess had begun to relax again, as much as she could do so in her current state. She was grateful the attention was no longer on her for the time being, and she took this opportunity to calm herself down. She had not realized that her heart rate intensified with the threat of having unbearable memories called upon, and she raised a hand to her chest to feel the beating. Looking down at herself, all she could concentrate on with any real urgency was her need to once again be clean. She could not recall a time where she had ever been so filthy, and in so much pain. Her various aches and pains had dulled into a conjoined numbness which paralyzed most of her body.

"Viscountess…" Orel spoke suddenly, once more, "I want to address… some of the things you said… before we were taken aboard this ship…"

The Viscountess's heart froze. *Nothing. I said nothing! Stop this; stop this right now!*

"She spoke?" Gwendolyn said, blinking her large, froggy eyes in disbelief.

Even Rivkah nodded, seeming to believe she had spoken as well. The Viscountess could feel her senses beginning to shut down. She could not stand the idea of anyone knowing more about her than she did, herself. She began to rock on her knees, clenching and unclenching her dirty and bloodied fists. *Stop, stop, stop, STOP…!*

"You remember… don't you?" Orel urged her. "You said—"

Everything went white, like a soundless flash before her eyes that swallowed all of her senses. At least for these few passing seconds, she was safe, and nothing could harm her in any way. She was in her own void; a protective space where she could feel weightless and free. Nothing mattered now. She would float here without subsistence for an eternity; through perpetuity. She felt one with the universe, and she would neither need nor want for anything else, ever again.

Suddenly, the flash of white was gone. She was back in the cell, standing over everyone around her. They were all still seated on the metal flooring, each looking up at her with shocked expressions plastered on each of their faces. She looked down at herself again. Her clothes had been stripped and discarded around her, along with her boots, as she stood only in the nightgown Bern had given her to wear. When she looked up, she was greeted on the other side of the bars by Gertie's ugly golden grin and the same two pirates who had accompanied him before. There were a few rusty clicks as the bars separated once more, the door of the cell squeaking open.

"Why, 'allo there lovey," he said in his deplorable, deep and scratchy voice. "I'm afraid yer gonna hafta come with me. The Cap'n's lady wants to sees ya'…"

CHAPTER 16

S. S. Beulah

The Viscountess somewhat limped on a stiff left leg as she was escorted by the two taller pirates in much the same way as the two guards from Fyndridge had done. They dragged her along, Gertie walking a few paces in front of them. Though her peripheral vision was blocked by each man on either side of her, she could easily see over Gertie's head, in front of her. She tried to memorize the layout of the ship with each turn they made, while also taking mental note of each pirate they passed by. This ship was so much bigger than her father's, the crew at least three times more crowded. Still, she continued to silently count heads.

It was difficult for her to get a good feel for the ship's design, but she tried to keep her mind on the task set before her. The ship was made up largely of wood, and as she looked up, she could not see a single spot of sky around the massive sheet canopies that sailed high above them, ballooning out around miles of thick, taut rope. She suspected by the ship's size, hot air produced by burning coals would not be adequate enough lift to keep it aloft. Then she recalled Gertie mentioning something about gas, before. *Hydrogen…?* She sniffed the air around her.

"Heh, looks like the retard done got a whiff of herself," the pirate to her left said with a smirk.

"I can smell it, too," the other pirate sporting the scratches on his face, from Rivkah's nails, replied. "*The* Amadeus... Can ya' believe it?"

The Viscountess tried to ignore them as she continued to take in the odor of the air, catching an array of strange scents; from engine oils, to gunpowder, to musky man sweat. She did not smell the sulfuric trace of coal, and in its absence, there was no replacement. She presumed a heavy flow of hydrogen gas, permeating all around them. Her mechanical mind was at work now. She knew there was no way the ship could sustain the weight of enough metal cylinders filled with compressed hydrogen gas to offset the heaviness of the ship. How were they even in flight?

What methods were they using aboard the ship to produce a continuous flow of such an odorless gas? All of the skylark ships she had ever seen in her young age were largely powered by coal. She went over the chemical reactions she had read about from her father's collection of books, in her head. She remembered how to reform steam by reacting methane with water, but this would also create enough carbon monoxide to be problematic to the crew, so she scratched this as a possibility. She remembered reading about the introduction of a reactive metal; the alkaline earth metal, to water.

That method is also unfeasible, she thought quietly to herself. *Unless the buffoons enjoy explosions, which I wouldn't put past them, all things considered...*

Then the idea struck her. The electrolysis of water. Hydrogen gas could be produced by the passing of an electric current through a small body of water. Could this be how they were managing so well without coal? These thoughts swam around in her head with reflexive strokes, invigorating her body by the power of her mind turning gears alone. As they walked over the deck of the ship, a light gust of wind swept up her fiery mane and rustled the folds of her nightgown. The light of the sun shone through the sheet canopies from overhead, which provided a pleasant shade. At this level of elevation, the temperature was cool and soothing.

She found it difficult to focus now as her mind wandered back to her days aboard her father's ship, as a child. There was nothing she loved more on the planet than the sky in her hair on a cool, sunny day. She especially loved flying over oceanic waters, the few that were left relatively untouched by the nuclear war. It left their world in ruins, but somehow the aquatic world was getting by. So much pain and suffering she would never have to know. She could smell the salt of the ocean as her mind took her back, and she remembered how she would spread her arms far out around her and pretend she were not a bird, but a dolphin. With her head in the clouds, she already felt rather birdlike.

She would tell her mother this, and her mother would smile with her little mouth and laugh with her sad eyes. She always thought her mother was one of the most beautiful women she had ever seen. Whenever anyone would tell her how she looked so much like her, it would fill her with pure joy. She did not put much stock into appearance at such a young age, but when she looked at her mother, she could see only the warmth. Only the love. Only the goodness, and the selfless abandon. She wanted to be like her father, in all his mechanical genius; but like her mother, in her deepest capacity to care about the world in its endless expanse, and everyone in it. The Viscountess had lost sight of that somewhere along the way.

When her mother died, so did the warmth, and the love, and all of the goodness in the world. When she was no longer there, neither was the desire to interact, and connect, and exist in a place where the ugliness of people could not be outweighed by the sheer beauty of a heart that bled for them all. Her mother was not a martyr, but a ferocious protector. Her life was forfeit for the life of her child, and for the betterment of the world in which her child would live. The Viscountess somehow managed to have a childhood in the midst of ruin, and it was only because her mother had shielded her from all of the pain; like the pain she would endure the night she—*All Mother, I can't!*

As the Viscountess banished the thought of her mother from her mind, she realized she was supposed to be counting pirate crew and memorizing her surroundings. Which she had not been doing. She had no idea where she was now as the pirates continued to drag her along, trailing close behind Gertie who was coming upon a cabin door where a tall woman stood. Her arms were crossed over her chest, and she wore elegant, silken hooded robes that hugged around her curvaceous form. She was voluptuous, like Bern, but without the lean muscle to accommodate her curves. Instead, it was apparent that this woman simply loved croissants.

"What is all *this?*" she said, her voice smooth and rolling, overlapping a throaty whisper which had come of her words. It reminded the Viscountess of a rolling pin over floury dough that had bits of crushed sugar mixed into it. She hated baking.

"Milady!" Gertie exclaimed dramatically, throwing himself at her feet in an awkward bow. "I have brung to you the daughter of the widower, Amadeus!"

She only turned her nose up at him, her obscured, dark face contorting in disdain from underneath her hood. "Do you not allow the prisoners sufficient trips to the toilet?! And she is dressed so immodestly! What *is* this? Is this a trick?" she coldly replied.

The Viscountess turned her gaze to the floor, shamed and angry.

"Milady...?" Gertie said, looking up at her from his stripy knees on the deck's floorboards.

"*Bathe* her!" she boomed. "I will not have foulness on this ship, is that perfectly understood?!"

"Y-Yes, Milady."

"This better be a trite joke, because if this is the manner by which you seriously conduct the simple tasks you are given then I will have to discuss with *my love* what members of the crew we are to dispose of. Take her to the bath at once, and no more of this funny business! I do not find it the least bit amusing. Have I made myself perfectly crystal clear?"

Gertie scampered to his feet hurriedly as he nodded his head in acquiesce. In an instant, he was scurrying away, both men on either side of the Viscountess following closely behind as they firmed their grips around her arms. She winced, but appreciated the sudden urgency in their step. The sooner she could get cleaned up, the better. They went down several flights of stairs along the side of the ship. The wood railing was thin, and the wind was a little more severe than when she had been directly beneath the canopy on the deck. The men on either side of her once more served only to block her view, though were they not there, she suspected the rickety railing alone would have made her nervous. What if she bumped her body into one of them, she wondered?

There was little time to find out, as they were moving very quickly, often lifting her off the ground completely with each stairwell descent. Finally they made it to the ship's base, passing through a door and into a pitch black cabin, shutting the door behind them. The Viscountess was growing increasingly uneasy about this situation.

"I keep forgetting," one of the pirates said. She could feel him blindly groping around her. "Where's the light in here?"

Gertie flipped a switch. There was a flicker of light, illuminating the cabin from the ceiling. Following the light was a strange whirring sound that reverberated throughout the room. The Viscountess could see pipes running up each corner of the small space; the source of the odd noise. As she looked up, she noticed an electric light fixture; a globe, that was attached overhead. She was awed. Her eyes trailed over what appeared to be a very large steel tub next to a rounded board with a latch, in the middle of the floor. There was another board with a latch directly above the tub. It was attached to a piece of rope which Gertie now held firmly in one of his hands.

"Let 'er go, boys," Gertie said with a look that was not quite a sneer, but not quite a smile. She did not know how else to interpret this expression, but she knew it made her uncomfortable each time.

Both pirates complied, releasing her arms. She crossed them over her chest, rubbing them with her hands, indignantly. As they stepped away from her, her eyes fell over Gertie who was looking at her very hard. She wondered what he could possibly have up his sleeve.

"Well? What'cha waitin' fer? You gonna get in the tub, or are we gonna hafta force ya' in it?" Gertie glowered.

The Viscountess was reluctant to step toward the tub, but knew she did not want their grubby hands all over her either. She meekly obeyed the round little man who reminded her of a nugget, and swung her legs over the steel of the banister. It was caked with soap scum from the inside, and she could feel a thin layer of it between her toes. She cringed. The empty tub almost came up to her waist, when standing.

Then he gave the rope a fast, solid tug. The Viscountess looked up to see the latched board above her suddenly snap wide open. Down came a cascade of soapy, scalding hot water that washed over her head and swept the feet out from under her, instantaneously making the grime lining the tub very slick. The water burned her face, shoulders, and arms most of all as her sunburns reacted to the stinging heat. She wanted to scream with the pain, but her mental block coupled with the undertow of the rushing overhead current kept her from crying out. For the moment, she was pinned to the inside bottom of the tub, her legs kicking uselessly over slick, soapy surface.

The sheer nightgown floated up around her under the rushing water, along with her long, thick mane of hair. When the last of the hot stream had fallen upon her, she groped around desperately, thrusting her hands out of the water to grab the sides of the tub. She pulled herself up, gasping for air as her head surfaced from the full, steaming tub. Her eyes welled up with tears as soundless sobs shook their way out of her body. Gertie was doubled over on the ground, hacking and wheezing with hysterical laughter. The other two pirates were slumped over each other, cackling and pointing, and carrying on just as well. The Viscountess felt an overwhelming hatred rise up from within her.

She gritted her teeth, shaking with pain and blinding rage. She could feel herself slipping into a white bliss once more, phasing out of reality. Why did this keep happening to her? What form of *magic* was this? She could not make sense of it, and she could not control it. She merely let it wash over her, as it did not scald like the water. It did not scald like the thought of watching her mother die, or watching her father die, or the way they all laughed at her. It did not scald like being pushed away by a great love, or the betrayal of a friend, or the anxiety of no longer being able to hear out of her left ear.

In the blink of an eye, she was dressed in rich purple robes, silky and soft as they fluttered in the wind. Her hair, her wounds, her skin— all clean. They were back on the stairwell along the side of the ship with the rickety, thin railing. It was broken. Gertie was shaking her by the shoulders and screaming things at her. There was only one other pirate with him; the man with the scratched face. He was looking down over the side of the railing, shouting incoherently. His face and neck were red with strain, contorted with incomprehensible emotion. It was clear to her what had happened, but not what she had done. Her eyes fluttered with startled confusion. She could feel sputter against her cheeks from Gertie's mouth as he shouted at her a few inches from her face. His gold ingot teeth flashed in front of her with each exclaimed profanity.

When both men were done yelling, the Viscountess was snatched up by the wrist and led up the stairs. It was all a sort of blur to her, as she tried desperately to make sense of what was happening all around her. Eventually she found herself in front of the tall woman dressed in silken robes once more, and she was thrown to the floorboards before her feet. She could only look up at her, frightened and exceedingly disoriented.

"That is *much* better," the woman simply said, from underneath her hood. Her voice was much the same two overlapping tones, as before. "She is a scrawny little thing; it is good that my oldest robe fit her. I wondered about that when I had one of the other crewmen run it down." She sounded so strange, and ethereal. The Viscountess wondered why she cared so much about her presentation when she was only to be treated this way.

Gertie looked as though he were about to explode. He was quivering, extending his finger downward to where she had fallen. "Milady, she done *shoved* wunna the crew clean off the side a' the ship! The railing's broke by the loopty loo. He's dead! She *killed* him…!"

Killed…? the Viscountess repeated the word in her head. She had never killed anyone before; not in her entire lifetime. She could not even begin to fathom doing such a thing. Surely, it could not be true. She glanced up at each face above her, from Gertie's horrible crooked mug, to the man with the scratched face as he glared back at her, silent rage boiling beneath the surface of a hardened veneer. Try as she might, there was no predicting what the tall, robed woman was thinking now, her rotund body blocking her already shrouded features.

"That will be all," she replied, dismissively.

"But… But, Milady, she—!"

"*That's* all." Her inflection reminded the Viscountess of two piano keys, one falling shortly after the other. She repeated herself almost derisively, as though a small simplifying of her words would better serve to get the point across that she was quite finished with him.

Gertie bared every last inch of his gleaming, gritted teeth. Scornfully, he turned on his heel and stormed away. The taller pirate followed suit, closely behind him. As they each stomped off, the Viscountess glanced around the area of the deck for the first time. There were no other pirates going about their business in view, though she could hear the sounds of bustling activity from all around her. Tall pillars held up the mast of the ship, which made up the all encompassing canopy overhead. The deck was wide and open, though obstructed by various ropes and poles running the width and length of the outer perimeter. The cabin entrance had circular windows all along the walls, its standalone placement kept separate from the living quarters of the rest of the crew.

"Rise, girl," the woman said, still standing over her. She motioned for her to climb to her feet, with overturned palms. The skin of her hands was as smooth as her voice, without the sugary crunch. They were dark like rich chocolate, playing striking contrast to the white of her robes.

The Viscountess hesitantly obeyed, head now downturned as gusts of wind gently whipped the purple silken robes out of her way. Her legs were creamy and bare with a collection of various scrapes and bruises, as the robes she now wore, and even the damp, ragged nightgown underneath, parted from her lower body. She quickly tugged the fabric closed around her. *You find this to be much better…?* she scowled, somehow feeling more naked than she had when wearing just the nightgown.

"You actually clean up rather well," the woman noted, moving one of her dark fingers to coil around the knotted waves of the Viscountess's hair. It blew loose in the wind through the woman's fingers, and the Viscountess flinched back reactively at her cool touch grazing her cheek. "You are something of a dog to look at still, but I have never before seen such a shade of red… Your hair is really quite remarkable."

The Viscountess was uncertain of how to respond to this, so she just solemnly looked up at her through lowered lashes. She could not figure this woman out. In the short time she had observed her, all she perceived were an array of irregular behavioral patterns. What did she want with her? Who was she to the man who killed her father? Did it not matter at all that the Viscountess supposedly murdered a man; a member of Demetrius's crew?

"Now come with me," the dark-skinned woman said, turning to open the door to the cabin. She stepped inside, motioning for the Viscountess to follow. Hesitantly she complied, trailing behind her into the room. It was a spacious living quarter, with pipes running up each corner in much the same way as the cabin with the tub. There were light fixtures along the ceiling as well. She could tell they were powered by electricity just the same; no candles, lanterns, or fire of any kind as far as she could see. For now though, the light shone in through the cabin's circular windows, casting elongated waiflike rays into the room. Particles of dust floated around in the light like hundreds of tiny winged fae. "Have a seat, if you please."

The Viscountess looked further into the room, following the much taller woman's extended arm with her eyes. She gestured toward a wicker loveseat padded by soft, cushy pillows. The various furnishings around the room consisted of a heart-shaped double bed, a deep oak desk opposite the wicker chair, and a massive rug flooring the center of the moderately sized space. Everything was in soft pastels, like the painted flora of her mother's favorite dress. She slowly crossed over to the chair and carefully sat down, adamant not to wince in spite of her body's pained protest. The tall, curvy woman positioned herself on the other side of the desk, standing before her with her long, piano key fingers resting over its surface.

"My given name is Beulah Wilhelmina Mildred Smith."

None of those names were good. Beulah, especially. It reminded the Viscountess of the retching sound she made when she vomited all over the floor of the holding cell.

"My love is heavy-handed," she continued, "and by this, I do not refer to a philosophy all my own. I speak only of the captain of the ship; Demetrius. He can be somewhat of a tyrant at times, but he means well. He wants only to restore the earth by the power of the key; I know this to be true in my heart. To do that, we must find the castle. If you are Rose's daughter, you would know of what I speak. The key belonged to her, but *oh*! How Amadeus forbade her from using it."

And just what do you know about my parents...? the Viscountess wondered, clenching her fists in her lap as Beulah spoke.

"I've known Rose for some time, as she was the bearer of the key! I met my darling Demetrius through his *relations* with her... He tells me not of the nature, or manner in which he had come to know her. He much prefers to live here, in the present—with *me*."

The Viscountess's fists continued to clench. She began to dig her nails into her palms once again. *What are you suggesting, exactly...?*

"He lamented her death; truly. But once he knew she'd had the key all along, well... let's just say he had quite the thorn to pick with Amadeus after that. Whatever deal they made, I *do* apologize on his behalf that it had to end in your beloved father's demise. My condolences."

She imagined plunging Demetrius's jagged dagger into the fleshy slabs of fat that made up the many layers of her body, starting from her breast, cutting down and across. She imagined opening her wide like a great feast bird, letting her entrails spill out over the surface of the desk in heavy, meaty chunks; her white robes, drenched red.

"Perhaps you are wondering why I would be telling you all of this now," she said, reaching up with her hands to bring down her hood. As she swept it back and away from her face, her features became more defined. Large, lush lips set under a wide button nose, and high cheek bones which accented exotic catlike eyes, violet in hue. Gone from her otherwise striking appearance were eyelashes, brows, and even hair on her head. She was bald in every sense of the word, the shape of her skull like a perfect bulbous globe, gleaming within the sunbeams coming in through the windows. "The answer is simple, really... Demetrius now knows he needs each of the twelve gemstones if he is to find, and unlock the castle. What he does not know is how to operate the key. You do. Your mother told you what you needed to do before she died, did she not? That is why you've been holding it! You must tell him. A favor for a favor, yes?"

A favor...? You honestly believe you're doing me any favors?! You are mistaken; my mother has told me nothing of the castle beyond its existence! You are wasting your time.

There was a brief pause. "Come now; we *all* want the same thing. We *all* wish to harness the castle's restorative powers to revitalize this earthen wasteland. Simply tell him. You can save yourself *and* your friends a world of suffering. You need only cooperate, and I'll see to it that my love does not inflict any further harm upon the each of you. That sounds good, now doesn't it?"

The Viscountess sat fidgeting; wringing the silken fabric of the robes she now wore, in her fists. Aside from this, she was very still. Her eyes narrowed ferociously as she looked the dark-skinned woman over, defiant and resolute. *There's no way I would ever help you. Either of you,* she glared, watching as Beulah grew increasingly rigid with each passing second the Viscountess sat there, unmoving; unspeaking. She reaped a certain satisfaction from the still, deadpan anger she felt rolling off Beulah's façade in steady waves. The waves only grew more volatile as she sat there, receiving them in perfect silence. Under other circumstances, this would be very uncomfortable for her. Instead, it only made her feel all the more steadied—*powerful.* Only if for a moment, she felt in control. She relished every second of it.

"Alright then, have it your way," Beulah frowned. Her violet cat eyes faded as she stood, very calm, but radiating the heat of an anger so vicious, the Viscountess could feel it fueling her own. At least for now, she was boldly unafraid. The taller woman in her white silken robes was as the eye of a storm, tranquil amid an aura of staggering chaos.

"I tried to be nice," she said, moving around the desk and stepping toward a closed vent on the wall that the Viscountess had not initially seen. "I gave you a chance. You've been cleaned, clothed, and I've even offered you amity! Keep that in mind for when you are writhing around in whatever agony my love so chooses to put you in!" She opened the vent with the push of a button, putting her full lips up to its aperture. "Demetrius; are you finished with the miner?"

After a few passing seconds, Demetrius's voice echoed back through the vent. "I'm still busy down here. What do you need?"

"That little *brat* spawn of Rose still refuses to speak, even after my offer! And, my love, she threw one of the crewmen overboard the ship; I saw it with my own eyes! She's not a weak little thing as she would have us believe. You need to come up here and let her in on the spot of conversation you've been having with her *loverboy*..."

"I see. I'll be right there."

The vent reclosed as she released the button. She turned to face the Viscountess once more, and as she did so, the Viscountess thought she could feel the frenetic energy flickering its way through the woman's very pores. There was a glint behind her violet eyes, like hot metal lights flashing through an electric stream. As calm as she was, it was still clear she was absolutely livid. It was a while before she spoke again, just standing there, staring.

"You've no concept of the pain he can, and *will* impose. Even if the answers need to be extracted from you by force, he *will* get them. For the good of the world, as we know it! Your insolence will not hinder us, and it will not keep us from our goal – just as your mother's didn't."

My mother's... My mother's insolence?! the Viscountess fumed, slowly rising to her feet. Any aches she felt were washed away in that moment with her building rage. *How did you come to know her? How could you have met my father's murderer through her?!*

Beulah returned the Viscountess's reaction with a mean smirk which came more from her eyes than the rest of her face. It made her feel uneasy; as though the rotund, dark-skinned woman were more mad than angry. "You are a lucky girl, being useless as you are..." she said ominously. "You should see what he does with the men who prove ultimately uncooperative."

Demetrius stepped through the cabin entrance in that moment. The Viscountess was somewhat startled by how quickly he emerged, standing in the doorway with his arms at his sides from underneath his cloak. His metallic hand clutched a fistful of scraggly brown hair. Once he stepped forward, the rest of Roland came into view as he dragged his limp body toward her.

Oh my All Mother; Roland!

She charged at him. The single thought cycling through the Viscountess's mind now, was a dire need to get Roland away from this insidious cloaked monster. Her sudden burst was met only with thousands of electric volts surging through her body. The shock came out of nowhere, and as sudden as her own impetuous mad dash. She felt every muscle in her back convulse and spasm as she stiffened up, eyes bugging out at the ceiling as she involuntarily arched her neck back. The *ceiling*—these few fleeting seconds felt like an eternity, the muscle tissue surrounding each of her ligaments feeling as though they were being torn apart.

In but a sudden flash, the ceiling had changed. White square tiles had replaced wooden ship planks. There were white bright lights everywhere. Humanoid figures were hovering over her, wearing strange masks and gloves that smelled faintly of disinfectant and sterilized rubber. They wore white coats; everything was very *white*. The Viscountess became aware of her own quick, erratic breathing, her heart feeling as though it would burst from her chest at any moment.

There was something in her mouth. There was something cold and hard on either side of her head; a pressure above her ears, over her temples. She was restrained by bands, each of her arms and legs strapped down to a lightly cushioned surface she could feel behind her back. Try as she might on reflexive instinct alone, she could not free her wrists from the bindings, her arms firmly secured at her sides.

"Her pupils are dilating, Doctor," came a faraway, distorted voice that somehow still rang through her right ear. "It looks like she's finally coming out of it."

"Good… Increase the voltage; let's do it again," another replied, the similarly distorted voice coming from the closest figure standing over her, basked in the white light. "Let's not lose her again, now that we have her."

No… No, no, no…! the Viscountess screamed, in her mind. She tried to shake her head, but her attempts at moving came through as short, violent twitching which sent a twinge of pain up the back of her neck. It was as though she had pinched a nerve. *Please…!* she cried. She was terrified. What was happening to her?

"*Clear*, in 3… 2… 1…!"

Another shock surged through her; this time, the sensation of the electric current concentrated in one place—all throughout her head. She could feel the volts pulsating into her temples, where they met between her eyes. Were they even open? The whiteness of her surroundings seemed to blend together as pressure built behind her lids. The muscles in her arms and legs tensed and contracted in response to the electricity trailing down the rest of her body. The smell of disinfectant and rubber left her senses, as with the sensation of a surface beneath her. She could feel the cold, hard pressure surrounding her head dissipate, and once more she was lost in an abysmal state of listless confusion.

Finally, the voltage stopped, and she collapsed to the ground in a twisted heap. Everything seemed to be back to 'normal' again. When she collected herself enough to look up from the floor, her eyes followed the causative source of her full body shock. There stood Beulah, her fingers extended toward her. Her nails were secreting wafts of smoke. It occurred to the Viscountess then, that this woman may have the power to alter ones' perceptions of reality.

Demetrius flung Roland to the ground beside her. He looked badly beaten, in much the same way as Orel. One of his eyes was swollen and bruised, his jaw was cracked, and his nose looked mangled as if a dog had used it for a chew toy. He was still dirty from the mines, his shirt ragged and torn, with coal smears and blood stains coating the clothen fabric. His eyes were closed and his breathing was labored and wheezy as he exhaled through his mouth. He was drenched in sweat. The Viscountess gently cupped his face in her hands as tears streamed down her face. She had cried more times now, than she had over the course of her entire lifetime. The guilt she felt was crippling.

I'm so sorry, Roland... I'm so sorry for everything you've had to go through, because of me... Please; please, forgive me. This was never supposed to happen! I only ever wanted... I only ever wanted to make you happy...!

She covered his body with her own, enveloping him in rolling cascades of fiery red hair as she buried her face in his chest. She could smell the coppery intermingling of sweat and blood on his clothes, the faintest hint of cayenne just barely still distinguishable beneath other scents. He was cold and clammy, his tanned skin now pale; sickly. *Please, be okay,* she cried.

...Just be okay.

She felt a sudden, sharp tug around her hair that wrenched her head upright. Her body followed with it as she painfully felt herself being pulled away. Her hands rose up to grasp around the metal of Demetrius's wrist. As he violently dragged her off of Roland, the Viscountess felt a rough hand fumble around her legs.

"Let... Let her go...!" Roland stirred, straining to draw her nearer. It was no use. As he struggled over the hard wood of the floor, the Viscountess's robes slipped through his fingers.

CHAPTER 17

A Hero's Sacrifice

Demetrius held the Viscountess in front of Roland, keeping a few feet of distance between them. She tried to struggle against him, but the cloaked man was too strong for her to slip away. He held her arms firmly behind her back with his metal grip; his other hand, wrapped with dark gauzed fabric, clutched tightly around her neck.

"Now we'll try this again, boy," Demetrius snarled in his husky voice, squeezing up into the Viscountess's throat. She gulped back, just as she felt her air passage tighten. "When I sent you back to that pathetic little town of yours to inquire as to the *whereabouts* of that woman, I know someone told you something! You're gonna tell me, or you're gonna watch me as I *squeeze* the life from this girl's body!"

The Viscountess felt him squeeze tighter around her neck as he uttered the word. She gagged slightly, and as he steeled his grip she felt a strange sense of déjà vu; as though something similar had once happened before. Roland grinded his teeth as he writhed on the floor, clearly pained and in a state of panic. His whole body shook, his face contorted with deep inner turmoil. As she watched him, she felt an overwhelming empathy sweep over her – she knew that turmoil.

"I... I *told* you...!" Roland grimaced. "No one knew what direction she went! I asked the guards back in Fyndridge, and they *would have known* when she returned! They would have known if she *hadn't*, and still came out of the mines alive, because guards are constantly patrolling the surrounding area. Someone would have seen her on foot, before she ever made it back into the desert... Just let her go!"

The Viscountess could feel Demetrius grin evilly from over her head. "Let *who* go? Amadeus's pretty little daughter… or the woman who has *my* key?!" He tightened his grip a little more. The Viscountess was beginning to feel lightheaded.

"My love," Beulah interrupted, "I do *not* think her that pretty…"

There was a sudden banging on the door.

"Damn it; what now?!" Demetrius raged, loudly.

"Sir! We have stowaways aboard the ship!" one of the pirates could be heard from the other side.

"What?!" both Demetrius and Beulah were as three separate voices cried out in unison. Between Demetrius's husky thundering by itself and Beulah's smooth booming, overlapping an ethereal whispery rasp, the Viscountess could see how the two might somehow be intimately involved. The moment of understanding was short-lived, as Demetrius, the monster and not the lover, threw the Viscountess back to the ground several feet from Roland.

She landed over the rug covering part of the wood floor, watching as both Beulah and Demetrius bolted out of the room. Beulah turned to give the Viscountess one last terrible glare. "We haven't finished with you wretches yet," she said, pulling up her hood. She locked the door from the outside, as they left.

The Viscountess redirected her gaze over Roland, whose eyes were like murky waters, gently casting waves of light over a stony surface underneath. He looked tired and defeated. She crawled over to him, off the carpet and onto the hardwood floor, throwing her arms around him as he embraced her. She could feel the stubble from his chin softly graze the nape of her neck, just slightly off her shoulder. His body convulsed with small shaking sobs, and she held him close. She wanted only to comfort him.

"Arnie," he said, "Arnie; he can read! I could have asked him…!"

Shhh, it's okay… I understand…

"I could have asked him what your name is! We could have had you write it out, and he could have told me what it said! I didn't, Viscountess… I didn't, because I… I was upset. I didn't want to know your name, then. I didn't want to know, because I thought you might have been *prejudiced.* It… It bothered me, and it was petty, and… All Mother, I'm so, *so* sorry…!"

I was. I was prejudiced. It's okay; I know…

"I don't want you to die without my ever knowing your name. I've never opened up to anyone like this, and I have problems; *serious* problems! I'm not a very good person, inside… I hate myself *so* much sometimes and I'm always angry, and… and I must be going out of my mind!"

The Viscountess could feel the bitter nip of tears welling up behind her eyes all over again, as Roland spoke. She could feel the cool wet trickling of his own tears over her shoulder, as his emotions intermingled with hers. For once, she was unafraid, and she could think only of pouring into him. She wanted to know him; to know his body, and his mind – to seep into every dark crevice and fill it with light. She wanted to be the sun to his moon.

"Damn it; I just want to be *strong* for you!" he said, pulling away from her suddenly. He must have felt her tears drizzling over his shoulder, as he took her by the outside of her arms and lifted her off of him. "I don't want to be pitied! Don't *pity* me, Viscountess; I am unworthy! Don't you see?! I'm a *crazed* man! I'm not well. The awful, terrible things that go through my head on a regular basis; they haunt me to my core! I would only taint you…" he sobbed. "I would only *mar* you with my poison…!"

He pulled away now completely, moving his body backward on his knuckles over the floor. He dragged one of his legs, and the Viscountess realized then that it must have been broken. She crawled toward him once more as he retreated.

"No! Don't you come *any* closer!" he shouted. She flinched back, as he held up his finger. "I'm worthless to you now; I'm not strong enough. I never was! It was all a façade because… because I *selfishly* wanted you to like me! Don't you see how selfish I am?!"

The Viscountess was pained by his words. Her tears poured forth like liquid from a stream.

"How can I ask you of that…?" he continued, softly. "How can I ask *anyone* of that, when I ask so much just to be considered normal in spite of the horrible things I've done?! You don't *know* me! If you did, you'd—"

The Viscountess defiantly slapped his finger away from her face. While his hand was batted off to the side, she moved herself within his reach, laying herself along the inside of his other arm. He looked aghast; conflicted, as she forced herself unto him. She clutched the torn fabric of his shirt in one of her tiny fists and sobbed with him. She did not care what he thought of himself, because she knew what she thought; what she felt. She needed to feel him, and for him to feel her in turn. She wanted to be with him.

Roland was silent now, as he carefully moved her hair back behind one of her ears. He used the hand she had batted away. He held her in his other arm, his bicep curling around her securely. She looked up at him, and she could see that his eyes were tired and deadened; glazed puffy and red, traced by his sorrow. There were thin lines down his cheeks from his eyes, in clean liquid streaks, which divided the thin layer of dried dirt on his face.

"...I don't think you know what you're getting yourself into, with me..." he said, solemnly.

I have nowhere else to go, but with you, she replied softly, in her head.

"I... I've killed, before. I'm a *murderer.*"

The Viscountess's blood ran cold. Her heart was like a heavy icicle in her chest, the weight of it threatening to plunge downward, falling through her to bury itself in the cold snow of her bare feet. Her eyes widened to meet with his piercingly empty gaze. There was no light behind his bright blue eyes, as though he were removed from himself completely; like a war-weary man in the face of his own execution at dawn. But she wanted to be the dawn to his eve.

She reached up and touched the side of his cheek. Her fingers bade to caress the outer lining of his jaw. As she gazed up at him, open and vulnerable, she watched the spark slowly return to his strong, wolflike features. His brows furrowed with distress as he appeared to realize, only then, that he would not be rid of her; nor would he be rid of the emotions he so struggled with. She would not be denied.

She kissed him. Or, perhaps he kissed her. Her eyes had shut before she knew what was happening; what she was doing. With both her hands now lining his jaw, she felt his arms wrap tightly around her waist, his hands coarsely meeting at the small of her back. His lips were both rough and soft; his skin, both hot and cool. A shudder of tremors wracked through her body with his commanding touch. The kisses came deep; visceral, and fast. She could feel his tongue slip past her lips. She was overwhelmed.

Waves of emotion washed over her, none of which her rational mind was able to process. It was as though by sheer force of will, her lucid consciousness had been cast out in favor of the diabolical liberties

Roland had taken with her lips; with her body. His hands moved over her through the silk of the rich purple robes she wore, with the ferocity of a raging brushfire. He enveloped her in heat, impassioned, as he laid her over the floor and moved on top of her. His touch did not scald.

"I think I *love* you," he said, his mouth gently parting from hers. He worked his way down her neckline, nipping at the dip where her neck and shoulders met. She shuddered.

She laced her fingers to crown at the nape of his neck in turn, draping her arms over his shoulders and drawing him nearer. Her tears continued to flow freely. *They say that I've killed a man,* she cried, her whole body shaking with fear at the mere thought she could even be capable of such a thing. *Please help me; I don't know what to do! I... I can't disprove it! How can I not know whether or not I've killed someone before? I'm so horrible; All Mother, how could I do such a thing and not even know it?!*

She held onto him for dear life, and he only continued to kiss down her body, wrapping her securely in his arms. "It's okay now," he said, his words spoken smoothly between each of his kisses, "I got'cha."

Her heart fluttered. It amazed her how the simplest of words could set her at such ease in the midst of so much chaos. Perhaps if he had the capacity to love—perhaps if she had that same capacity—it could somehow be okay that they each be capable killers, just the same. It had to be okay. What would her good mother think of her, having killed; the satisfaction that it could bring? What would her sheltering father think of his little girl being ravished on the floorboards of an enemy ship, with a strange common man? She did not know – but she did not want to think about her parents, right then, either.

She refocused her attention on the man hovering over her, as he appreciated every last inch of her body. His touch would make her ache, with pleasure, as well as pain. Her body was ragged, and so was his. It was okay, though; it was all okay. He had her now, and he was never going to let her go. She knew this to be true, because he was crazy and *she* was crazy, and he was finally letting her in. Perhaps this was why he would push her away so quickly, each time someone walked up on them. Perhaps he simply did not want to show anyone else how he could be vulnerable. She could relate with that.

I got'cha, she repeated his words in her head. She liked it. In its beautiful simplicity, it said so much. It was so inviting; so all encompassing. In the same way she felt enveloped by his arms, she felt enveloped by his words. *How I wish I could tell you... I need you to know that I think I love you, too...*

Roland stopped for a moment to gaze back into her eyes. She smiled up at him, through her tears. Meagerly, he smiled back. "I don't know how, Viscountess," he spoke softly, "but I'm going to get you out of this. If... If you can still kiss me, even after knowing that I... that I'm—"

She stopped him, raising her thumb to his mouth, her other fingers curling around his cheek. He gently kissed it. Her longest fingers grazed the lobe of his ear. "Listen," he said, "I do know where Bern went. Alasdair... he's a dayshift guard! He told me he saw her walking northeast into the distance; far from the town gate. I told him about the attack, and what was happening. He said he'd get help!"

The Viscountess looked up at him worriedly. She had mixed feelings about him knowing this information, but could not put her finger on why this sat ill with her. He saw the sudden look in her eyes, and his voice softened as he continued to speak.

"Don't worry... Watching that bastard *hurt* you..." he gritted, "...It was driving me crazy. I... I think that if he hadn't been called away, I might have gone mad if it had gone on any longer. And I would have told him, before it did. I just can't stand to see you hurt. I'm only sorry that I let it go on for as long as it did. Please, forgive me."

This made her feel much better. She felt like he knew her better than she knew herself. At the same time, she could not help but feel somewhat guilty for wanting him to give up the same information he had been beaten for, so that she did not have to endure any suffering comparable to what he had been through; even if only in part. What kind of person did this make her? Still, she pushed the thought from her mind, for the time being.

"...I wish I could hear you say it..." he said, suddenly. This caught the Viscountess off guard, and she looked up at him, confused. He pushed up off the floor and climbed off of her, sitting upright as he did so. She sat up too, as he sighed weightily, running a hand through his already tousled hair. "I wish I could hear you say you love me. I know I only took advantage of your being mute, at first; opening up to you, because you couldn't talk back. But I feel like... I feel like you're a good person, inside. I feel like you're so good, and I'm so *bad*, and... and, damn it, you fell out of the sky—and now you're in my life. I... I don't want to lose you, now that I've found you. And I don't want to be bad anymore."

You never were! she voicelessly replied, again cupping his face in her hands. *How can you think yourself so bad? I do love you! I've only known you for a few short days, but I really do love you! Please, believe me...!*

She looked deeply into his eyes, urging him; compelling him to *see* the love in her heart. She wanted so badly for him to see. If that is what it would take to get him to realize he was not bad, that she could really and truly love him, then she knew what she had to do. She tried desperately to remember when she had been crying uncontrollably. She remembered the holding cell with Rivkah, and the two other women she had just met. Gertie had just doused her in ice cold water. She tried to remember the involuntary sounds she made with her throat; the ghastly, sorrowful sobs that ricocheted out from deep within her, to meet with the stagnant air.

Roland watched, his expression slowly shifting from troubled uncertainty to eager anticipation once it dawned on him what it was she was doing. "Viscountess..." he started to say. She just glided her fingers up either side of his head, running them through his scraggly brown hair. She got the sense that he particularly liked this, since it so easily interrupted him speaking. Wistfully, she cut the air between them as a shooting arrow from a recurve bow. Powerfully, she shot her eyes through his, like hot metal bowling out the barrel of a fondled trigger gun.

The Viscountess knew exactly what she wanted; what she felt. Her lower lip quivered as she tried desperately to express that to him, in words. Surely he could see the want in her eyes, her brows narrowed with determination. She swallowed back, aiming to break her own silence once more. Warily, she got the vibrations in her throat started, trying to formulate some utterance of speech. *Illl,* she strained.

...Illlluh...!

"No, don't," Roland softly, and tiredly smiled. "Don't further stress yourself; I... I think I feel you. It might sound crazy, but I really do think I'm *seeing* you. Really seeing you, y'know?"

She felt relieved, but she so desperately wanted to say it, all the same. It would be just as much affirmation for her, as it would be, for him. She continued to strain the words in her head, thereby transforming them into a declaration; a verbal admission of her surrender. She had already given herself up to him in mind and in heart. She knew she could construct sound at her lowest low; so why not when she felt her utmost high?

Roland stopped her with another intense, ravenous kiss. It did not matter now. The world around her was slipping away, in much the same way it had whenever she would phase out of consciousness, if but only for a moment. She was in the moment, now, with him. There was nowhere else she would rather be. *Is this real?* she thought silently to herself.

"There are stories I want to tell you," Roland said, his lips gently parting from hers once more. "...I sometimes wish I could write, because I just have this mental image; this picture in my head. It's hard to describe exactly. Sometimes I get these sudden flashes, in my mind, and I see a future; my aspirations—*our* future. That, maybe you're what I've been looking for all this time."

The Viscountess's heart fluttered as he spoke. Did they really *have* a future? Together?

"It came to me in a dream... And we're there, on a barren, windswept plain, and I gently push you behind me. You wrap your arms around me as I steel my nerves and take a terrible brunt, like some invisible volley of arrows. I just hold on, knowing that I am shielding you... and I can see you, gently touching me in an afterward kind of effect, soothing small cuts and wiping away blood. And just..."

Again, her eyes began to well up with tears. What an insipid crybaby, she was.

"...of knowingly choosing to endure pain to spare you from it... and you helping to soothe me and cradle me afterwards."

With his words, the Viscountess felt as though she were falling through the wood of the floor. Or, perhaps her feet had fallen asleep. Either way, she could have sworn she were as light as a feather on the wind, and would only drift downward past the floorboards, through the other cabins of the ship, until finally she had fallen all the way completely through. She would drift aimlessly down, falling, and falling; falling deeper in love with each breath they shared. In spite of all the pain, she felt a great peace.

"There's another image I have..." he continued.

Anything. Tell me anything; I want to know you.

"Us, in the kitchen... my kitchen, actually... You're standing over the stove, and I've half-snuck up behind you, and I wrap my arms around you, and you smile, sighingly... I kiss your ear and place my hands over your stomach, and you place a hand over my hands as you continue to stir."

Well, at least this image did not involve her baking. Perhaps she could learn how better to cook. She recalled the couple of lessons she had taken with Madame Beatrice, aboard her father's ship. She was not a very good student and made it abundantly clear by way of her own body language alone, that domestic skills took the backburner when compared with her burning desire to someday pilot her own ship. Suddenly, it occurred to her; could she cater to the man she loved *and* captain a vessel all her own? Would it be possible to do both, despite the unorthodox of following two radically different dreams at once?

Another dilemma; there was no way she would ever be able to express to Roland, in words, what it was that she wanted. She could not express what her passion was; the one thing that had driven her since far back as she could remember. Her mother's romance novels instilled in her an understanding of her own tender heart, whereas her father's books on engineering and piloting served as a means to follow a far more personal passion; one that could not be shared in another. Only she, and she alone, could be the captain.

Just then, there was an abrupt click at the door. In an instant, it burst open, and Beulah rushed into the room. She was raving with maddened rage. "You *fools!*" she boomed, her voice overlapped by an otherworldly screeching that shook the Viscountess to her core. Roland shoved her away from him, and she fell backward just as Beulah had let loose a shockwave of electric current straight into Roland's chest. He made a horrible gagging, gargling sound; deep, and guttural with the force of the blast. It threw him back against the wall adjacent her. His body crumpled onto the ground, spasming with electricity still coursing through him.

The Viscountess watched in horror from across the room as her eyes fell over his tongue, flicking out involuntarily; his whole body twitching just as Orel's did, but with far greater magnitude. White foam filled his mouth, followed by a gusher of blood which seeped down the sides of his jaw. She screamed in terror. Once the shock had finally subsided, Roland's body fell limp; eyes open, as he laid there. All the light had gone from his bright blue hues, once and for all.

CHAPTER 18

Dark Fugue

No longer wearing the purple robes, the Viscountess reawakened in the holding cell with a start.

"Hey! Hey; take it easy, you're alright now!" she heard Ovocula say, as the woman clutched her shoulders, trying to hold her down. She was thrashing around, not conscious of her limbs, and she had not realized until after the fact that she almost kicked the makeshift bandage from Orel's already knocked-around head. "You're safe for now. You haven't been out for very long."

It took her a moment before her mind was coherent enough to register her surroundings. She stopped thrashing, gently easing herself up off the ground. *Lost time... Lost time, again...* she dwelled, gazing around the cell. *What happened? What happened to me?! ...Where's Roland? What is happening?!* she was hysterical and wide-eyed, gripping Ovocula by the shoulders, in turn. *Oh All Mother, I'm losing my senses...!*

"Shhh, it's okay. You're alive. You're back here, with us," Ovocula soothed.

The cell remained unchanged from when she had left it. The dried remnants of her filth were still in the center of the metal floor, as were her discarded filthy clothes. Rivkah and Orel were still side by side along the far end of the wall, and Gwendolyn was still seated upright in her respective spot, just the same. Her perpetually startled gaze shone like diamonds between the shadows cast through the cell's bars.

"Miss Ovocula," she said, musically, "Perhaps it might be in the Viscountess's best interest if we filled in the blanks for her, as to what has happened. Starting with just before she was escorted away, a few hours ago."

A few hours?! So much time... I'm losing so much time! The Viscountess's heart was pounding. *This is a nightmare. All Mother, what is happening to me...?*

Ovocula nodded, in agreement. "Yes... Yes, for once, I think I am in accord with you."

"*Miss* Viscountess," Gwendolyn started. The Viscountess cocked a brow as she looked to her. "Might you have any recollection of what you were doing... what you were *saying*... before the pirate men came and took you away?"

The Viscountess slowly shook her head, her hands loosening their grips and falling away from Ovocula's shoulders. She felt moderately dejected, being unable to remember these things people were telling her.

"Okay, then. Let me help," Orel curtly responded. "Do you know that the only reason you're alive right now, is because Roland is *dead,* and now Demetrius doesn't know whether he'll be able to find Bern and the key, without you?" He was abnormally stilled as he spoke. His words were as steady as his body, propped there on the floor in the corner of the cell.

He... He's dead...?

"Your mother was an enchanting woman, Viscountess," he continued. "In this case, the apple has fallen far from the tree as can be... Who *are* you? I mean, who are you *really* – are you even aware of yourself? The way your narrow-mindedness; your self-centeredness, hinders you?"

I'm sure I haven't the slightest idea what you're talking about! Roland can't be dead; he just can't be! I refuse to believe it...!

"I helped you, because I had faith in you. I didn't know what it was about you that stirred such a feeling in me, until I'd seen the symbol on the back of your neck. I didn't realize you would *shrink* from your responsibility. You are *failing* your family by allowing yourself to become so distracted from your legacy... and for what?"

As he spoke, the Viscountess felt short of breath; as though her senses were all shutting down while each of his words struck different chords deep within her. She felt shamed, indignant, and utterly angry. He was beginning to sound like her uncle. How could he talk to her in such a way? *You don't know anything; you don't even know that Roland can't be dead! How would you know something like that, being locked up in here?!* she gritted, clenching her fists.

"They said Roland's heart stopped… They said Demetrius threw him overboard. Demetrius has killed most everyone on your parents' ship. He's cut out Rivkah's tongue. He's probably torturing Alasdair and Kael right now, as we speak!"

Alasdair, and Kael…? They were the stowaways?

"…And for *what*—all so that you could distract Roland from taking advantage of the diversion they tried to make for you?! A few selfish moments, and now he's *dead.*"

Stop! Stop saying that! she covered her ears. Slowly, she could feel herself once again beginning to lose control. *It isn't true! Not true… not true… not true…!*

She could feel everything around her gently fading from drab darkness to white absence. Slowly, she was slipping back into her place of safety, where she could not be reached. She would be alone again, but she would not be lonely. She would be one with the universe; one with everything. What was physical was once more falling away, all around her. As each of her senses began to shut down, she heard Gwendolyn suddenly; "Your eyelids are so heavy," she said. "You are growing very sleepy…"

What is this…? the Viscountess thought. She could hear Gwendolyn's voice, but nothing else.

"So very… very… sleepy… On the count of three, you *will* fall into a safe slumber; but you will remember all that is missing. Take us through… Show us the way… Tell us what you see…"

I…? What are you—?

"One…"

"How do you know this is going to work…?" Ovocula's voice distantly echoed.

"Two…" Gwendolyn continued, without break. Her voice was close; clear.

…?!…

"…*Three*…"

The Viscountess opened her eyes, no longer the girl whose heart shown the stability of a rabbit in retreat, but a lion unleashed, as she stood. Her feet were grounded like roots burrowed deep beneath the soil; planted firmly on the bit of earth between the tracks of the mine floor. Before her paused four creatures, sizing she and Bern up in the mere seconds that had passed. They were mutated humanoid beings she had only encountered once before – the night her mother perished.

But she had long since pushed this far from her conscious mind, reading about these creatures only in post-war texts and overhearing her father and her uncle discussing skirmish strategies with the rest of the ship's crew. Now, here they stood before her. In the flesh, once again.

These creatures were human, with not a trace of humanity left in their bones. Their infected bodies were wrought with the radiation which accompanied the virus coursing through their blood. They were ravenous beings, and with a single bite, they spread their taint. They were the *degenerates*; subterran men and women whose mutations reached far beyond their bodies, to take over their brains. They were a much further cry from the earth dweller, overexposed to the atmospheric corrosion; the ultimate victims of nuclear bombing.

None of that mattered now. The Viscountess had succumbed to her self-perceived psychosis, and she was just as far gone as the beasts she now faced.

"It is time we abscond, Bern," she said, turning to the woman at her side.

Bern returned the Viscountess's words with a startled half glance. "Wh-...What?"

Immediately following the Viscountess having spoken (and during Bern's bewildered utterance), the degenerates started in on them in a maddened sprint, shrieking and snarling inhumanly. Without a moment's hesitation, both she and Bern whirled around and shot off like bullets in the direction of the light beam, still following the key's marked objective.

"That little trick you tried to pull on me earlier won't work on these," the Viscountess shouted, so as to be heard over the degenerates' loud, frenzied screeching. "You cannot manipulate a mind where there is none... just as you cannot do so, using a gemstone which matches the birth of your target." She watched her feet as she spoke, careful where she ran. The unevenness of the ground threatened to send her tumbling toward it.

"Who *are* you?!" Bern shouted back, running right alongside her.

The Viscountess smiled, blackly. "It mattered little to you, then. It matters less, now."

The light led them down a tunnel where the smell of sulfur was noticeably less abrasive. The Viscountess glanced up at a steam powered fan, a fixture ventilating the air and sucking it through toward the surface. There had to be another way out. As they ran, a wagon filled past its brim with coal came into view straight ahead. There would be little room of getting around it, the ground to track ratio disappearing with the mile long drop on either side. The Viscountess and Bern exchanged quick nods with one another, communicating only with their eyes.

Near simultaneously, they maneuvered by the wagon, the Viscountess weaving around the side as Bern dove over it. Immediately, both women rammed themselves against its outer rim. The wheels squeaked, but beyond that, there was not a single budge. They each slumped up beside it, defeatedly. The wagon alone must have weighed a quarter of a ton, and filled with coal, it was completely immovable. The Viscountess glowered at Bern, who cursed loudly with panic. Without hesitation, the Viscountess snatched at the key strapped to Bern's back, her hand over the gemstone as she forcibly pointed it at the wagon.

"*λογία povis!*" she bellowed. A wave of energy exploded through the key, followed by a blinding white flash. She could feel the key throb with power as it erupted mightily against the wagon. The wagon teetered on two of its four wheels toward the fast approaching degenerates. "*Now* you push."

With one giant heave, they both followed through, pushing with all of their strength to tip the wagon over completely. It came crashing loudly to the floor of the tracks, the coal spilling out over what little path there was like an avalanche of boulders. The four degenerates stumbled over the rolling bits of coal, two of them falling altogether and plummeting off the edge of the trail. The other two regained their balance, making it to the toppled wagon and attempted to scramble over it. Bern swiveled the key around her body by its strap, taking it up like a bludgeon. She wound it back as she had done so once before, in preparation to swing.

The first degenerate whose monstrous face came into view over the other side of the wagon would be turned inward like a keyhole molded to the key's bit and pin with Bern's anticipated force. As both creatures' arms came into view, their dried, bony fingers wrapping around that which obstructed them, they each began pulling themselves up and over to get at their prey. One had successfully lifted itself on top of the wagon, and just as soon as the Viscountess could see those crazed yellow eyes hungrily staring back at hers, Bern unleashed a violent, swooping batter ram of a swing, connecting solidly with the side of the degenerate's head.

A loud crack resounded like the bang of a fired pistol, as metal met with skull. The degenerate slumped off to the side, falling limply over the mound of spilled coals. Now the frenzied cries of but one remained, it too pulling itself up and over the toppled wagon. Bern wound back another swing, letting loose what remained of her full strength. Again, the key closed over a degenerate's head, and again, the creature fell limp, this time dropping off the side of the tracks to meet with the others. Seconds later, a dull thud was distantly audible as it struck rock bottom. As if by some mechanical function, the key's light resumed course, and the silence that followed was deafening but for the faint hum of the active gemstone.

The Viscountess and Bern panted to catch their breath, Bern looking perplexed and deflated. Her hazel eyes read that she had much to say, without the means to say it.

"Of any commoner I've come to know, only *one* has proven herself trustworthy, and reliable; I see that now," the Viscountess said, breaking the silence. "And now she is gone."

"I *saved* your **life**!" Bern shot back, defensively. "Of any aristocrat I've come to know, *all* of them have had this unwarranted superiority complex! Your petty, classist presumptions—"

"You saved my life, *Bern*, to see what more I had to offer," the Viscountess gritted, her voice gradually getting louder with each word. Still, she maintained her gathered demeanor. "You stole my property, and then kept me around for no other reason than to somehow soothe a guilty conscience letting your sister die... or maybe you *killed* her, yourself...!"

Bern flinched back with the Viscountess's words, her bottom lip quivering, eyes wide and glossy with the pain of the weighty blow she had just been dealt. Her emotions seemed to wash over her in a single convoluted wave which came to pass only moments later. As quickly as the tides of her defiance carried these emotions away, the Viscountess was able to dissect them mechanically, through the shocked expression dawning Bern's hardened features. She knew she struck a nerve.

"Th-The world *depends* on me!" Bern cried out, almost pleadingly. "I do what I have to, for the sake of those around me! I am *entitled* to pass judgment as I see it best, because I *know* my cause is just! How can I truly know this of other people?! How can I protect them if they only sabotage themselves; you *tell* me!" She was nearly screaming.

"Do I still look like her, Bern? Your sister?" the Viscountess goaded, going very quiet. "…Or just when I'm angry? What did you *do* to her, Bern…?"

"I *loved* her!" Bern shrieked.

Her voice carried far throughout the tunnels of the coal mines, echoing off walls and bounding into distant space where the key's light did not reach. It took but a second's passing for another series of hideous, screeching groans to make it down their passageway, the chilling intonations seeming far away, but close enough that the Viscountess knew it was Bern's cry that had alerted more mine wandering degenerates of their presence. Bern was visibly losing nerve, her eyes darting all around, and then falling to rest on the Viscountess once more. Without uttering another word, she took off in a sprint in the direction the light guided her, still determined to find the buried gemstone.

The Viscountess gave chase, refusing to let her out of her sight for even a second. "You martyr yourself *not* for the good of the world," she called after her, "but to justify your own denial! You feel guilty, and it's eating you alive inside, isn't it?! It's glory you're after!"

"No! You don't know me! You don't *see* me!" Bern screamed back at her.

"Give me back my key, Bern…!"

"It's *not* your *key*! It belongs to *no* one! Only *I* should harness its power; only *I* can be trusted to do right by everyone because **everyone is broken**! You understand *nothing!*"

Bern was faster on foot than the Viscountess was, who struggled to keep up in the tattered, newly soiled floral dress she wore, and even then, Bern was by far the better athlete. Despite this, the Viscountess felt only one thing as emotions ran high for her traitorous counterpart—fixation. *Get the key at all costs.*

She operated as a kind of machine in this altered cognitive state, hindering emotions such as fear and rage simply not an option for her. Her analytical mind had gone into overdrive by this point, dictating her every move. Her conscious emotions, though banished into the back of her psyche, were the archetype; the building plans which mapped out what she needed to do. Her *atlas*.

The Viscountess could hear frantic echoing footsteps from all around, though she was unable to tell where they were coming from. She knew many other degenerates would be upon them soon. Bern rounded another corner in hot pursuit of the key's light, the hide of her sleeveless duster billowing out behind her as it caught the musty air. As the Viscountess rounded the corner after her, she felt a gust of wind followed by a loud crack, the sound popping in her ear. Then, the pain. The Viscountess collapsed to the ground, falling over the tracks as her leg was knocked out from under her. Bern had swung the key into her left thigh.

With the Viscountess effectively immobilized for the time being, Bern deftly unfastened the knapsack she carried on her back, dropping it to the ground momentarily to sift through it. She quickly pulled out the bundle of strange-looking tubes with string attached, then reached into her pant pocket for a match. It took her striking it over the side of one of the tubes a couple of times before it finally caught fire. The footsteps were growing louder; the ghastly screeches, more abundant. She handed both the lit match and the tubes to the Viscountess.

"I'm sorry," was all she said.

The Viscountess watched her gather up the knapsack – and the key – and take off after the light which continued to lead her deeper into the mine. She watched her until she disappeared from view. The key's light gradually began to leave with her, the shadows that filled every last corner and crevice of the mine beginning to return. She knew she would soon be left in complete darkness, the further away Bern fled, left only with a single burning flame smaller than the nail on her smallest finger. She looked at the tubes while she could still read the painted lettering on the bundle—*Dynamite*. Were these bombs?

The screeching and the footsteps grew louder, still. The Viscountess saw shadows moving over the walls, and then soon, figures. Before the darkness enveloped her surroundings completely, she held the match to the string coming out from each of the tubes. A spark ignited from the flame, hissing down the string fast. She watched it a moment, before hurling it as far as her arm could throw in the direction of the shadowy figures growing along the walls. She saw the spark bounce and flicker against rock, just before everything went pitch black.

Moments later, a huge fiery burst engulfed everything in its radius.

Suddenly, she was face to face with Demetrius and his buccaneer crew, digging her nails into her palms until her knuckles were white and blood was drawn. Her eyes were on Rivkah, bound and on the ground near Roland, who had gold-toothed Gertie's knife to his throat. The hot morning sun was beating down on her as she continued to take in these surroundings.

•   She shouldered her way away from Orel, who was propping her up against him to support her. Limping, she stepped forward, closing the distance between herself and Demetrius who only stood there, watching. All eyes were on her, just watching. The other pirates, including Gertie, began to draw on her; each with swords and daggers, and Gertie's gun.

"I regrettably must inform you that you have been *beaten*," the Viscountess spoke, her words venomous with hate. "Someone stole what *you* were trying to steal, already! Several hours ago."

She stopped short, just a few feet in front of Demetrius. Rivkah and Roland each stared at her with wide eyes; Rivkah, moreover. In the many years she had known the Viscountess, never once had she heard her speak. The evil sneer twisting Demetrius's lips into toothy disdain slowly dissipated into a volatile frown. The Viscountess stood tensely on edge, anticipating the man's next move. She could tell her implicit issued challenge had provoked him.

"Put away that gun," Demetrius said, blankly. He threw Gertie a sidelong glance, warningly. "Your trigger-happy finger is what got us into this mess, you *fool*."

"Aye, Cap'n..." he conceded, with an ugly scowl. Gertie's face really irritated the Viscountess.

Demetrius started in on her, further closing the distance between them.

"Don't you touch her," Roland snarled, savagely. He repeated himself; "Don't you *touch* her!"

Stopping a foot in front of the Viscountess, Demetrius ignored Roland's words. His aura was very dark; dire, as he stared her down. She stared up at him in turn, glaring into his thick, veiling hood where she could just make out the faintest outlines of his obscured face. They each stood in silence, the Viscountess unwilling to stand down from Demetrius as he loomed over her, dauntingly. A few moments passed. The Viscountess remained composed, detached, and completely unmoved. Tension was building.

"Viscountess—" Orel started to speak, but she cut him off.

"You should leave here now, while you can, and not kill any more innocent people," she said, her voice deadpan. She continued to stare up at him, watching as he shifted his weight slightly.

Without warning, he wound back and punched her across the side of her head, his closed fist slamming into her left temple. The impact of the blow produced a loud metallic crack against her cheekbone. He had used his machinelike right limb.

"No! *Noooo!*" Roland shouted, his voice throaty and deeply growling as he twisted and thrashed against Gertie's knife which dug further into his neck.

The Viscountess saw him snap as she tumbled to the ground, catching herself with her hands. She skidded over loose dirt, trying to regain her footing as Roland kicked and roared, shouting obscenities and convulsing around in the sand, wild with rage. By this point, he had shaken himself free of Gertie's grip, but two other men pounced on him to keep him restrained. She was crouched over, balancing herself with her hand on the thigh of her right leg. She pushed off from the ground, using her other hand, and rose to her feet once steadied.

She could hear Orel breathing heavily, almost hyperventilating, behind her. Rivkah looked on, her screams gargling from her mouth, in the absence of her tongue. Roland continued to shout with his arms held behind his back, until one of the pirates came up beside him and kicked him solidly in the ribs. He grunted, coughing, as pain visibly washed over him. Strangely enough, the Viscountess felt no pain, though a fresh gusher of blood began to spill from her left ear. The ringing sensation only came from her right ear now, her left ear having since gone completely deaf. She felt a tingling sensation that took up the entire left side of her face, though to a much greater magnitude from when she had previously been slapped.

"Let's try this again," Demetrius said, disdainfully. "Either you tell me where the key is, or everyone dies. Starting with your *ex*-crewmate, here." He gestured toward Rivkah with an idle wave of his bandaged left arm.

The Viscountess straightened herself out and brushed off her dress uselessly with a patting of hands. Her eyes trailed up the inside of his hood once again, to meet with his obscured face. She wanted to see into his eyes. Just as the Viscountess had never been struck, she also had never raised her own hand in violence. Operating on her impulses alone, she threw all of her weight into a shot of a punch that hooked into Demetrius's jaw; the only feature of his face that she could see. His thick hood came flying off his head with the force behind her blow. The impact hurt her thumb, tucked awkwardly under her knuckles, which also cracked and split. She had a feeling it hurt her more than it did him.

She knew the consequences for what she had done would be severe, but at least for now, that did not matter. Only seconds would pass that she would relish this moment – while it was still hers. In these mere fleeting seconds, all chaos broke loose. Several of the pirates charged toward her, bumping around the tied up Rivkah, bound on the ground. The pirates restraining Roland pushed his face into the sand, twisting his arms, with one of their hands clasped around the back of his neck. Orel had grabbed the Viscountess around the waist from behind, with both his arms. He pulled her around him, stepping in front of her protectively. She was surprised by his sudden burst of courageousness, having mistaken the nervous, lanky man for something of a coward.

The pirates fought around Orel, striking him to the ground by the hilts of their daggers, stomping and kicking him as he fell. Two of them rolled him over on his chest, stepping on the backs of his shoulders. They each took hold of his forearms, pulling up and twisting until there were several audible pops and cracks. He screamed horrifically. The Viscountess watched Demetrius. He was still standing, the one red eye she could make out, staring her down vilely. The rest of his face was covered in burns that healed over his bald scalp and left eye, which was just a covering of pale, gruesomely scarred skin. He calmly pulled his hood up over his head, once more.

"Stop!" he bellowed deeply. The bustling pirates heeded him, and fell back. Even Orel's agonized screams reduced to shaky whimpers as he convulsed on the ground, unable to stand.

"Even if you find the key, you barely know how to operate it," the Viscountess spoke, projecting her voice so as to be heard by all. "Only I know how to properly harness its power, and it's been stolen. You will kill *no one*, because if you do, I will not help you. You need me alive, so take me, and leave them."

Something new was at work, inside her. She needed the key 'at all costs,' the only expenditure she could not abide, being her allies. Although presently unhindered by her emotions, she could not ignore their ultimate role in finding the key. In the midst of her mother's passing, the most valuable lesson she had learned from her was to protect her loved ones 'at all costs.' Her objectives were clear. She would find the key, and she would protect her loved ones.

Demetrius seemed to consider her words for a moment, falling very silent under his hood. He stepped to her, again coming within a couple of feet in front of her. "I know that in order to operate the twelve gemstones, I need twelve signs of the sun; twelve children to twelve stones," he said, calmly. "…I'm missing a few."

With that, he snatched up a fistful of her hair with his metal hand, ripping it loose from the torn piece of lace which held it up in its messy bun. A fragment of a second later, her legs flailed up off the ground in a cartwheel as she was sent spiraling down. He had flung her limply, headfirst and careening. He forcibly laid her out over the sand. She felt strands of her hair break away from her scalp as her backside connected with the earth beneath her. Then he closed his black leather boot down over her neck, asphyxiating her. She thrashed and kicked, her hands instinctively rising up to grasp around his ankle. Weakly, she pulled and clawed to no avail.

She could feel a cold rush to her brain, the oxygen blocked from her lungs. Unable to control her mouth pumping open, she gasped and gulped like a fish on land. Her eyes jutted out, round and wide. They started to get blurry, and everything around her seemed to be getting distant and faded with her vision. Soon, a feeling of weightlessness, followed by the increasing expanse of white. It was no source of lighting, but nothing at all; had her eyes rolled back into her head? Even the ringing in her right ear had faded.

Soon, the white dimmed to black. She found herself back in the cell with Orel, Ovocula, Gwendolyn, and Rivkah. Orel was saying something, but she was not really listening. "You said that… you were the only one who knew…! Th-The only one who knew how to… to harness the key's powers, properly," he said, wheezing from injuries sustained both prior to boarding the *S.S. Beulah*, as well as after. She caught the tail end of his words, haphazardly as she tuned into what he was saying. "How would you… know something like this? Your mother would have had to've *known*… Wh-When did she tell you…?"

The Viscountess shot him an angry glare that he would not be able to see through his swollen, blackened eyes. "As she lay *dying*," she replied, venomously.

There was a brief pause, as each person around the room seemed to be taken aback by her having spoken. Nevertheless, she continued, her mind ablaze with the bitterness in her heart.

"I stayed with her, through one—final—*fairytale*. One final story wherein she would reveal the various magical properties the key possessed. Least of which included the colors of each gemstone; of each sign, and how they correlate with the children of their respective stone. How these stones even give off their own unique scent! At such a tender age, I couldn't possibly even *begin* to fathom the importance of her words; what they would mean, not just for myself, but for the future of the world! But... I never asked for this. I never asked for *any* of it, and I resent you even bringing it up."

She looked down at herself, climbing unsteadily to her feet. She looked at the mess of herself she had made with disgust, and began to shamelessly undress. She fumbled with the string of her corset from behind, deftly slipping her fingers between the loops and loosening the constrictive garment to the best of her ability.

"You... You resent that I should... bring it up...?" Orel retorted, an air of incredulity to his words. He seemed particularly off put by her callousness. He began twitching, uncontrollably. "Surely you don't... mean to tell me... that you shirk your responsibility, as the rightful wielder of the key...?"

The Viscountess returned his words with a defensive glare. She continued to remove articles of soiled clothing, stripping off her corset and proceeding to strip off her dress. "...I... I think I may have found something *better*... I don't deny that Demetrius must be punished for his crimes against my family, and so many others. I don't deny that I need to face this thing, and I am no less anxious to see him *dead* for what he's done; to nullify the threat, as the only one who best knows what the key, and the gemstones, are capable of...!"

"You are very angry, and bitter, Miss Viscountess," Gwendolyn said, suddenly. The Viscountess turned to look at her, as she kicked off her boots and began slipping out of her torn, grubby stockings. Gwendolyn only smiled back pleasantly with her eyes. "But you do not appear this way when you do not speak. Almost as if there are two completely different sides to you. One, perhaps, more closely taking after your mother; the other, a result of your having lost her."

"You don't know an *All Mother* damn thing about *mine!*" the Viscountess shot, angrily. Her emotions were surfacing, even on this elevated plane of thought. Despite her mild flare-up however, she remained fundamentally analytic. "Look – I haven't the slightest idea what you *common* vermin are all about, but those of a more 'high society' nature have taught me that this world is *insane* and you have to take from it whatever you can get. There are no free handouts for the daughter of a skylark captain; the man who wanted only a son!

There is no one supporting the girl in anything much beyond cooking, and baking, and how to properly lace a blasted corset! I taught myself everything *of value* that I now know!"

"And what of... your mother...?!" Orel erratically wheezed, clearly worked up by her words. Ovocula and Rivkah just silently watched, wide-eyed and visibly displeased. Their emotions beyond that were otherwise unfathomable to the Viscountess, who only threw down her soiled garments against the ground with a wet, grimy splat. "What of... everything your mother... has taught you... for the good of... the people...? How can you be... so self-serving?"

"My mother," the Viscountess glared, "is *gone*. If she is gone, then so is everything! Unless... Unless I can find my *new* everything...!"

"Viscountess—!" Ovocula started to speak, but she must have decided against it upon seeing the look in the Viscountess's eyes. She returned her utterance with a glance, unchanged from the glare which hardened her features.

"You... You *selfish* little—!"

"I think you suffer a split personality," Gwendolyn interrupted, before Orel could get the rest of his words out. Another pause hung in the air with her allegation. "I think that whenever something happens to you, and it turns out that you simply cannot handle it, a *shift* occurs. Then suddenly, that is when the dormant warrior inside you takes over. You are then brave enough to speak, and confront all that is bad, and suspend hindering emotions – all in favor of protecting both your physical body and the part of you which desperately clings to her innocence."

Her insightfully voiced thoughts, though spoken with offhanded inflection, bowled the Viscountess over like a tidal wave. How could something like that even be possible? From there, she faintly heard the sound of a door abruptly open and close, followed by the approach of clunky footsteps—*Gertie*. It was not until then that she became consciously aware that she was seeing events long since already panned out. Not only seeing, but feeling; experiencing. All that lost time, and how she would have sworn on her life that she had not once spoken, in spite of what everyone around her seemed to believe.

With these answers, came so many more questions. She wanted to see more of a past she had all but blocked out; from the Fyndridge guards she had maimed and eluded, to the pirate she most undoubtedly killed. What caused her to be this way? How was she now seeing these shades of her memory? *Gwendolyn,* she thought. *Could she be a... a sorceress?*

Soon, her surroundings dimmed to complete pitch darkness. She experienced a moment of weightlessness settled into a cold, rigid sensation against the span of her whole backside. As she breathed in deeply and sighed, she slowly began to open her eyes, soon realizing that she was still in the holding cell. No longer was she reliving events forcibly pushed into the forefront of her mind. It took her but a few seconds to fully recover her mind, catching up with her.

"So... will she be able to speak now, then?" she heard Ovocula's voice.

The Viscountess's eyes stared up at the dark, barren ceiling of the cell. Her vision was blurred as she squinted to refocus, laying flat over the cold metal flooring and wearing only the ragged nightgown she had previously worn under the purple robes. Parts of the ceiling were splotched green with mildew and rust. It made for a rather bleak contrast within the shroud of shadows. At any rate, these depressing surroundings did nothing to help her mood. Perhaps Roland truly *was* dead. And perhaps she truly *had* failed her family. All she wanted to do was lie there for an eternity, until she too was nothing more than a splotchy growth infused into the corroded metal which encased them.

"As I have said, my uncle was a psychologist," Gwendolyn softly, musically replied. "All I have done was influence the Viscountess to recall things she had suppressed from her memory. I get the sense that the split is a new development for her, if only for the fact that she was so very susceptible to the techniques I would overhear my uncle using on far older patients. I supposed it was worth a try; I did not think it would be quite so easy to... break *into* her, as it were."

The Viscountess had no idea what they were talking about, but still they carried on as if she were not even there. She would think she should have gotten used to this by now. She did not care. Nothing mattered, now.

"...You did very well, Mister Doctor Orel," Gwendolyn continued. "I cannot help but feel there was quite a bit of truth to the emotions you projected..."

"You said we ought to get a deliberate rise out of her, so that she would slip back into her *supposed* altered state," he simply replied. "I might be an old fool of a man, but I know what it means to have loved, and to have lost..."

CHAPTER 19

Interlude to Remnants of the Past

"She isn't going to speak,"

Ovocula said finally, after a very long silence. The Viscountess had not been paying attention to anyone around her for quite some time. She just lay there, staring up at the ceiling. She felt like something inside her had broken, as if she were a windup doll whose key had been wrenched from its backside. She felt empty; listless.

She could hear the ever so slightest smile in Gwendolyn's voice. "I would imagine having everything one has ever had to deal with called up from the forgotten recesses of ones' mind would be rather taxing – for one," she sweetly sang.

She felt like a failure. No matter how she tried to look at it, the Viscountess could not do anything besides lay there and feel sorry for herself. She could not even call up enough energy to hate herself for feeling sorry for herself. Was she really giving up? Orel had every right to be mad at her, whether he was deliberately trying to get a rise out of her so that Gwendolyn could enter her mind, or not. That was another feeling she could not shake – she felt somehow violated; as though her darkness had just been laid bare in the light, for all to see. It was a darkness she never knew she had, and yet they only scratched its surface.

As they continued to talk among themselves as though the Viscountess was gone from the room, her thoughts drifted toward her uncle. She tried to recall times where he had influenced her; instances which led her to being so unable to see past herself. She knew the fault rested only upon her own slender shoulders. She tried to picture his face in her mind, from his bushy furrowed brows to his deep, inset brown eyes; from his long beaklike nose to the thin distinguished braid of hair pulled back behind his head, his receded hairline made that much more noticeable. She had hated him so. But then, perhaps she hated a lot of things. Perhaps she hated a lot of *people*.

And all that energy spent hating and brooding; resenting and judging – it only dragged her further and further down. The return of the stinging in her eyes, from bitter tears. What right did she have? She had felt just as entitled to her prescribed way of living; her own hand of judgment, as Bern. This was before she was able to catch a glimpse of herself, and what she had become. Just then, she felt a hand curl around her palm, and gently squeeze. Startled out of her dwellings, the Viscountess abruptly turned her head and came face to face with Rivkah, who had crawled up beside her and gazed at her now with a soft, reassuring smile.

Rivkah, the Viscountess sighed, looking at her now through her blurred vision. Her beautiful golden brown eyes were so soft in the dim light; so comforting, and accepting—*forgiving*. They shamed her. She gently squeezed her caramel-mocha hand back, blinking away the tears flowing freely from her eyes. She did not deserve the kindness she had shown her; not after she had been so hateful. How could such a common woman as she still have any care left for her?

"Man, Orel; you look like hell… What did they *do* to you…?!"

The jarring, high-pitched squeak resounded in the single ear the Viscountess could hear out of, stirring her from her state of melancholy. She sat upright with surprise, recognizing the voice as none other than Blythe's. He stood on the other side of the cell's bars wearing the same grubby clothes he had worn when the Viscountess first met him at The Rogue Musket. His shoulder-length dirty blonde hair looked as though it had been licked up the side by a horse that may have confused him for a bundle of straw.

"Blythe!" Orel responded, sightlessly. "You're… How did you…?"

"You *know* this person, Mister Doctor Orel?" Gwendolyn chimed in.

"I snuck onboard with Alasdair and Kael," he replied. "We hid in the cargo area of the ship, next to this cabin. I ducked in here for cover. Didn't expect you to be here, though! Is this where they've been holding you…? All Mother, what did they *do* to you?!"

"The same thing Demetrius is probably doing to your other friends, right now," Ovocula said, flatly.

Blythe flinched with her words. He seemed to scan the inside of the cell with his eyes, but the back corners were far too darkened with shadow, where Ovocula preferred to linger.

"It's been a couple of hours since his men found you," she continued, "and I doubt he would have only *just* started torturing them for information. With all the chaos that's been going on, I would imagine he'd be far less concerned with keeping either of them alive. That being said, the sooner we get out of here, the better."

Blythe shakily fumbled around his pockets. He looked like a muddled sack of potatoes as he patted himself down. After a few seconds of frantic searching, he produced a ring of silvery keys. "I found these! When Alasdair and Kael were caught! They fell off that short fat man."

"Oh, my!" Gwendolyn sang. "Gertie is usually so careful with his keys. How lovely of you to have picked them up, mister lady ma'am sir!"

Ovocula immerged from the shadows in that instant, climbing to her feet and coming up to the bars. Blythe flinched back, once more, with her approach. "Here's the situation," she said forcefully, wrapping her fingers around the bars next to either side of her face. She got up as close as could be. "On my last escort to the loopty l—…the *toilet*, I counted what I believe to be the last of the crewmen, *not* including the captain or his lady. In total, that's thirty-six men! Of our group, I'd say Gwendolyn, myself, and Rivkah are in able enough condition to assist you in rescuing your friends and taking over this ship!"

The Viscountess's heart sank with her words, as no one vouched in her favor or seemed to protest. As Rivkah's hand slipped away from her own, she felt utterly alienated and hopelessly ineffectual.

"Thirty-six men versus four of us; that means we *each* have to either kill or detain nine men! And this is assuming your friends are not in any condition to fight alongside us, as I would suspect will be the case."

"Miss Ovocula!" Gwendolyn cooed. "You have suddenly become so proactive! And I had not realized that you were such an *accomplished* mathematician!"

"That's all astrology is," Ovocula snapped at her, her words coming out abrupt and quick. "Astrology uses mathematical equations to compute the locations and alignments of the planets in relation to the constellations, all in accordance with the time and location of your birth."

"Whoa, whoa, whoa… Wait a minute, here," Blythe said, taking another step back with the ring of keys clenched tightly in one of his fists. "You can't *possibly* expect me to—… I mean, just look at me! Look at all of *you*! How do you expect to take over an entire ship?!"

"Blythe," Orel said, wearily. "About enough time has passed for Gertie to have realized his keys are missing. We need to act fast. Did you see any weapons of *any* kind in cargo?"

"Some. But I don't know how to use—!"

"Just let them out. I can't go anywhere, in my condition. This is the last chance we have."

Hesitating a moment, eyes darting between Orel and Ovocula, Blythe reluctantly stepped forward toward the lock fixture on the other side of the bars. As he shakily tried each key, his eyes glanced quickly to fall upon the Viscountess, with scorn. She watched him with matched malcontent, knowing full well the esteem he held Bern in. The Viscountess could no longer trust her, and she did not like *this* little weasel since the very moment she laid eyes upon him.

"I think it's the short rusty one," Ovocula said, pointing to a small key on the ring in his hands.

"Yes," Gwendolyn smiled. "I do believe Miss Ovocula to be most accurate in her assertion."

Blythe grumbled with agitation. Finally, he slipped the key into the lock and turned it open. The bars emitted a rusty squeak as they fell away from each other, once more materializing into an unassuming door, now ajar. Ovocula impatiently pushed it the rest of the way open, picking up her extravagant black dress as she stepped over the threshold and out of the cell. Rivkah shot up and followed close behind her, and the bare-footed Gwendolyn was soon to accompany them.

The Viscountess started to climb to her feet, but Blythe slammed the cell door shut before she could pass through. He eyed her smugly as everyone looked on. She could feel her heart pounding in her chest, as anger bubbled up within her and curdled into hate.

"Blythe, what are you doing?!" Orel exclaimed, with furrowed brows.

"That nightgown she's wearing," Blythe said, his eyes piercing. "It belonged to Bern's *lover*."

CHAPTER 20

Insanity

The next thing the Viscountess knew, she had her hands clutched tightly around what she thought was Blythe's neck. Upon further reawakening from whatever fugue she had slipped into, she realized that the neck belonged to Beulah. She did not look pleased.

"Glk... lkkgghh...!" Beulah gagged, as though she had just finished saying something. Her eyes were bugging out of her head, her hands clutching the Viscountess's wrists, desperate to be released. Why was she not forcing electric current through her body? How had the Viscountess gotten so close to her in the first place?

As she gazed around and took in her surroundings, she realized they were on the deck of the ship, just outside Beulah's living chambers. It was dark with nightfall. Rain was pouring all around, harsh winds blowing the rainwater at a slant, which washed over the deck's floorboards. They were soaking wet, and so were the ballooned sails which kept the ship aloft, high overhead. Suddenly, the Viscountess felt a firm hand clasp around her shoulder.

"That's enough, Viscountess!" Ovocula shouted over the sound of rain against mast. She glanced over her shoulder at the woman. Her green eyes shone in moonlight, made dim, between matted strands of dark wet hair. The ship sank well below the clouds with the building water weight. "She told us what we needed to hear, and we *need* to *hurry.* Just let her go for now; she's secure where she is!"

The Viscountess turned to look Beulah over more closely. She was chained to one of the thin wooden pillars holding up the ship's mast, one of her chubby ankles bound by a padlocked cuff link; the other cuff, fastened around the pillar itself. She was coughing, barely able to utter her disdainful obscenities as both women took their leave. The Viscountess tore her attention away as Ovocula snatched up her wrist and pulled her along. They ran the expanse of the deck together, and as they made their way, she could barely see through all the icy rain beating against her forehead and washing over her shoulders. The white nightgown she wore was soaked, and clung to her slender body like a second skin. She was appallingly exposed and yet unable to stop to acknowledge even an ounce of indignity.

"I've learned the layout of this ship pretty well," Ovocula yelled back to the Viscountess, maintaining her grip around her wrist. She carried the folds of her heavy, sopping wet dress in her other arm. "I'm not *entirely* sure, but I think Demetrius's interrogation chamber is this way! Stay close to me – and watch my back!"

Watch your back?! the Viscountess repeated, in her head. The very notion seemed so surreal to her. *Just what makes you think I'm capable of—?*

Just then and all at once, she became very aware of the sheathed sword strapped to her waist as it knocked against her hip with each bounding stride. There was no time to ponder what was happening, or how it came to be that she would brandish a weapon she had no knowledge of how to wield properly. All she could do was fall in step behind Ovocula as she led her along.

"This rain is as much a curse as it is a blessing," Ovocula yelled back at her. "It's weighting down the ship, but so long as it keeps raining like this, that *castlelark witch* can't utilize her energy to shock us with volts of electricity; not without also shocking herself, let alone the whole ship!"

Castlelark…? the Viscountess repeated to herself. *She's from the Castle in the Sky?!*

The ship teetered with the storm as both women ran; Ovocula in her elegant black ladies' boots and the Viscountess, barefooted. Thoughts were careening through her mind like a hurricane crashing over the plains, and uprooting all life in its path. She was finding it increasingly difficult to make sense of anything anymore, reduced to being led around by the arm, where before, she at least had the freedom to think for herself, if only under the noses of her father and uncle. She could not even do that much, anymore. It then occurred to her that Ovocula was probably unaware that she once again blanked out, and had since returned from another dissociative episode.

When is this going to end? she grieved.

They continued along, and as they made their way, lightning crashed amidst the pouring rain, illuminating the floorboards and fallen bodies of pirates—presumably all dead. How did this happen? It was as though time had slowed down, suddenly. There, another bloodbath massacre set before her eyes, but this time the tables had been turned. She felt strangely detached from it all, as though she were not truly there. She felt the icy cold rain on her skin and the tremor of shivers which followed. She felt her heart pounding in her chest with sharp, relentless palpitations. She felt the rebound from the rough stomps her feet made against wooden planks, the cold water splashing over her calves and thighs with every stride she took.

She could physically feel these strong sensations, and yet somehow there was a perceptible disconnect. She was confused; perhaps terrified. Undeniably overwhelmed. Even so, there were no other emotions she felt. What few sights she took in, in her frantic state of mind, were a blur as she passively pondered this. It was not long before she found herself coming upon a heavy door, slightly ajar in the near distance, with Ovocula still leading the way. It knocked against the jamb as the wind and rain pushed against it. Ovocula did not slow down, despite the Viscountess's immediate inclination to do so. With a solid burst out from under her soaked black dress, Ovocula booted the door with startling force.

The door came off its hinge, having been damaged considerably before they had come. Rigidly, it came crashing down. Ovocula simply ran over it and into the room while the Viscountess took to standing in the doorway. It was the first time the woman had released her wrist since she pulled her off of Beulah. As the Viscountess looked into the darkened room over Ovocula's shoulder, another crash of lightning lit up a ghastly scene.

"Oh, All Mother...!" Ovocula gasped.

Alasdair was seated over an upright chair in the small room's center, his arms bound to the wooden armrest with wire cord. There were no fingers on each of his hands. The rest of his body was bound by this same cord, which cut deep lacerations into his paled, discolored flesh. His clothing had been stripped from his bloodied body, and so had evidence of his sex as the Viscountess's eyes immediately zoned in on the space between his legs, which pooled dark blood into the seat. It had poured down the legs of the chair and all around the floor. She had never seen so much blood in all her life. She knew this was Alasdair before it occurred to her that she could not see his face. His throat had been slit so deeply that his head was almost entirely severed, hanging over the other side of the chair, mostly unseen, leaving the fresh gaping wound on gruesome display.

Ovocula retched, turning to vomit. The Viscountess remembered that the woman had not eaten in a while, a fact which casually crossed her mind as she watched her bend, dry heaving, her face as white as Gwendolyn's. *Where was Gwendolyn?* she thought, her eyes carelessly scanning the rest of the tiny space gone black once more. The stormy weather withdrew the light from the thunder clash. She heard whimpering in a corner of the room. With that, her eyes fell over a collection of shadowy figures hovering around another in a chair cast in shadow. It had fallen on its side, the male body strapped to it quivering uncontrollably.

Another clash of thunder followed the lightning. With the sudden burst of light, the Viscountess could clearly see the faces of Gwendolyn and Rivkah, both standing over a weeping Blythe who had draped himself around Kael's body in the chair. Like Alasdair, Kael was completely bare though relatively intact. He sustained some noticeable cuts and bruises, but seemed otherwise physically well. His mental and emotional state were another conundrum entirely which the Viscountess chose not to dwell on, for fear that any acknowledgement she allotted to the horror of the scene would send her spiraling into another bout of lost time.

Just breathe, she told herself with detached conviction. *This, too, shall pass.*

"All Mother, Kael, what have they done…?" Blythe sobbed. "Alasdair is *dead.* Thank All Mother they didn't kill you, too…"

"Excuse me, mister lady ma'am sir," Gwendolyn ineptly interjected, "but it would do you well to keep in mind that the captain of the ship, Demetrius, is solely responsible for the tortures he subjects his prisoners to. Given the nature of this awful spectacle, I would be curious to know the psychology behind his actions."

The Viscountess raised a brow at the woman's words, still so musical in their delivery. How could she maintain her *only* seeming composure in the midst of such horror? The blood; the gore – it was everywhere. How could she stand it? She was not the only one perturbed by Gwendolyn's aloof whimsy. Blythe turned, in that moment, and faced her. Again, the clash of thunder ceased, the lightning in its wake flashing fiercely before leaving the room black.

"Psychology?!" the Viscountess could hear Blythe snap, his high-pitched voice screeching with incredulity. "I *fail* to see how that 'hocus pocus' nonsense matters right now! Kael needs physical aid, immediately! We need to get him to Orel!" He was hysterical.

"Orel's arms are broken, and both his eyes are swollen practically all the way shut," Ovocula replied. Her voice sounded weak, as she gulped back the last of her empty retching. "...Or don't you remember?"

"Well, we have to do *something!* Damn it, we could have gotten to them sooner if you all hadn't let that *bitch* talk you into letting her out; she's done nothing but hold us back!" Blythe was screaming now, as another flash of lightning illuminated his face. It was contorted in furious anguish like a child's, his finger pointed menacingly at the Viscountess. "Alasdair wouldn't be dead right now; Kael wouldn't be in the condition he's in—if *you* hadn't led us to this!"

Led us...? the Viscountess repeated his hateful words in her head. Had she taken charge, somehow? She looked down into Kael's wide, listless eyes. The man's body was shaking within Blythe's arms, still strapped to the toppled chair which shook with his own involuntary movements. She felt a strong sense of empathy for him as he lay there, realizing then that she was strangely unaffected by Blythe's rage. There subsisted a peculiar detachment from everything else happening around her, except for this unconscious connection to Kael's plight; a sort of sickly vertigo.

She began to move further into the room, stepping toward him as darkness once more engulfed them. She was somehow drawn to his unresponsive state of shock and unspoken despair; the horrors he undoubtedly borne witness to, forced to watch as Alasdair had been gruesomely murdered before his very eyes. His once spirited personality had all but cleared away, like rolling smoke from quenched flames. In this moment, the Viscountess could think of nothing else but to offer him the comfort in knowing that she understood him; what he was feeling. She had blocked these remnants of her past from her memory, but inherently she had known them well.

Another flash of lightning. "NO! You stay *right* where you are!" Blythe screeched, standing to meet her.

The Viscountess felt somewhat startled by his sudden outburst, as though she had snapped out of a trance. Her attention was now redirected upon Blythe's face, his delicately boyish features twisted into a demonic, visceral hate. She stared back at him now, the empathy for Kael which she had felt only moments before, washed away with an air of quiet annoyance. It was as though by the light of the thundering flash, only she and Blythe remained. Their surroundings and comrades were no longer present; only their mutual disdain.

"Ever since Bern brought you to Fyndridge, you've been nothing but trouble!" he spat, the light from the flash once more disappearing. "You come here, and you think that just because you sort of resemble the likeness of a loved one that you can manipulate *everyone* into thinking you're good – but I knew the truth the moment I laid eyes on you! You're *not* good; you're a taker! You'll just take, take, and *take* and everyone will hand you everything on a silver platter because they're all too stupid to see you for what you really are! Well… Well I'm not gonna let you take Kael away from me, like Roland took Bern's *only love* away from her!"

What…? The Viscountess gaped, trying to make the least bit of sense of what he was saying. Her blood felt hot. She could feel it flush her face; a mix of discomfiture and general resentment rising up from within. *Bern's love… Her sister…? No—she wasn't really her sister,* she thought, the pieces coming together for her in that instant. *She lied to me. But, why?*

"I don't know what she saw in you! I told her it was a mistake; that she was only trying to rekindle what she had lost to Roland… What he had taken away from her!"

Is that why she didn't kill me at once, when she discovered my key…? She… She tried to kill me in the mines! But… perhaps she wasn't the one who killed that other woman, after all…

The Viscountess's mind swirled with newfound perspective. *How did she die?* she wondered. Perhaps she was not murdered, at all. It was unfathomable that Roland ever be capable of taking the life of a lover; not when she felt the things she had for him. Not when he would go so far out of his way to remove her from harm's way. The very notion was preposterous.

How could he be dead?! It's not true; it can't be!

"I won't let you take away Kael!" Blythe continued. "He... He's *mine!*"

A brief silence resounded through the darkness of the room before anyone finally spoke, once more making known the presences amid the shadows. It was Gwendolyn who cut into Blythe's focus on the Viscountess, with her words; "Could it be that you *love* him...?"

Her softly melodious voice seemed to startle Blythe's attention away from her. Though the Viscountess could not see his gaze in the pitch blackness of the room, she could somehow feel his concentration break and draw away. "He..." his voice sounded hoarse. "He prefers the company of women to the likes of me. Said so, himself."

Suddenly, there was another flash of lightning, but the thunder roared and burned so hot the Viscountess had to turn away from the room as she stood there near the busted doorway. She turned to face its source, behind her. It was Beulah, her fingers ablaze with electric current coursing through her nails. Before the Viscountess could so much as question how the woman managed to free herself of her shackles, she was struck by thousands of volts of electricity. She felt it pulsate all throughout her body, racking her head and knotting her nerves, limbs locked and jerking. It was with this blast that she suddenly felt the wooden planks beneath her bare feet fall away from her. The thin muscles in her body pulsated painfully, her teeth clenching involuntarily. There was something in her mouth.

She was strapped down, her vision blurred by her own tears. She could make out the white tiled ceiling as before, strange masked figures looming over her once more. Everything smelled of disinfectant and sterilized rubber; everything was very clean and very *white*. What was this? She could feel the panic rising up from within her, as she tried in vain to free herself of her bindings. She twisted frantically, the straps cutting into her ankles and wrists. The surface she was lying over, sprawled out and vulnerable, felt hard and uncomfortable despite being lightly cushioned.

"Her pupils," came a distorted voice. She heard it ringing through her right ear. "They are dilating again, Doctor. She is coming to!"

"Let's make certain it sticks this time," another replied, voice distorted as it echoed over her. It came from the figure hovering closest, directly above her. "This is dangerous enough a procedure as it is; we don't want her brain fried, we just want it functioning properly."

What's wrong with my brain...?!

"Yes, Doctor. Discharging another fifty-five volts, at two-tenths of a second..."

The Viscountess felt the pressure above her ears intensify over her temples, presumably in preparation for another shock. Her heart raced. She clenched her teeth, surprised to discover the plush, springy texture of what had been in her mouth; a terrycloth rag? An oversized cotton swab?

Stop! There's nothing wrong with my brain! All Mother, what are you doing to me...?!

"*Clear*, in 3... 2... 1...!"

A blinding light filled the room and washed everything away, the whiteness of her surroundings engulfed in an even whiter flash. Her senses were overwhelmed with a steadfast sense of being. It was like her many other blackouts, but rather than become the universe for all intents and purposes, she instead, became *aware* of 'the universe.' Something outside herself. Something which interrupted the ebb and flow of her very subsistence. What a strange and foreign feeling it was to her; a feeling which made her look past herself and see a clearer image in her head. It was a feeling which forced her to acknowledge her own plight.

...Something she had denied all along...

"Ovocula? Did you hear me?" her uncle said. She opened her eyes to Acanthus's disapproving frown. He wore an eggplant-purple suit jacket with a white button-up shirt, and black necktie. His glare was discerning, as though to deliberately make her aware of how well he truly knew her. Had he known, the whole time, what goes on in her head?

She realized then that she had still been lying down, but no longer bound and restrained. *I am not Ovocula!* she thought, craning her neck to look up at him. *Don't you recognize your own niece?!*

"I asked you a question," he replied, seated cross-legged in an armchair a few feet away from her. "How many of you are *in* there...?"

CHAPTER 21

Crazy Little Sad Loose Cannon Girl

T he Viscountess slowly sat upright, realizing then that the surface she had been laying over was now a couch. It seemed just moments before, she was strapped to what felt like an ironing board. She was still in some way restrained. It took her but a moment to survey her surroundings, paying no mind to Acanthus who sat adjacent to her. The couch was rich, Victorian velvet in a deep scarlet. There was a loud whirring noise she would have otherwise tuned out completely, if not for her uneven distribution of hearing and the fact that the room was otherwise so quiet.

She followed the sound of the whirring noise with her gaze, realizing then that it was coming from a ventilation source overhead in a far corner of the room's ceiling. *Air conditioning*, she thought. Her eyes fell over the gaudy floral wallpaper; very busy-looking, with thick, dark lines which made up the outer layer of each flowery design. The colors were as bold and thick as the borders surrounding them. It was not the least bit aesthetically pleasing, and the Viscountess could not help but feel somewhat nauseous, the wallpaper dizzying her tired eyes.

A brief chill ran through her. The conditioned air in the room was almost *too* cool, and it was not until she tried to rub her hands over her arms that she cast her gaze down, seeing the straitjacket covering her body. She wriggled firmly, out of impulse. Though she was no longer immobilized, it became clear to her that she was still a prisoner of sorts. Under this, she still wore the nightgown; faintly stained, but otherwise clean and dried. *Where am I...?* she wondered.

She continued to glance around the room, eyes trailing over the plain carpet that seemed to match the color of the couch—the drapes, too. There was only one window on the far wall, below the vent in the ceiling. It was firmly barred shut; the glass, on the outside. Around the room, there were bookcases filled with books, thick and thin, which looked as though they had not been touched in years, but for one; *Airship Engineering for the Sky Captain of Tomorrow.* The thin layer of dust over every surface served as indication that this room was not often used. The cool air was stuffy. She smelled mildew somewhere.

In contrast to the wallpaper which was louder than the constant humming of the ventilation system, the objects and furniture around the room were very plain. The chairs, the globe on the desk, the neatly stacked papers, the perfectly lined up pens and pencils; all of these odds and ends seemed somewhat placed, and seldom disturbed. The room, though simple, still seemed cluttered. As the Viscountess sat upright on the couch and pivoted her body to face her uncle more directly, the distance between them grew. Her surroundings made her feel claustrophobic, mere feet apart from Acanthus.

He frowned disapprovingly, adjusting his posture slightly in his armchair. He seemed to be moving back a ways from her. The distance she felt was more the result of his perceived negative feelings toward her, than anything else. She met his eyes. His contemptuous gaze pierced right through her, brown eyes darkened beneath those low, bushy brows.

"I suppose I should take it to mean by your silence, that I am no longer speaking to Ovocula?" Acanthus said.

The Viscountess stumbled over his words as they echoed throughout her troubled mind. Her confusion transformed quickly into anger. *Of course you're not speaking to Ovocula!* she fumed, eyes narrowing with bitter disdain. *You spent enough time making certain I was always under your thumb! How can you not know who I am?! Am I just some kind of object to you; a possession you begrudgingly keep?*

Acanthus smirked, acknowledging her gaze. "Ahh... The girl who plays the perpetual victim, yet stakes no claim in her role as *antagonist.* Welcome back, my dear."

...What are you talking about?

"Are you aware of what you've put your family through? The sacrifices we had made—*all* for you? Do you know that it was your recklessness that cost your father his life, and possibly your mother's as well?"

The Viscountess could feel her heart rise and fall, blood boiling; anxiety building. *Me?! How could you possibly blame me for that?!* she gasped, trembling angrily within the constraints of the white jacket which encased her.

"If not for your depraved involvement with the mental patient whose escape you assisted, your father would still be here today. The staff at this ward; they would be alive, as well. If not for *you*."

…What…?

Acanthus's expression softened, suddenly. "Even when you were being transferred from Fyndridge for your violent behavior, I held onto the hope that you could still be helped. That maybe the treatment from a more restrictive asylum could somehow *fix* you."

Fyndridge? An asylum…?

"…That you would not become a permanent resident here, at Galvinsglade."

The Viscountess's eyes drooped as she tried to make sense of her uncle's words. Within the distance of her thoughts, she wandered her gaze around the room and took note of details she had missed before. The bookcase, her uncle's armchair, the base of the globe; letters etched into the wooded parts of each piece of furniture. She turned her attention to the plaque over the front of the desk. The lettering read the same way, wherever she looked; *Property of Galvinsglade Institute for the Criminally Insane.*

A foreign sense of clarity shocked her system. For the first time since her mother's passing, she realized where she was—whom she had become. "I…" she stammered, eyes welling up with tears. "I truly *have* gone mad. Haven't I…?" Her whole body shook with the death rattle of her sheltered ignorance, and slowly she rocked. Through glassy eyes, she looked up at her uncle's face. He looked somewhat startled to realize it was *she* who had spoken, and not another facet of her being; a personality she was not presently conscious of.

"Ahh," he said, resignedly. "Finally speaking for yourself, after all these years? I've always told Amadeus you harbored a *dark* side… even before Rose's passing. In all my years evaluating you; meeting with you for your mental health, I did not realize there were numerous others.

The same question I posed to Ovocula, I will again, ask of you—how many?"

The Viscountess flinched. "H-How many what...?" Her voice sounded so strange and unwelcome to her; like an old friend who had abandoned her amidst the chaos, only to return in the aftermath. She did not like the sound of it; deep and raspy, yet softly pitched. Her inflections were meek, and untrained – quite the contrast to Acanthus's nasally, yet refined and assertive diction. She wondered whether it was his words, or his manner of speaking which infuriated her more.

"You are not a *stupid* girl; you are spoilt, and you are lazy! So much so, that I wonder whether it was for that reason alone, that you allowed your accomplice to cause most of the damage." Acanthus's voice raised in volume as he spoke, as though to rile her with his poised vehemence. "In the end, he abandoned you though, didn't he? Left you here to take the fall... If you had more drive, what do you suppose you would *do* with it?"

No... Roland loved me! He said so himself! she thought. *He came for me once, and he'll come for me again!* Her teeth gritted, tears streaked down her face as she narrowed her brows angrily, every ounce of hatred she felt pouring unto her uncle like a stream of molten lava.

"And there's that anger... Perhaps you would allow me to speak with that girl inside of you, once and for all; the one handling the *dirtier* work of your subconscious will..."

"...*What* girl?"

Acanthus's lips parted in a grin, more gum than tooth. She felt as though he were mocking her. "There is much you don't know... Much of yourself, it would *seem* you are unaware..." Again he shifted slightly in his chair, leaning forward a little more so as to look her in the eyes with a shrewdness not previously present in his gaze. "It was horrible, what those hooligans did to your mother. It was even more horrible that you were there to watch. Your father, I fear, neglected your mother; let *you* run amok—until you became what you are, now."

"No!" the Viscountess shot back, with a snarl. "It was always *you* who held me back! *You* kept me from following in my father's footsteps! You... You influenced him against me! You made him believe I needed to be watched carefully, and that I needed to be sheltered! You—"

"Your perception of reality truly *is* warped, isn't it?" Acanthus interrupted her, flatly. "Even if you were ever able to tell us *exactly* what happened to your mother, how could I believe it to be true?" His grin

faded suddenly, the muscles in his sunken face relaxing, replaced with
a stony gaze. He looked almost weary. "Even as a young girl, you had
a penchant for tall tales. At first, I suspected you to be a rotten little
liar. It hadn't occurred to me that you might actually *believe* your own
absurdities. You perceive reality so differently from how it truly is...
but *why?* Can you not handle the truth?"

The Viscountess fell to her silence, once again unsure of what to
say, or how to respond.

"What do you really *know* of the truth?" he continued. "Do you
know that of all these personalities living inside you, the *one* worthy of
living was the one he took away? Was the one he killed?"

Who killed—?

"That *boyfriend* of yours who caused all this trouble with you...
Bern, I think it was? She informs me that *he* is to blame for the death of
your innocence, and thus the *birth* of your... malignance. Now there's
a word," he said, the hint of his smirk returning only briefly. "Are you
aware of its meaning?"

"What are you saying?!" she sobbed, anger and hopelessness
blended together as her body shook from within her bindings. "You
think I'm evil...?! You're my uncle! How could you have treated me this
way? I... I thought you had died... You're the only family I have left,
and you treat me like I'm some kind of animal!"

"Yes, you almost had me killed, didn't you?" he replied, darkly.
"Just as you had your father killed. And even some of the people who
worked with him; friends, and colleagues—all dead. It was *Demetrius*
who dealt the blow, but *you*, with your mindless infatuation... *you* who
influenced him to kill. *For you.*"

Her heart stopped. She could not have wanted that. Could she
have? No.

"Do you not *see?* He wanted freedom! This key Ovocula talks
about, which unlocks some ridiculous Castle in the Sky... which
has as much relevance to a metaphysical astrologic phenomena as a
brick... was the *same* key to the holding cell you helped him escape
from. Perhaps the 'why' doesn't matter, at this point... It wouldn't
change what you did; make it any less horrible. That you wanted us
dead enough to play a part in such a despicable act in the first place...
that is more than I can stand to reason with."

"But... Demetrius... I... I have so much *hate* for him...! All
Mother, the things I wish only to *do* to him..." the Viscountess rocked

with her words, tearing her gaze from her uncle's abruptly, causing fiery strands of wild, loose hair to fall over her face. "How could I *ever* wish to help him?! You tell me that! If I am so bad, you tell me that!"

She was feral with rage—sorrow—*fear*. It was all too much to take in at once.

There was a silence not even the soft whirring of the conditioned room could break. Again, Acanthus spoke. "Some part of you must know," he said. "He, too, has many faces he wears."

CHAPTER 22

Remnants of the Past

She had built a world around herself; the two of them, together. When reality became too much to bear, she retreated inside herself to find solace in a fantasy world she had created. It was not long before the most all-encompassing love she had ever known had interwoven himself into her reverie, with one all his own. It was not until then, that she even realized their split personalities had created a sort of mutual realm, where they both resided in this alternate universe…

At least, this was how she was now making sense of things. She would like to think that their love was just too big to fit into one space—one world. Lost memories began flooding into her conscious mind, all at once. Memories long forgotten and blocked out now filled her up with a sense of lucidity. She had known him long before she had met him…

"Your father tried to make a deal with me, the other day," came his voice, from a place locked within the farthest recesses of her mind. She was seated next to him on the curb of some sidewalk on a sunny day. The pavement was cool under the shade of an old oak tree. There was green grass all around; something she had not seen in quite some time. Soft, happy music chimed as a colorfully painted truck went by. It was a particularly hot day, but he had brought her a sugar cone with two scoops of ice cream; vanilla, and strawberry. As he spoke, he handed it to her. His, was chocolate.

"...He told me not to see you anymore. That I'm a bad influence on you..."

She remembered how angry she felt when she heard this; how strongly she suspected that her uncle had something to do with it. After all, it was through her uncle that she even met him—during one of his sessions, while she was cleaning his study in Galvinsglade. Since her own admission into the asylum, her uncle's workspace had gotten dusty; *moldy*. She remembered that it was she, who kept it clean. How could she have forgotten where she first met the young man who stole her heart with but a single sidelong glance?

He sat on the same couch she had reawakened to find herself on, but he was then allowed free mobility of his hands in the absence of a straitjacket. He was eloquent and gestured expressively as he spoke, all the while stealing quick glances at her as she went about her business of cleaning. Sometimes her uncle would forget to close the door all the way, which separated the study from the room where he spoke to his patients. The young man's looks were always accompanied by a barely detectable crescent smile, and always with her uncle's attention split between the notepad upon which he wrote. His looks always made her heart race. It was not long before he would approach her, slipping her a note after one of these sessions with her uncle.

"*You* don't think I'm a bad influence on you, do you?" he asked, returning her to the curb, seated next to him.

She had vigorously shaken her head. *No! You are the best thing that's ever happened to me...!*

"Well, that's good, because I won't stay where I'm not wanted," he curtly replied. His tone was harsh, bushy brows narrowed as he glared at her. She remembered this moment as the first of many, in which he had hurt her.

I want you... Of course, I want you... How could you even doubt that...?

Something about him always made her feel shy at the thought of reaching for him, or looking him directly in the eyes for long. He was always so forceful with her; from his impassioned pursuit of her, to his occasional angry outburst. She knew he did not mean it. She overheard many a session between he, and her uncle. How could he be held responsible? She knew he struggled with multiple personality disorder, and she had plenty of issues all her own. She wanted only for him to feel appreciated, accepted, and *cherished* when he was with her.

"…Your father said I can either stop seeing you, or he'll get me readmitted to Fyndridge. I just got out of that hellhole. I… I'm *not* going back. But I'm *not* losing you, either."

Her heart fluttered. She relished the thought of being possessed; of feeling a sense of belonging. She hated it from her father and uncle. She could not make sense of how it was any different coming from this man she had not even dated a full year, but somehow, it *was*. His domineering, controlling nature captivated her in ways that made her feel *guided* for the first time since her mother's passing—something she still blocked out. She felt as though her father and uncle kept her, whereas her mother led her. Her mother was encouraging, rather than domineering; a distinction she could not make, then. She was merely happy to be led.

Her lover's face darkened, suddenly. Her flutters turned to chills. "…I think we should kill him," he said. It was so matter-of-fact. So simple. His upper lip curled into an 'off' smile as he took in a mouthful of his chocolate ice cream. She lost her craving.

There was more talk; a plan, of sorts. He had it all worked out. He had his own 'street gang,' after all. They would fight each other for sport, and for play. They would bet, and gamble. Her entanglement in these endeavors served as the last straw for her father, who knew very well what was going on by her uncle's disclosure. Her father had all the power, being that he and his staff oversaw much of what went on in both asylums—Fyndridge and Galvinsglade. All she had to do was signal to her lover from the window.

Her mind fast-forwarded to a month or so later. She was home, and it was her birthday. Acanthus grabbed her arm just as she had made a brief hand signal, indicating it was time; her love and his entourage could then make their move. She knew they were hiding somewhere outside in the bushes, though she was unable to see them as dusk was just beginning to fall. As her uncle pulled her away from the window and into the next room, she looked over every vaguely familiar face at the dinner table. They were all colleagues of her father's. She had not a single friend, and she was not in any frame of mind to deal with her own terror.

And so, the blackouts had begun. How could she have consented to what was a short while from happening? Whom could she have confided in, engulfed in her own silence? This was a horrible nightmare from which she could not awaken. All she could do was forget. All she could do was send another part of her psyche to deal with the situation for her. She lit a candle in her bedroom, some time much earlier. She had the presence of mind to leave her window unlocked—so the intruders could get in. They would pour gasoline all over the wooden floors; the wooden walls; the wooden furniture. Within the hour, her father's rustic home would be up in flames.

Her mind jumped to a few days prior, standing in the middle of her lover's tiny apartment, made even smaller by the trash and clutter built up over the years. The memory alone assaulted her every senses. The wallpaper was wrought with black mold, and peeling. Cockroaches weaved in and out of the cabinets. The sink was infested with hundreds of ants, amid the stacks of dirty dishes which spilled out over the countertops. The sour stench of garbage intermingled with ammonia was so strong it made her nose burn. This was misery.

"You walk out that door, you're gone for good!" her lover screamed. Who was he this time? Demetrius? Roland? No—she had not yet met Roland. His voice came at her in a growl. His bare chest was heaving; fists clenched and knuckles white as he stood there before her. "No one could *ever* love you more than *I* love you; do you hear me?!"

She *did* hear him. Every time he said it, she heard him. By now, she had had enough. Her tear-stricken eyes danced over the knob of the door to her right, several feet away. She remembered how terrified she was; how the last thing she wanted was to leave him. Every fragment of a second her eyes lingered on that handle, her fast-beating heart throbbed all the more painfully in her chest. Could he really let her go so easily? Perhaps she could just leave for a short while; just run, then come back after he calmed down. Maybe then, he would not hurt her.

Too late. She found herself suddenly swept from her feet as he seized both her arms, forcibly digging into her flesh. She could barely let out a small whimper before the back of her head and spine connected solidly with the wall behind her. She could not even cry out in pain, fear and shock overcoming her. Immediately, her gaze melted into his. She remembered those icy blue eyes nearly buried beneath his bushy brows, tense and contorted with blind rage.

"No!" he shouted. He was mere inches from her face. She could feel particles of saliva fly against her cheeks as his guttural roar escaped from his mouth. "No! Don't you think it; don't you leave me! You stupid bitch! You stupid *fucking* bitch!" He was shaking her now, knocking her head against the wall. He released one of her arms and slapped the left side of her face.

Demetrius.

Silently, she sobbed as he pulled a pistol from his back pocket and held it up to her chin. She felt the cold steel pressed into her jawline as he grabbed up a fistful of her hair, jerking it down so that her head was forced back. All she could see at this point was the glazy popcorn ceiling through the tears which now streaked her face. The yellow glow of the dim lighting in the apartment served only to further impair her vision.

"You see what you made me do?!" she could hear him scream at her, between sobs of his own. The gun muzzle trembled as he clicked back the safety. "...You think I *like* hitting you?!"

It was so strange, reflecting back on this moment she had blocked out in her mind; how lonely she felt, even in the arms of the one she loved most. There were a great many captivating qualities which drew her to him, in the beginning. How could it be that their world would collapse into the desolation it was then? Her arms were rigid at her sides, her fists opening and closing at odd intervals; a nervous tick. She quivered uncontrollably as she felt his body pressed up against her own. She could feel his heart beating powerfully through his chest.

Quietly; voicelessly, she had hummed in her mind the lullaby of her mother's mandolin. It soothed her. It took her far away from there—if only for a fleeting moment. Perhaps then, she might tune out the sound of the cold steel clattering with each shaky jerk her lover made. Perhaps then, his aching sobs intermingled with her own quiet whimpers would be obscured by the memory of her mother's sweet singing. She tried only to focus on her memories, shutting her eyes tight; waiting for him to pull the trigger. But even this moment was just a memory.

He pulled away from her suddenly. Her head reflexively tilted to face him once more, as he backed away and held the gun to his temple. He was breathing heavily, face streaked with perspiration, tears, and saliva. She imagined there was little difference in how she, herself looked. "Maybe I should just blow my brains out, here and now," he said, shifting his body weight erratically; dancing from one foot to the other. His whole arm trembled with the muzzle of the gun disappearing into his matted hair. "You want to leave me... They *always* leave me..."

Her eyes grew wide; panicked. She moved herself off the wall, stepping toward him. *No*, she thought, shakily. *No, no, no... Please... I'll stay. I'll stay for you. Just don't hurt yourself, please.* Tenderly, she raised her hands to his face, cupping his cheeks in her palms. Her fingers grazed over light, rough stubble, sliding through his hair to meet with the cold metal of the gun. Gently, she eased it down, his arm following to drop at his side. He enveloped her into a warm embrace, and they shared a kiss to melt away all of her fears and doubts—all of her pain.

How could she have been so stupid? So easily manipulated, and used?

At least she was smart enough to equip herself with a bullet-proof vest after that little stint. It saved her from Gertie's bullet, but not from the first-degree burns the flames had caused her. She wondered whether her uncle would still have tried to get her out of there, begrudged as he was, had he known initially what her part in this had been. Surely he would not have scorned her father, once given reason to further scorn her. After all, it was *she* who was at fault and not Amadeus, as per his imparted 'deal.' She wondered what her uncle had even known about it.

It took her father dying at the hands of her lover for her to finally realize how wrong this was; all of this—from the dark fantasy they wove, to the twisted things it made the each of them do. How unhealthy, and sick their love was. And she felt just as at fault, if not more so. She took the key and ran; the master key to the asylum. The mark of freedom and power her mother once held so dear. The power her father would see turned over to her. She would stop at nothing to keep it from the man she loved, in that moment of confusion and chaos. She suppressed the urge to run back to him, by forgetting him completely.

Again, her mind jumped. How saddened, and angry she was at the thought of her lover courting one of the nurses at the asylum; Beulah Smith—administer of all the electroshock therapy she had endured. It caused her so much pain and discomfort. How was it his aim to seduce this woman, as he had done so with her? Was she not enough to satisfy his desires?

"Relax," he would tell her. "I don't *really* love her... I just can't break us out of here, by myself. Of all your father's staff, she was the easiest target. How many men do you know would truly take an interest in a woman who's *bald?* Just trust me."

Beulah was robust, and voluptuous; quite the contrast to her own small, bony frame. It made her feel inadequate. She wondered whether Beulah had told him of her humiliating experiences; how the staff neglected her, leaving her to writhe in her own filth for hours. How they all mocked her, the daughter of the murdered asylum owner. How, rather than champion her father's legacy, her destiny was to be committed. Were he still alive, he would never have allowed this to happen to her—not to his own daughter. How could her own uncle have signed her away? How could this be her fate? She was wrought with self-pity and despair.

It had not occurred to her just how bad things truly were at Galvinsglade. This was not a place where patients went to get better. Fyndridge; *maybe*. Maybe there would have been a chance. The moment she was transferred marked the moment her life became forfeit.

"I don't *really* love her..." she repeated his words in her head. Yet, he made it seem so real. Had he really loved *her*? Or was she just another object to be controlled? After all; he had escaped the asylum, and she was all but left behind. He abandoned her, just as her uncle had said.

So, where was she to go from here?

She snapped back to the present, many questions left unanswered; many memories remaining unearthed. Her uncle was standing now to leave the room. She thought he might be retrieving what staff was left at the asylum, or perhaps other authorities to take her away again; someplace worse. It made little difference to her as she lay there, looking up at the ceiling. There was a large ceiling mirror she had not noticed before, and her reflection left her aghast. She barely recognized herself. Was this truly what she had become?

Her fiery red hair was loose and wild, like the mane of an untamed lion; a great, flocculent mass all about her head. Her brown eyes were dark, with deep circles which told the tales of wakeful madness. She had not seen the light of the sun in a long time, her skin ghostly pale; freckles sunken into her complexion as distant marks from long ago memories. One of her bare legs hung awkwardly off the side of the couch like the limb of a broken marionette. She was very thin, almost skeletal. Her high cheekbones and angular features curved sharply under soft, porcelain flesh. As she stared back at herself, her only thoughts were that of self-loathing.

I'm done, she thought. *It was all a lie. All of it. And I can never take any of it back.*

She gazed into her own eyes. They looked dull and tired. The expression on her face was on the verge of contortion, breaking down with more tears. It was almost as though there was something behind it, keeping her from doing so. Something that opposed her giving into total despair. Her expression slowly changed, her deep brown eyes lighting up with a spark of hope. An internal conversation she would have with herself, manifesting not in words, but in sheer emotion; talking herself up, and preparing her for trials to come.

Her eyes began to harden with a slow-building resolve. As she focused on her reflection in the mirror overhead, her whole visage began to change. The glass seemed to ripple, like waves in a pool of water. Bern now stood before her, donning her sleeveless brown duster. Behind the woman was a barren wasteland, not unlike the one she had traveled upon her escape from the wreckage of the *Wild Rose*; her father's ship.

"I've been looking for you, Viscountess," Bern said, key in hand. The gem at its base glowed that soft, brilliant blue, the light encasing the frame of the mirror slowly expanding into the room. Soon, the room was engulfed completely by the light's gentle rays as she extended it outward, almost as though drawing her in. "It seems you've been awfully lonely lately."

The Viscountess could no longer tell whether she was still lying over the couch, feeling nothing behind her as the gap between she and the ceiling mirror closed. The experience was very surreal. She wondered whether she may have been drugged.

"...You tried... to *kill* me..." she weakly voiced, traces of scorn coating her words.

Bern's deep hazel eyes softened into a look of remorse. "...I'm sorry. I didn't want to. You exhibit a certain naïvety and innocence all your own, that I wish we could keep... but you were holding me back. I left you, to continue the search for the gemstones on my own. There are terrible things out there, Viscountess... Things, that if you saw them, would only cause you to become more jaded. I know it, because I *feel* it. In you; in all of us."

She realized then, that if this were true; that if she had these other *people*, all living inside of her... the ceaseless inner turmoil she faced could only mean that she was truly at war with herself. Each one of her personalities, all highly critical of the next, judged each other based upon their own individual belief systems. She was constantly at odds with herself. She felt the presences of Bern, Ovocula; even Gwendolyn. She could only speculate where the lines between fantasy and reality blurred for her—who was 'real' and who was not.

"I came back looking for you," Bern continued, "because once I'd found out that you had survived, it occurred to me that you were stronger than I initially gave credit. You've made a lot of progress, and you've come a long way. You're even consciously speaking; do you realize that? What an important accomplishment that is!"

The Viscountess felt numb to the praise. "How had you come to realize I was not dead?"

Bern lowered the key, moving forward through the surface of the mirror. "I saw Roland, again, just before he'd left," she replied, solemnly. At the mention of his name, the Viscountess felt a sharp stab in her chest; as though her heart were being squeezed when she drew in a breath. "Viscountess... Did you know these gems we're searching for hold a great many powers? Somewhere in you, you *must*. Roland is alive, and he has escaped. There's only one way we can right these wrongs, and it isn't with you, sitting in a small padded room for the rest of our lives, our minds deteriorating..."

"You're not *real*, Bern!" the Viscountess cried, flinching within the confines of her straitjacket.

"Bullshit. To say I'm not real is to say that *you're* not real. To say that *what you've been through* isn't real. If we are to have any sort of integration in the future, you're going to have to trust in me. In yourself. Don't you have any confidence; any faith in yourself at all...?"

"...Integration...?" the Viscountess repeated.

Bern sighed, weightily. "...It's going to take some time. But you're going to have to work through it; sort yourself out. That means, coming into the person you wish to be. Some of us are going to get left behind along the way. Others will become a much greater part of you. Integration... *Absorption*... becoming more whole, by—"

"...By the signs," the Viscountess said, in unison with her thoughts coming to conclusion, once and for all. "It's like what Ovocula had spoken about, before. What Orel sought to refute. You each represent different parts of me; my astrological makeup. I can't operate the gems without all of you. None of us can, without each other. Am I right...?"

Bern nodded, reluctantly. "...It's what I'm slowly beginning to understand... I *do* need you. I can't go it alone anymore. So, what say you slip out of that straitjacket, so I can give you back this key? I've kept it safe for you. You won't be able to escape from Galvinsglade without it."

The Viscountess drew a deep breath. She glanced down at herself, the jacket securing one arm over the other, both crossed over her chest. The jacket had buckles over the sleeves, and she could feel more cutting into her skin, from behind. She knew what she had to do.

"Bern…" she said calmly, though her heart was racing with apprehension. "I know you took my brooch. The one bearing my family insignia. It was gone, when I looked for it with Orel… Storage compartment, for room *642*. *My* room. You're the only one who could have taken it."

Bern's face suddenly became very stony. Her eyes were dire; serious. "Viscountess… Don't you remember who *gave* you your insignia? Who *branded* you…?"

Slowly, she shook her head. She had forgotten. Perhaps it was something she actively wanted to forget, as a small child. "How would *you* know?" she shot back, defensively. As she spoke, she began working her right arm against the fabric of the straitjacket; loosening it as best she could, in preparation.

Bern frowned, darkly. "…Your uncle… Does he still smoke his cigars…?"

The Viscountess's heart skipped a beat. She pushed her right arm forcibly towards the opposite shoulder with as much strength as she could muster. She bit her lower lip hard, to keep from crying out in pain as her right shoulder audibly dislocated from its socket. She did not want to hear the rest of Bern's words. She did not want to remember.

"He quit a long time ago," she responded, through gritted teeth. "A-Around the time I started seeing him for psychiatric evaluations…"

"…He put it out on the back of your neck," she continued. "It was your birthday. You detest birthdays, don't you… I remember, because I was there. Your *burn*; the day I took over, for the first time. The day you willed me into existence. You had just turned four, as I recall. I am that many years younger than you."

The Viscountess feebly brought her right arm up over her head, gritting her teeth against the tremors of pain that shot through her shoulder blade and down her back. Tilting her head forward under her arm, she was able to free both her limbs, her right arm dangling a bit lower than her left as she dropped them at her sides in exhaustion.

"Do you know how old you are now? How long you've been

here...? Or, has the concept of time escaped you, along with your memories?"

She did not want to think about it. She ignored Bern's words, wincing as she shakily raised her arms to her mouth and began unfastening her sleeve buckles with her teeth. However long she had been kept at this asylum; however long it had been since the fires swept away what remained of everything she had known and cared for; she at least knew it was recent that Roland had escaped. There was still time.

Then it occurred to her. *Still time, for what?* She stopped with the thought, just as her buckled sleeves came undone. Her eyes focused on Bern's, who seemed to realize what had crossed her mind in that moment. The turquoise gem in the key glowed brighter in a brief flash, the room still obscured by the brilliance of the light. It was hypnotic.

"When we find Roland again, Viscountess," Bern said, "...you must try to be mindful that while he may be the one you love, he shares his body with others; Demetrius, who cannot be excused for what he has done. Not just to you, but many others. The *Governor*, whom *I* cannot excuse for... for how he *used* me..." her voice choked as she spoke. "What we seek is bigger than retribution, and self-discovery. Do you understand that?"

The Viscountess nodded, slowly. "...The Castle in the Sky... the lost language of salvation... the power to restore the earth..."

She watched Bern smile as she used her free hands to unfasten the top and bottom buckles of the straightjacket, more with her left arm than the other she had just injured in order to free herself. She would have to pop it back into place soon. Bern sifted through a pocket in her knapsack, which hung off one of her shoulders. She withdrew a small, sapphire brooch; the one the Viscountess had worn when they first met. It smelled of lavender.

"I kept it safe for you," she said. "It so turns out that you had one of the gems on you, all this time; given to you by your uncle. I recognized it instantly when I saw it. He fashioned it into this brooch, did he not...? He had given it to you shortly after the burn... Even as a child, in your heart, you never forgave him. Though you'd forgotten about the incident, as well as the origins of this gift, completely."

The Viscountess stepped onto the material of the jacket's left sleeve, tugging her body out of its canvas cloth prison, the buckles clinking loosely as she let it fall to the floor.

"Roland has a gem," Bern said.

The Viscountess smiled. "That must be how he survived the fall, when he was thrown overboard the *S.S. Beulah*. It must be how *I* survived… The Stone of the Sage. My mother's gem."

Bern returned her smile, extending the key toward her. "Come. What say we take it from him then, shall we? We'll meet up with the others. They're waiting for us."

The Viscountess touched a hand to the base of the key, running her fingers over the smooth, bulbous surface of the glowing gemstone. "We have a long way to go," she said. "Do you really think we can do this…?"

Bern said nothing, in turn.

The Viscountess followed her through the mirror.

Photo by Jennifer Smith

About
TAVERSIA
təvû(r)zhə

Taversia hates "about me's" because she doesn't know what to say. She's actually writing this right now, in third-person narrative. Here are a few facts; a mix of details which have very little to do with who Taversia is as a person, as well as some things that do:

- This is Taversia's first novel.
- When Taversia graduated from high school, her name was spelled wrong on her diploma.
- Taversia has never been to college.
- Sometimes, Taversia cries late at night about her life.
- She thinks it's hilarious.
- Before writing Viscountess, Taversia worked as a model and stage performer, and occasionally waited tables.
- The chapter, "Crazy Little Sad Loose Cannon Girl" was named for a direct quote by Fiona Apple in an interview, where she described peoples' perceptions of her.

TAVERSIA'S FAVORITE THINGS:
- Movies: Donnie Darko, Amélie, Labyrinth, and Ever After.
- Music: A Perfect Circle and Florence + The Machine.
- Flower: Tiger Lily

Well, that's all she can come up with right now. For more stuff, you can probably visit her internets. (www.taversia.net)

CPSIA information can be obtained at www.ICGtesting.com
Printed in the USA
LVOW06s1419120114

369099LV00001B/1/P